The Diamond Device

M.H. Thaung

This is a work of fiction. Any similarity to real persons, living or dead, is coincidental and not intended by the author.

ISBN-13: 978-1-912819-14-0 (print)
ISBN-13: 978-1-912819-15-7 (ebook)

Cover by Creative Covers

To my mother, Dr Khin May Sein (1935-2020).

You are no longer with us, but your memory shines.

*In my mother's land of birth, "Sein" means "diamond."

Chapter 1

Alf hunched his shoulders as he limped along the pavement, but rain still trickled off his flat cap and down his neck. He shoved his hands deeper into the misshapen pockets of his workman's jacket. If only he could afford a pair of gloves.

He scowled at the fancy detached houses he was passing, their cheerful porch lights mocking his mood. They lay on the route from the docks to his home in the labourers' residential district. Tonight, the area even boasted a patrolling constable, who eyed Alf suspiciously under the glow from the gas street lamp.

So what? It wasn't a crime to walk along the street, and snooty residents had no right to complain he spoiled their view. He even had an honest job.

At least, he had until today.

Bloody scientists and their inventions. For the last eighteen months, Alf had operated cranes at a factory that made naval supplies. After a recent change in ownership, the boss had brought in new technology. The machines needed little human input, so most of the factory hands had been laid off. The boss *claimed* it was his patriotic duty, freeing up men to sign up for the armed forces. But he'd be raking in more profits too.

And where did that leave Alf? He was no paper-pusher to be kept on in a desk job, and he wasn't one of the foreman's golden boys. His workmates had been quite happy to seek jobs elsewhere as sailors, soldiers or even airship crew.

But no, not Alf. His false leg barred him from even applying.

A steam-powered carriage chugged past, wheels rolling through a puddle and sending up spray. With a curse, Alf stepped to the side. His dragging foot caught on an uneven paving stone that sent him stumbling. He clutched a nearby lamp post.

The constable strolled up with a hand on his holstered truncheon. "Everything alright, sir?"

"Uh, yeah." The copper probably thought he was drunk. Alf released his grasp, then wiped grimy hands on his trousers. "I have a gammy leg."

The admission stuck in his craw. After the accident at his previous workplace–driving a steam-powered digger–they'd offered him a choice of prosthetic legs. He'd picked the clockwork model, simply because it was worth more than a wooden one. The mechanism needed to be wound each morning, but it let the ankle flex more naturally when climbing stairs. Problem was, the power didn't last all day. By evening, the leg was a dead weight attached below his aching knee.

"Right you are." The policeman adjusted his peaked cap and regulation waterproof cape, obviously waiting for Alf to move on.

Fists clenched, Alf progressed up the street. As more street lamps flickered into life, his stomach rumbled. It was nearly suppertime. What was Mum going to say about his lost job? With her arthritis, she couldn't work long hours. Alf had been the main breadwinner for the eight years since Gwen's dad passed on. And as for Gwen? With her engineering studies, she wasn't bringing home any money either.

A door opened just ahead, illuminating a neat garden path flanked by carefully tended flower beds. Silhouetted in the doorway were two figures. One was female, her curves beginning the slow decline towards sagginghood. The other was tall, lean and male. He held a top hat and cane.

"Lovely to see you. Do come again, and soon." The woman's voice was plummy, although a touch breathless.

"It's been a pleasure!" said the man. He leaned over her hand.

Alf stopped to stare. He'd read in the weekly rag that nobs kissed women's hands, but he hadn't believed it was true. And in full view of the whole street!

"God's blood, it's wet!" Donning his hat, the man bounded down the steps and along the path.

"I'll send the butler out with an umbrella."

"No need. I see a cab." He raised his cane in farewell, and his long stride took him past Alf with barely a glance.

Alf ducked the swinging cane as the scent of ginger cake taunted his nostrils. He glowered at the young man's smirking profile. Bloke probably didn't have a care in the world.

A battered cab ground to a halt in a cloud of steam. Before the driver could climb down from his perch, the toff yanked the door open and jumped in, calling, "Parlay Square, and make it speedy."

Bloody toffs, always acting like the world revolved around them, just because they had money. Meanwhile, hard-working folks like Alf–

A wave of freezing water drenched him as the cab sped off.

Bloody toffs.

Tossing his battered top hat on the worn leather seat, Rich

leaned back and frowned. His visit hadn't gone nearly as well as he'd hoped. Certainly, afternoon visits to ladies of a certain age–while their husbands were out–deflected suspicions from what he was really doing. But he'd been so sure that Mrs Sadler's house would promise rich pickings for a night-time burglary. Instead, he'd found tasteless gaudy ornaments that would be impossible to fence, and well-maintained security automata of the latest design. Turned out that Mr Sadler was a munitions manufacturer, so he was more conscious of household security than most gentlemen.

Rich shrugged. One couldn't win them all. For his clandestine activities, he tried to pick affluent targets who weren't in the public eye and who weren't known to each other. There was still some guesswork involved, but careful preparation paid off. So far, his one burglary per month didn't stand out from Ironfort's background crime rate.

Where should he try next? He ran a hand through his thinning hair–an unfortunate trait shared with his father. Mrs Sadler's fulsome reception suggested no inkling that he was down to his last handful of crowns. He didn't dare give that impression, which was why he'd called a cab rather than walking home. If word got out that he was nearly broke... With a threadbare silk handkerchief, he mopped his brow. He was at risk of losing the name of *Lord* Richard Hayes and, more importantly, his seat on the Council of Lords, the governing body within Lesser Grenia.

The vehicle rocked as it hit a pothole. A curse from the driver floated through the hatch in front. Rich suppressed a similar curse as a spring poked his backside. He missed the days when his parents kept a private horse-drawn carriage.

When Mother and Father had set off on a trade mission

three years ago, Rich had promised he'd hold the family seat in the Council of Lords. He hadn't expected to lose all contact with them. Since then, political tensions with neighbouring Calesia had steadily increased, although diplomats on both sides still feigned cordiality. With the Hayes fortunes tied up in ventures abroad, Rich now had no way of accessing foreign funds. Practically speaking, all he controlled was a dairy farm in the country and the Parlay Square townhouse, a mouldering chunk of real estate that would require tens of thousands of crowns to modernise.

Smoke and steam from the carriage's engine seeped through the window and made him cough. He waved it away, catching a glimpse of an army recruitment poster.

Even worse, Rich's parents were Calesian, albeit more successful than their fellow immigrants. Their investment acumen had earned his father a noble title. Although Rich had been born here, if he were convicted of any wrongdoing, the weight of the law would fall more heavily on his head. Not to mention being branded as a potential traitor.

"Sir?" came the cabbie's voice. "Just turning into Parlay Square. That'll be six pence."

Reaching into his woefully empty coin pouch, Rich found a florin. When the carriage stopped, he handed it over with a smile. "Keep the change, my good man."

While the belching carriage moved off, he donned his hat and sauntered along the street towards his house. His precarious living depended on presenting himself as a confident man of means.

By the time Alf arrived home, he was soaking, starving and in a filthy mood. He stomped down the uneven stone steps to their rented basement flat. The warped communal door didn't fully close, and water pooled on the concrete floor. Bloody greedy landlords. Before he could use the latchkey, his apartment door swung open. A blast of warm damp air hit him, scented with cabbage, bacon and onions.

"Wotcher, Alf." Gwen grinned up at him from a pixie-like face, marred by a yellowing black eye. "Busy day?"

Alf stepped into the main room, and the stresses of the day eased. He tugged Gwen's honey-blonde fringe, smirking as she batted his hand away. Her hair was several shades lighter than his and a good deal fluffier, although they shared Mum's muddy brown eyes. "Yeah, it always is. Any grub left for me?"

"Naw, we got tired of waiting." She stuck out her tongue when he scowled.

"Gwen, don't tease your brother so." Mum's querulous voice came from the kitchen at the back, accompanied by the clang of a spoon in the pot. "He's been hard at work. How was your day, Alf?"

"Oh, fine. Just a normal day. No problems." He forced a cheerful smile. After taking off his sodden coat and hanging it up, he sat on the couch that doubled as Gwen's bed, trying not to knock over her stack of books. He clumsily rolled up his left trouser leg. His clothes would take days to dry out properly.

"Let me help." Gwen knelt and undid the laces on his right shoe and pulled it off, along with his soggy sock.

Alf wiggled his toes against the worn carpet with a frown. Gwen wasn't usually so attentive. "Did your classes go alright today?"

"Sure, we had lots of fun." She tossed his sock into the laundry bag. Mum's laundry job meant they didn't need to wash by hand.

"No more 'accidents'?" His frown deepened. That black eye wasn't the first.

She flinched slightly. "No, I just keep my mouth shut, even when the posh students are talking tripe."

"I'm sure it'll sort itself out in the exams." Alf sighed. He could never think of encouraging things to say. "You'll show them up when it really matters."

"Um..." She picked at a loose thread in the carpet. "We had a spot test today."

That sounded ominous. Sliding a hand down the side of his prosthesis, Alf prodded the switch that released the vacuum. The cuff hissed and then loosened. He slipped it off, then massaged what remained of his leg below the knee. After checking his cane was in its usual place by the wall, he eyed the still-silent Gwen. "And?"

"I tried! It's not my fault they make things so complicated."

Great. Even though Mum had stopped Gwen from running errands, she still couldn't keep up with the lessons. If only she'd stuck with cookery school, or even that carpentry course. Though at least college was now free, unlike when he'd left school fifteen years ago. And her homework was more interesting these days. "Maybe you should think about–"

"I'll be fine! Just need a bit more time to get my head round things. This is definitely the right choice for me." Settling herself on a floor cushion, Gwen tapped the prosthesis. "Oh, we took one of these apart today."

Mum hobbled in with a tray, which she set on Alf's lap. It bore a steaming plate of hash and a mug of sweet, milky tea. "Let your brother eat in peace. I'm sure he's been working his fingers to the bone. He doesn't need you wittering on about all them fancy devices."

"I don't mind." Alf picked up his fork and dug in. If he was occupied with eating, Gwen could chatter away all she wanted, and he wouldn't be expected to answer awkward questions. Today, he wasn't in a mood to argue about her schooling. Besides, the hash was dark and crispy round the edges, just how he liked it. "What did you learn about false legs?"

"Control systems. You have a special one, don't you?"

He nodded and swallowed. The hot food warmed his stomach. "Yes, a new type."

"So, ordinary false legs have springs and joints in the usual places, but you need to move differently, since they don't *know* what you're doing. They just passively rely on gravity and momentum. Your type has a clockwork-powered"–she frowned in concentration–"sensori-controller system that interprets your, uh, body signals, and moves more... with you, like."

Alf chuckled. "That's more or less it."

She wrinkled her nose. "Can it hear what you're thinking? Sounds a bit creepy, it doing something by itself."

"Not really by itself. It only listens when it's attached to me. And I like that it doesn't look so obvious when I'm walking." He suppressed his earlier uncomplimentary thoughts about the device, just in case it really could hear him. With it being a recent model, who knew what its creator might have added?

Mum returned with two more mugs and set them on the writing desk that held Gwen's notes. Alf had bought the desk from a neighbour who was moving out. Although it made the room more cluttered, Gwen assured him it helped her study. It had better not prove a waste.

After easing herself on to the stool, Mum cupped her mug with arthritic hands. The flat was never quite warm enough for comfort, so she slept in the kitchen, leaving Alf the bedroom. "I read in the paper today about all those new machines they're bringing into the factories. That anything to do with your work?"

Alf stiffened, a denial on his lips. But it would be easier to keep up a small lie than a large one. "Er, yeah, they installed some in my factory. Makes the place more efficient."

Gwen's eyes widened. "They taught us about that too. Technology can now do a lot of things that people were doing by hand. That means you need fewer people to do the same work, doesn't it?"

Alf squirmed inside. "That's right."

"Don't tell me they're laying people off." Mum pointed a swollen-knuckled finger at Alf's plate. "Why've you stopped eating? Is my cooking not good? Shall I go and make–"

"No, it's great!" Alf shovelled food into his mouth and took his time chewing, not even tasting what he was eating. Eventually, he swallowed. "They don't need so many workers. Some of my mates have signed up for military service. Doing their patriotic duty." Nice for them, moving straight into well-paid jobs when war was only a distant possibility.

Mum glanced at the wall, where she'd tacked a newspaper picture of King Michael and Queen Sylvia. "Good for them. And what about you?" Her brow crinkled in concern.

"Oh, I'm fine. Someone needs to oversee the machines." Damn, why had he said that? No way could he keep his unemployment from Mum for long.

"That sounds good for your prospects. And maybe a nice girl–"

Alf coughed as an errant piece of cabbage stuck in his throat.

After he took a gulp of tea, Gwen tapped his arm. "I'm supposed to do a project. All the other students got their parents to sort them out. Can I come to work with you someday?"

"No!" Her sullen face made him blurt, "I wouldn't want to push my luck, it being a recent promotion and all." Gah, even worse! What was he saying? Cheeks burning, he tugged at his collar. "I don't want to get in trouble with the boss. And... and, they have safety regulations about visitors and everything."

"Oh, poo." She brightened. "Well, how about increasing my pocket money allowance? And there are some books I'm sure would help..."

"Of course he will," said Mum. "Since you're going up in the world, it's only right to help your family."

"Uh, sure," muttered Alf, thinking of his meagre final pay packet.

Mum's cheeks crinkled with her smile. "That's my boy."

Damn.

Chapter 2

Rich's back twinged as he sat on a lumpy armchair, sipping stewed tea and eating burnt, unevenly sliced sponge cake. The Madeleys might have plenty of money, but they didn't spend it on hospitality. It would be a pleasure to return here tonight.

"As I was saying, Lord Hayes, it's such a delight to have you visit for afternoon tea at last." Mrs Madeley leaned across the sofa towards his armchair, wafting the odour of sweat and stale perfume in his direction.

Rich smiled, remembering last year when he'd burgled the other end of the street. "I'm sorry that other commitments have kept me from this pleasure for so long. I'm honoured to be here."

"Oh! No need to apologise. I'm sure you're *very* popular."

"I'm not sure I'd lay claim to that," he murmured.

Above the cosy fireplace hung an oil painting in surprisingly good taste. Its understated oak frame stood out among the room's clashing decorations like a pedigree racehorse in a farmyard.

Finally, something he could talk about with a straight face. "Is that an original Denoir? I particularly like how the sunlight reflects off the airship's cables."

"I don't know." She pursed her lips. "It was here when we moved in six years ago. My husband insisted we keep it on display, though I'd rather have replaced it with a portrait of our daughter."

Rich set down his teacup and spread his hands. "Maybe he had a momentary brain fever. I would always defer to the lady's preference. Was there much else left behind from the previous owners?"

"Plenty of other junk like this, ornaments, trinkets and so on." She unfolded a silk hand fan, which was even frillier than the antimacassars. "My husband's often away on business, so it hardly affects him. I finally put my foot down about sending the rest to storage. Currently it's taking up space in the back room, but it should be gone by next week."

How promising. Valuables that wouldn't even be missed. He chuckled. "Better find a use for the free space quickly, or else your husband will fill it up again. How long until his return?"

"Oh, he said at least three weeks in his last telegram."

"I see. Does he plan to enlist?"

"No. He's too old. What about you?" Mrs Madeley clasped her hands to her ample chest and took a deep breath. "I've no doubt you would look very gallant in uniform. So tall, unlike my husband."

Rich shrugged modestly. He could hardly help his height: standing out amongst other Lesser Grenians was more of a liability than an advantage, especially as it reminded people of his non-local origins. "Of course I will do my duty to our country, but I can better serve in my role on the Council of Lords."

Pink-cheeked, she waved the fan in front of her face, narrowly missing the beaded lampshade. "Oh, how silly of me! I hadn't exactly forgotten, but the Council don't publicise their work much."

"Not to worry." Although new laws required royal assent, the Council of Lords governed Lesser Grenia. Additionally, the nobles funded public services through paying their dues. So he was supporting the country financially. Or he would have been, had he had any money. Better not follow that thought too far. He returned his attention to his hostess. "Everyone does what they can."

"We all have to make sacrifices." With a conspiratorial smile, she lightly touched his arm. "Just between you and me, the tone of the area has declined. Can you believe our neighbours made their fortune in common trade?"

Where did the woman think goods came from? International commerce was the world's lifeblood, as long as someone intelligent made the decisions. Mother and Father's investments had earned them a place in the nobility. "Oh?"

She sniffed. "The Bergrim-Hoyts. Leo and Ina."

"Ah." Rich's eyebrows rose. Mr Bergrim-Hoyt owned factories down by the docks. The man was angling for a seat on the Council of Lords. However, it was the wife who enjoyed international notoriety. Professor Bergrim-Hoyt–a privately funded inventor–had developed the technology that allowed diamonds to generate energy. That meant less mass of fuel to transport, clean, practical generation of electricity and more precision when programming automata. If not for her discovery, Lesser Grenia would be forced to yield immediately if Calesia ever got round to declaring war. "Not quite so common now, perhaps."

"I suppose. One must be polite."

No, Rich wouldn't feel guilty about burgling this house. He put on an expression of embarrassed discomfort. "I wonder, might I make use of your facilities?"

"It's just at the back. I'll get the girl to show you." She

reached for the bell pull, then paused with a high-pitched giggle. “Oh, I’ve just remembered, I gave her the afternoon off.”

Better and better. He should have known from the state of the cake. He stood. “I’m sure I can find my way.”

In the industrial district, Alf limped along the pavement, blowing into his hands. The scent of canteen chips and vinegar hung mockingly in the air. If he got too hungry, he’d nip into the workers’ charity mission for a cup of hot soup. But then he’d have to sit through a sermon on gratitude and brotherly friendship. Too high a price to ease an empty stomach.

He’d toured the docks earlier, but none of his old mates had job openings: they’d turned him away with pity in their eyes. After that, he cold-called at factories where he didn’t know the staff. Of course, many workplaces were in the same boat as his previous one and laying off workers. Owners who could afford new machines would be laughing while others went to the wall. The factory two gates along from his old one had already closed, its equipment being broken up for spare parts.

One foreman disdainfully suggested he try patriotism and visit the military recruitment office. Stung, Alf turned his collar so that his industrial injury badge was prominently on display. The man then spluttered and made some weak excuse about wanting able-bodied workers. The encounter had left a bitter taste in his mouth.

Today’s pay so far was a measly ha’penny. He’d helped a cabbie load a carriage with coal, getting his hands filthy in the process. That would hardly pay the rent. He hadn’t yet gathered the gumption to admit his unemployment to

Mum. And where would that leave Gwen? What use was studying if they were thrown out on to the street?

Leaving the industrial area behind, he walked along a residential terrace and glowered at the houses' ornate façades. What did their occupants know of being out of money? They'd no idea what it meant to strive for an honest living. And that bloody scientist with her inventions. Why couldn't she have left well alone?

It was too early to go home, so he should keep looking for work. Factories were out, and he didn't have the learning for a desk job. As he passed a wrought-iron gate, his lip curled. No doubt its owner had paid a pretty penny for it, all for the sake of showing off to the neighbours. He paused, pride wrangling with need. Much as he despised the toffs, the point was that they had money and he did not. And they'd pay people to maintain their homes. Perhaps he ought to ask if they had any temporary work.

Could he just go up and knock? Was that how they did things? He racked his brains. These houses had two doors, didn't they? One for posh visitors and another one for deliveries and domestic staff. Typical toff behaviour. They were all going into the same house, so it was a waste of a door, not to mention also losing heat. Still, he'd better try a side door.

He walked on, not quite sure what he was looking for. A house that wasn't too posh, but that looked in need of extra help. Ah, what about that one on the next corner? Straggling weeds adorned the flower bed, but smoke puffed out of the chimney, and a cheerful glow came from the front room window. Even better, its side door was ajar, almost as if it were inviting him in. It must be fate.

Alf limped through the open gate and up the overgrown

side path. Bah, if deliveries came up this path, why not make this wider, with the narrow path for nobby folk?

At the open door, the scent of well-cooked sponge cake met his nose. His stomach rumbled as he called, “Hello?” Would a sympathetic maid answer, or would a snobbish butler tell him to be on his way? They might take him for a beggar, and he couldn’t fully blame them.

Nobody responded.

His brow wrinkled. Surely somebody was in, but he didn’t want to shout or else the neighbours might think him a drunkard. If someone called the coppers on him, that would really take the biscuit.

At a hissing sound, he poked his head around the door. The cluttered kitchen was unoccupied, but his eye was drawn to a kettle on the range. The smell of burnt iron suggested it had been overlooked. He lifted his false leg carefully over the sill and stepped inside. After finding a tea cloth to wrap around his hand, he removed the kettle from the heat, wincing as he left streaks of coal dust on the linen. Then he inspected his surroundings.

In the centre of the room was a table, on top of which lay a plate of sliced sponge cake. Alf’s mouth watered. Where was everyone? He glanced longingly at the cake, but pilfering food would ruin his chances of seeking work, not to mention being plain wrong. So he’d better seek one of the domestic servants.

Stepping through the internal door, he found himself in a hallway. A gleam of light came from the front door to his right, and the clink of china from a doorway. Alf started to sweat. He couldn’t bother the owners! He’d better find someone else. On the basis that servants would be at the back of the house, he turned left and shuffled down the hallway, softly calling, "Hello? Anyone?"

He blundered into a storeroom, and his eyes widened. Dusty boxes and cloth-covered picture frames were crammed into the space. Bloody toffs, so much stuff they had to put it in storage. What did they keep in those boxes? He reached out–

"What are you doing?" An authoritative voice sounded from the doorway.

After drying his hands in the privy room, Rich sauntered towards the front of the house, pausing at the storeroom he'd previously located. A second, closer look would give him a better idea how large a bag–

What in the blazes? He gaped at the rough-looking chap pawing at the wrapped and boxed-up items. Surely he didn't work here, not wearing that flat cap indoors.

Nostrils flaring, Rich drew himself up to his full height. "What are you doing?"

The man's head jerked round, and he stumbled, clutching a picture cloth with a sooty hand. It slid off to reveal a rather attractive seascape. A box toppled off the pile and on to the floor with a crash. Silver cutlery spilled out. That would be worth a bob or two.

The man straightened up. His gaze darted around the room before settling on Rich. "I... uh..."

"Lord Hayes, are you alright?" Mrs Madeley sashayed down the corridor, unflatteringly silhouetted in the light from the door. "I heard–Oh!" She clutched at Rich, her crimson nails digging into his biceps. "Who's this?"

"That's what I was wondering." Rich wished he had his cane, though fortunately the man didn't seem aggressive. Prising his hostess' fingers off might be more of a challenge.

"Not one of your domestic staff, I suppose. Gardener?"

"No, no." Mrs Madeley went pink, and her chin wobbled. "I, er, gave all the servants the afternoon off before you arrived."

Perhaps this incursion was saving Rich from an awkward social extrication. He frowned. "Well, fellow? What do you have to say for yourself?"

"Terribly sorry sir, ma'am," the man mumbled, snatching off his cap. "I was wondering if you had any odd jobs."

That was a patent lie. Rich opened his mouth to challenge him, then paused. How excellent. This chap would make an ideal scapegoat for a burglary tonight. Time to plant some seeds. "And what's wrong with military recruitment?"

Scowling, the man pointed at his lapel, which bore a work injury badge. "I lost my leg in a factory accident. They won't take me."

Mrs Madeley batted her eyelids at Rich. "Oh, what a sad story."

"I suppose so." Lack of funds could certainly lead to desperation. "But look here, you mustn't go wandering around respectable people's houses like that." With an internal wince, Rich pulled a florin from his pocket. "Here's something to keep you out of trouble. Now be off with you."

Rich and Mrs Madeley stepped back while the intruder limped into the kitchen. After watching him safely on to the street, Rich closed the external kitchen door, taking the opportunity to inspect the lock. A simple one. Waving away Mrs Madeley's embarrassed protestations, he then insisted on tidying up the storeroom himself. While he replaced the fallen cutlery in the boxes, a few pieces found their way into his pocket. His efforts ensured that when more went missing later, it would be easy to blame the stranger. If he had any sense, the man would make himself scarce.

Hmm. Perhaps Rich could turn the situation even further to his advantage. He returned to the sitting room, where his hostess was waving her silk fan around. "Mrs Madeley, it belatedly occurs to me that the man might not be so innocent."

Her kohl-rimmed eyes widened. "Should we call the police?"

"I don't think that would help since he's gone away now. I do apologise. Perhaps I can make it up to you by offering some help with planning home security?"

"In what way?"

"Well, why don't you tell me about your anti-theft arrangements? For example, are your security automata the newest models?"

She chewed her lip. "Oh dear. We don't have any."

Rich hid a smile by taking a sip of his now-cold tea.

Chapter 3

Bloody toffs. After his peremptory dismissal, Alf stumbled down the street, barely aware of where his footsteps took him. Who cared, as long as it was out of the area? His scalp prickled under his cap, and he tugged the brim lower to hide his face. The street's residents were probably laughing at him from behind their lace curtains.

A foghorn startled him out of his daze. He unclenched his fist to find a florin. Its edges had made ridges in his palm, he was clutching it so tightly.

Over a week's rent! Alf's heart leapt, and he grinned. The landlord wouldn't kick them out, after all. Then he lost the smile, remembering the toff's patronising tone and the woman's vacuous expression beneath all that paint on her face. Still, if the man wanted to show off to her by giving Alf money, that was good, wasn't it?

Street lamps flickered. It was dusk. He glanced up at the high factory walls before him and sniffed brine on the air. Crikey, he'd gone in the opposite direction from home. It would be a long walk. At least it wasn't raining tonight, although a chill was settling into his bad knee.

Ahead of him stood *The Hearty Sailor* pub. At the scent of gravy, his stomach rumbled. He regarded the coin in his hand. If he nipped in there for warmth and a quick bite to eat, Mum could have his uneaten supper for lunch tomorrow. He looked at the coin again. It might also stretch to a pint or two, just to settle his nerves.

◊ ◊ ◊

The front door of Rich's mansion squealed as he opened it. More maintenance he couldn't afford. At least pawning those spoons had covered his expenses for a few more days, but he'd need to do a proper job within the next fortnight. "I'm back," he called.

"Evening, yer lordship." Sally's cheerful voice came from upstairs. "Your supper won't take but a minute to heat up."

"No rush." He placed her modest wages on the hallway table and hung up his coat before going to his living room.

The floorboards were warped but carefully scrubbed, thanks to Sally, and the unlit fireplace held only a few logs. Although it was chilly, he'd rather use a rug than light the fire just for himself. He poured himself a snifter of brandy from his diminishing supply and stood by the window while its warmth spread through his chest.

Sally's light tread sounded behind him. She bore a polished silver tray and a covered plate. As usual, her black dress, white apron and mob cap were spotlessly clean, if displaying signs of wear.

"Good evening." Rich smiled as she laid his dinner on the table. She'd arrived fresh out of school as a scullery maid and had spent the last fifteen years perfecting her housekeeping skills.

Too perfect, perhaps. While he sat, she straightened the cutlery by an infinitesimal amount. A frown creased her brow. "Ain't right, sir."

Here we go again. Even though he was her employer, his one and only maid left him in no doubt who ran the household. "It's perfectly fine, Sally."

"Cabbage and beef dripping isn't suitable fare for nobs.

You can't say you've gone off smoked salmon and them fancy little tarts your parents used to love." Her expression grew dreamy. "And us servants had a grand old time afterwards."

"Ah, so that's the real reason you miss my parents." Their soirées had filled the house with cheer. He pushed aside the pang in his chest with a shake of his head. "My current diet's much healthier than I used to eat."

With an arched eyebrow, she filled his water glass. "Did your day go well?"

"Yes, thank you. Spent the morning reading over proposals to the Council of Lords." That claim at least was true.

"Anything new?" Brandishing a soft cloth, she rubbed a spot on the mirror.

"Not really. The usual demands for change that don't help anyone else." It was so tedious, watching council members try to outmanoeuvre their rivals at the cost of the public good. During Rich's time sitting at hearings, he'd emulated his father and spoken out against proposals that only profited individuals. Of course a man was entitled to strive for a better position, but with nobility came an expectation—nay, an obligation—to care for the lesser classes. It wasn't as if they had the education to make wise decisions for themselves.

The polishing cloth dangled from her fingers. "And how about the afternoon?"

Rich swallowed. Sally's curiosity was nearly as bad as his mother's had been. "Spent it at my club. It's always good to keep an ear to the ground."

"You're not the only one," she muttered.

"What?" He tackled a tough stalk with his knife before

giving up and pushing it to the side of his plate.

She flicked a speck of dust off her apron. "Last night, one of the girls at the boarding house introduced me to the lad she's walking out with. He's a doorman at your club. He says he only sees you there once a week."

Rich paused, fork partway to his mouth. After all this time, why did she have to challenge him now? "Well, there's no reason to go every day–"

"But you always say you spend your afternoons there. You can't keep pretending there's nothing wrong!" She waved at the nearly bare walls, now displaying only unsaleable family portraits. "I've seen the ornaments and paintings disappear, one by one. And you only live in this room, with dust covers over everything else. Plus, letting all your other servants go. Look, if you want help with–"

"Given the political situation, I should allow household staff to move on and prepare for more important roles." He'd made that claim often enough to say it with the ring of conviction. "And it behoves me to adopt a modest lifestyle."

"Bollocks!" She blushed. "Pardon me, sir. But I worry about–"

Trying not to chuckle, he held up a hand. "Sally, I appreciate your concern. And your discretion over the years. How I choose to live my life is *my* decision. As I've told you before, I will not be offended if you seek employment elsewhere."

"Oh, I couldn't do that!" Her apron wrinkled as she clutched it. "You're not going to fire me, are you?"

"What? No, of course not. I'm just reminding you it's an option. You'd be an asset in any household." He ate in guilty silence for a few mouthfuls. Sally had been with the family since Rich was a boy, but he couldn't understand her near-panic whenever he brought up the topic of her moving on. With her skills, she deserved to be a head housekeeper. "Er... and how was your day, Sally?"

She smoothed down her apron. "Usual stuff. Baked, cleaned... oh, the tax collectors came round."

"Tax collectors? Already? But–" His throat closed up.

"Sir?"

He gulped his water. How could he have forgotten the amended quarterly "seat tax" schedule? Every year, each member of the Council of Lords had to contribute to the city's coffers a tenth of the value of his or her Ironfort house. If Rich couldn't pay, he'd lose his seat. And probably the house too, letting his parents down. "What did you tell them?"

"I said you weren't available, and what was wrong with making an appointment rather than knocking on the door without warning?"

"Good girl." He winced at her offended expression. She didn't take guff from anyone. Rich's boyhood memories included sliding across clean wet floors while Sally chased him with a soapy mop. "I mean, thank you."

"They said they'd be back tomorrow morning."

"Damn!" He *had* to do the job tonight. He eyed her doubtful face. "It's such an inconvenience, changing my plans. However, I'll make sure to meet them. I don't need you for anything else this evening, so you might as well go home once you've cleared up."

"Enjoy your evening, sir."

"I'm sure I will, thank you. You too."

Alf smacked his lips and gazed around the smoke-filled bar-room. Since he'd never had much of a head for drink, he was taking his time over this second pint. The chatter of other patrons gave the place a pleasant background hum. At a nearby table, a couple of off-duty sailors tucked into sausages and mash. In the far corner, coins clinked on the table as workmen played cards.

The scent of gravy didn't help Alf's grumbling stomach. However, he'd decided it would be wasteful to buy any food, so the ale would have to do for now. It left him feeling pleasantly detached, which he needed after his encounter in that house. Obviously a life of crime wasn't for him. Well, not that he had *planned* to do anything criminal, but the temptation had been in front of him. "Bloody scientists."

The cauliflower-eared barman nodded sympathetically.

"Bloody technology. And using diamonds! Way out of poor people's reach. Life's not fair." He lifted his tankard and drained it.

"No, things are tough these days." The barman wiped the counter, muscles flexing as he did so.

"And bloody toffs too." Alf's voice rose, and he thumped his tankard on the counter. "My sis has to put up with them, just 'cos they got money."

One of the sailors sniggered. "Pay her well, do they?"

Alf spun, tripping as his foot caught a loose floorboard. "My sis is a good girl! She's got brains, she has. And she makes better use of them than you and your–"

"Now, now." The barman removed empty glasses from easy reach.

The sailor's grin disappeared. "No need to be so touchy, mate."

"Touchy?" Alf's face worked. "No wonder I'm touchy! Thieving bastards, that's all they are. His Bloody High

Lordship–"

"Shut it!" Placing a hand of cards face-down by his pile of coins, a paint-spattered workman glowered. "Can't we play in peace?"

"Peace? Peace?" roared Alf, stomping towards the workmen's table. He slammed a fist on the surface.

Cards and coins scattered over the floor.

The workmen leapt to their feet and closed in on him.

After Sally left, Rich extinguished the downstairs lights as if he was having an early night. At ten o'clock, he changed into dark, nondescript clothing with concealed pockets for his lock picks and grease.

Exiting his house by the side door, he set his cap at a jaunty angle and strolled casually down the path. He had previously taken care to cultivate a reputation as a lord with irregular habits. Just *what* irregular habits might have a visitor depart the servant's door at nearly midnight... He grinned. Well, it would deflect attention from his other actions.

The Madeley's house was a half-hour walk away. Although the air was chilly, the smog had lifted a little. That was another advantage of the new diamond-powered technology: less smoke from burning coal and wood. Of course, there wasn't enough of the new fuel for every need, but it was a start. New sources of diamonds would guarantee fame and fortune to anyone enterprising and lucky enough to find them. And here was Rich, tied to Ironfort with barely a florin to his name. He couldn't afford to travel, whether in search of his parents or of diamonds.

No point feeling down about the matter. Maybe someday he'd get lucky on a job. As he patted his lock picks, his gut quivered with anticipation: nights like this made him feel alive.

The route was generally quiet, other than late shift workers trudging home and the occasional street worker seeking a customer. But wait, someone was cursing quietly ahead, accompanied by tapping noises. Surely Rich wasn't about to witness a mugging? He might feel obliged to intervene, and then there would go his plans.

He peered through the smog as he walked on, and then relaxed. Outside a pub, a burly aproned man was trying to attach boards across a broken window.

"Evening," muttered Rich.

"Not a good one," grumbled the man, rubbing at a misshapen ear. "Bloody fight broke out in my pub, and by the time the bobbies had dragged the culprits off and stomped broken glass all over my floor... Here's me trying to quietly secure my window in the middle of the night. You ever tried to hammer without disturbing anyone?"

"Not exactly," Rich replied truthfully before walking on.

The Madeley's street was empty of pedestrians. An unmanned steam carriage stood outside one of the neighbouring houses. Rich smirked: they obviously had a visitor who didn't want a cabbie blabbing about their movements. These days, citizens were encouraged to retire early, so as not to waste power. The houses were mainly dark, although an intermittent glow moved in a few of the windows. Those would be from security automata's sensors as they patrolled the house or rotated in place, depending on how sophisticated they were. Rich's title ensured that security firms informed him of recent developments, even though he'd quietly sold his own automata last year.

Soon, that would all change. He ambled towards the Madeley's kitchen door but paused when a glint from the front window caught his eye. An automaton? But she said she didn't have one. Holding his breath, he peered through the window.

Damn! Not quite the height of a postbox, the wheeled column glided around the sitting room where he'd taken tea just that afternoon. Its dome-shaped head swivelled and cast a blue glow on its surroundings. He nearly groaned. His talk about home security must have prompted her to rush out and buy one. No wonder she'd looked so thoughtful when he left. If only he'd kept quiet.

He padded back to the main street and walked on. Now what? Ordinarily, he'd have given up for the night, but with the tax collectors on his heels, he didn't have that option.

A nearby door creaked.

Rich glanced around, wondering if someone would depart in that carriage, but the driveway remained quiet and dark. Hang on, a side door was open a couple of buildings further up. Even better, there was no tell-tale glow from any of that house's front windows. Rich had no idea who lived there, but surely it was worth checking out? He crept up the path and slipped inside.

Chapter 4

Rich squinted in the dim light from the side window and half-open exterior door. Unsurprisingly, he was in a kitchen. He sniffed. The scent of parsnip and carrot lingered in the air, as well as roast beef. Oh, and mango. He inhaled more deeply with nostalgia. The imported fruit told him that this household, at least, didn't stint on food expenses. Hopefully there would be good pickings.

He stepped carefully across to the internal door. After silently easing it open, he entered the hallway, thankful that this house maintained its hinges. One advantage of these not-quite-so-grand houses was that domestic staff didn't live in, so he wouldn't be blundering into some poor maid's bedroom. Not that Sally lived in either now: they couldn't afford *that* kind of talk, and so he'd had to give her a room allowance too.

When a dark, man-height silhouette loomed in front of him, Rich flinched. But it didn't move. He patted its solid bulk then chuckled at his paranoia. It was far too large for a security automaton, plus it had arm-like protrusions. Maybe the householder collected odd sculptures. Not that its nature mattered: Rich couldn't possibly steal something that size, no matter how much it was worth.

Where should he search first? The sitting room seemed best. It was unlikely the owners stored heaps of valuables at the back of the house as Mrs Madeley did. Luckily for him, not everyone was cautious enough to organise a vault.

He gave the statue a final prod before creeping past a

staircase towards the front of the house. The sitting-room door stood ajar. Rich eased it wide open until it gently bumped into some solid piece of furniture: an old-fashioned bulky leather sofa. Then he slid inside, taking small, cautious steps on the unfamiliar carpeted floorboards. A street lamp shone through the bay window, and bare trees cast grotesque patterns on the wall.

At least there was enough light to see. Rather than the usual display cabinets, a large desk dominated the room. Stacks of papers lay on its surface. The top sheet bore a line drawing surrounded by squiggles. Some kind of technical design? What a shame, nothing obvious that he could fence.

A creak came from upstairs.

Rich froze, his pulse increasing.

A male voice muttered something and got a reply. Damn! The occupants were still awake. Should he dive for the kitchen door, or take his chances and stay? Exiting through the window would ruin his clothing.

Too late! As heavy feet descended the stairs, he scuttled into a gap behind the sofa. Cursing his height, he crouched and prayed that nobody would enter the sitting room. He pushed the door part-closed and peered through the crack of the hinge, but the hallway was too dark to make anything out.

"What a palaver," grunted a hoarse male voice.

"Shut up. Let's just get the job done." The second voice was higher-pitched but also male, breathing heavily.

When the door banged into the sofa, Rich nearly yelped. He hunched over on all fours and pressed himself against the wall. The floorboards bounced under his trembling knees as someone strode into the room.

A shadow loomed on the wall. Biting his lip, Rich

tensed. Paper rustled, and the footsteps receded into the hallway, leaving an acrid smell behind.

The hoarse voice said, “Gimme a moment. I’ll grab the diamond from the security auto–”

“No, we’re not to touch anything else.”

“But–”

“Idiot! Boss’ll kill you.”

“Oh. Right.”

The footsteps shuffled off. The kitchen door clicked shut. Straightening up, Rich wiped sweat off his brow. He took deep breaths until his head stopped spinning.

A clunk outside made his heart jump, but it was followed by the rhythmic chug of a steam engine.

Of course, they were using that empty carriage he’d passed earlier. Trust him to wander into a house that someone else was already hitting. He’d be lucky if there was anything left–

Hang on, hadn’t one of those men said something about a diamond? There was a security automaton–surely the sculpture in the hall–powered by *a diamond*? It must be an experimental model that had malfunctioned. How lucky, and luckier still the burglars had opted not to steal its power source. Industrial diamonds were cut to a standard size, so it wouldn’t be recognised when he sold it.

Excellent. He’d remove the diamond from that automaton, then he’d go home. He’d pushed his chances far enough tonight.

In the darkened hallway, he sidled towards the automaton, his breath shallow and heart racing. His fingers stroked the chill metal casing, seeking a seam. What size prising tool would be best? If the diamond power removed the need for a clockwork winding handle–

Its eyes flicked on, glowing red. Steel hands clamped his arms. The house lights came to life, revealing his massive mechanical opponent. He struggled while it pulled him into a crushing embrace.

"Intruder!" The automaton's screech made his ears ring.

Alf's head ached, although he was pretty sure nobody had bashed it. He tentatively probed his split lip and glowered at the man snoring in the opposite cell. Other drunks who'd been rounded up had gone to sleep on their bunks as if getting arrested was routine. The crumbling wall at his back felt too real for all this to be a bad dream.

Ironfort's main police station was a well-known historical landmark, and Alf passed it daily on his way to the docks. However, he'd never expected to be locked up inside. The cells were in the basement, and his barred window gave him a view of a moss-covered wall. It was topped with railings, on the other side of which lay the street.

He lay down again with his prosthesis wedged against the wall. What was he going to say to Mum? What would she think when he didn't return home? His head throbbed even more at the thought of the money he'd lost: someone must have snatched it during the fight. So much for paying the household expenses. It was all that toff's fault for giving him the money in the first place. He glared towards his barred cell door.

There were four rows of six cells each, partitioned with decrepit brick walls to shoulder height. Obviously they weren't supporting walls, and bars extended above them to the ceiling. Alf's cell had two bunks, but he was the only occupant. He glanced at the chamber pot, which contained evidence of his distressing evening. At least he hadn't had to do his business in full view of other prisoners.

Going by the chimes from the clock tower, the night guard checked on the cells hourly. He only gave the rooms a cursory glance before heading upstairs again. That was a small relief. Each time the man's bald head passed Alf's cell, the scent of liver sausage wafted towards him, reminding him he'd not had any dinner.

Footsteps sounded on the stairwell. Alf's brow creased. Surely it hadn't been an hour already? Maybe he'd dozed off without realising. Keeping his eyes half-closed, he squinted through his cell door.

The night guard appeared, scratching his bald pate. Behind him, two constables with peaked caps escorted a single prisoner. The man was tall but skinny–a bit scrawny to merit two policemen, surely–and dressed in dark clothing.

The smaller constable glanced around the cells. "Pretty quiet tonight."

"Just the usual drunk and disorderly," said the night guard. "Still glad to be patrolling the streets, Benj?"

"At least I'm not getting fat," said Benj.

"Hey, I have to process this lot before the day shift starts. If you knew the paperwork–"

The larger constable cleared his throat. "Just make sure you don't release this one by accident. He's to be charged."

The night guard snorted. "I've been doing this since well before you joined the force." After consulting his notebook, he unlocked the empty cell beside Alf's, gesturing for the prisoner to enter.

The door clanged shut, and the lock clicked.

Benj said, "Right, I want my handcuffs back."

Chains jingled. "Sorry?"

Standing outside Alf's cell, the night guard rolled his eyes. "We're not barbarians. The cuffs come off now that you're inside the cell. Put your hands through the bars."

"Well, that's a relief. Much obliged."

Alf raised an eyebrow at the prisoner's refined voice. Who would have believed it? It wasn't only poor folks who landed in prison.

Chains jangled, and Benj stepped away, tucking the handcuffs into his belt. "Of course, we're hanging on to your lock picks and other belongings. Chain of evidence, and all that." He chuckled as the three policemen left the room.

For some odd reason, this new neighbour's voice seemed familiar. Alf swung himself upright. Since he couldn't sleep, he might as well have a look at the guy. He hobbled over to the bars separating the cells.

The man was sitting on the bunk, inspecting his boots. His fingers tapped out an irregular rhythm on his knees. As Alf approached, he raised his head.

That toff! Alf gaped. "You!"

After the policemen left, Rich groaned and ran his hands through his thinning hair. How could things have gone so wrong? He'd never heard of a security automaton catching intruders rather than simply raising the alarm. It had held him fast until a posse of constables arrived and dragged him away.

He'd given the police his false name, glad he'd set up a rudimentary second identity. It wouldn't stand up to deep scrutiny, but it would do for a minor thieving charge. And after the police found his tools, he could hardly deny his intentions. The only possible bright spot was that since

Rich technically hadn't stolen anything–being caught red-handed inside the house–he would only be convicted of breaking and entering. That was up to a month's jail time, less if he cooperated. All he needed to do now was create a fiction that Lord Hayes had left Ironfort on urgent business. Mere coincidence that Henry Duggins was in jail for the same amount of time.

"You!" came a growl.

Rich's head jerked up. He met the glare of a stocky man in the next cell. "Have we met?"

"Ha, you don't even remember. It's your fault I'm here."

Great, they'd put him next door to a madman. "My good sir, I assure you–"

"Bloody toffs."

"Toff?" *I need to be Henry Duggins.* He swallowed. "I'm not–"

"Your posh voice and everything. You gave me money, remember? Or maybe you throw florins at everyone."

Oh, of course. It was that chap he'd seen off from the Madeley house. "Look, I'm not really a toff. Yer mus' be mistaken, ay."

"So what *are* you?" The man scratched his head, leaving his mousy hair in disarray. "Lock picks? You're a *thief*?"

"Pipe down, you two!" came a grumble from a prisoner across the way.

Thoughts racing, Rich stood and approached the bars. His interrogator wore the same shabby clothes as earlier, but they were if anything more crumpled, and a split lip had been added to the ensemble. Drunk and disorderly, indeed. That meant an opportunity: a chance to get a message to Sally.

He tried not to wrinkle his nose at the reek of spilled

beer. “Well done, sir. Even after a couple of drinks, you have your wits about you.”

“Oh?”

“Yes, not only do you pay attention to your surroundings, you think about what you observe.”

The man rubbed his knee and then straightened. “Well, yeah, ignoring stuff can lead to accidents.”

“In fact, I could do with your help.”

The man’s eyes narrowed. “And why should I help you?”

“Can you keep a secret?” Rich glanced around, his gaze settling on his interlocutor’s lapel. For his injury badge, he’d picked the Lesser Grenian flag rather than the more neutral heart. “We wouldn’t want, ah, unfriendly foreign ears to pass this information on.”

“Hmm. You look pretty foreign yourself.”

“Of course I do!” Rich spread his hands. “How could I blend in with Calesians otherwise?”

“Blend in? Why would you want to–Oh.” His eyes widened. “I know how to keep my mouth shut. But this had better be good.”

“The thieving is a cover story. I’m a... secret agent. Working for the Council of Lords.”

A sneer met *that* claim. “Secret agents visit nobs for tea and then break into their houses?”

“Listen. The most dangerous dissidents are the high-status ones you don’t suspect. What better cover for traitors than in respectable neighbourhoods? It’s not as if they go around announcing themselves. I interview people openly, and afterwards I explore their environments”–he winked–“more informally. In most cases, I am pleased to say, my findings prove their loyal status. What’s your name, by the way?"

"Alf. Alf Wilson." Gripping the bars, Alf leaned closer. "Go on."

"Wilson? A name with a long history. And you're out of work, I think you mentioned?"

"Yeah. I was with Cummings Naval Supplies, then he sold the factory and we all got laid off."

Rich's mind flicked through council reports. Cummings had retired to the country. Using his name wouldn't cause any harm. "Ah, yes. I investigated him six months ago."

"And?" A frown crossed Alf's face.

"He's no traitor." Rich smiled internally as Alf's shoulders relaxed. "But he was under considerable external pressure. I hate to think what might have happened if he'd yielded. But with our support, he could do the honourable thing and retire. Of course, this kind of thing doesn't get mentioned in public."

"He was a decent boss, taking me on even with..." Alf waved at his leg.

"It would have been dreadful if Cummings had been forced into an untenable situation, and I'm glad we could nip it in the bud. So, Alf, can you appreciate the delicate work we do? Behind the scenes, so to say."

"Wow." Alf stroked his unshaven chin. "I had no idea it was so complicated."

"My current problem is, nobody will bail me out because officially we don't exist." Rich shrugged. "Of course, I could be telling you a pack of lies."

"That's what I thought to begin with." Alf chuckled quietly.

"And no wonder! But I'll give you my final proof. Once

they let you out, look at the morning paper headlines." Council papers included a brief on imminent news items, not that Alf would know that. "You'll already know diamonds are in demand. But now King Michael himself is offering a reward to anyone who can locate new diamond mines. The announcement will be tomorrow. Investors will be keen to send out expeditions, and they'll pay well. They'll have to recruit explorers and assistants, but with most folk already joining the military there will be opportunities for employment. You could even consider it yourself."

"Bloody diamonds." Alf looked thoughtful. "But they won't want a one-legged man. You get paid for this secret stuff?"

"Oh yes, the money's quite good." Rich suppressed a smile. "And we're always seeking talented new recruits. Given that you lost your job, it's only fair that I make you aware of what else is around. Favour for a favour, so to say."

"So... I look at the papers. Then what?"

"If what you read convinces you I'm telling the truth, I want you to do something on my behalf. If you decide I'm lying, you can let the constables know. They might even reward you for providing evidence."

"Well, alright then. What d'you want me to do?"

"Visit a house on Parlay Square and speak to a woman called Sally..."

Chapter 5

Alf slunk out of the police station at dawn, his leg dragging. His head pounded like it contained its own steam engine, reminding him why he ought to stay off the booze.

Fortunately, they'd released him with only a caution, and the fellows he'd been fighting with last night had lost their combative mood. They headed off in different directions with no more than a hostile glare.

His footsteps took him round the back of the police station and towards the docks before he remembered he wasn't going to work. Hoping that nobody had noticed his blunder–not that anyone would care–he looked around, wondering if there might be any chance to find employment. Given how he'd spent last night, he'd better make up for it with a productive day.

At this hour, the industrial district was still deserted. The motley collection of workshops included flag dyers, automaton builders and locksmiths. Alf frowned: he lacked the specialist knowledge to work there. However, ahead of him stood an idle crane, presumably for shifting heavy deliveries. His hands twitched. Perhaps he could return later and see if they needed a backup driver, but there was no point in hanging around. He hunched his shoulders against the cold and headed to the market district.

As he approached a newspaper stand, his steps slowed, and he huffed. How could he have forgotten Rich's fantastic story and request? With a nod at the paper boy, he checked the headline:

STAR SCIENTIST KIDNAPPED! CALESIAN SPY CAUGHT RED-HANDED!

Calesian spies in Ironfort? And their victim was Professor Ina Bergrim-Hoyt, inventor of the diamond-powered generator. Alf growled under his breath. The woman might have caused him trouble with her invention, but foreigners dragging her off was beyond the pale.

Still, nothing about diamonds. Bloody fake toff. Alf's ears heated at the thought of how easily he'd been taken in. Maybe he should tell the police what Rich had claimed. Though, given how smoothly the bloke had suggested it, it was probably another bluff and would just make him look even more stupid. Better forget the matter, head home and square things with Mum. He made a face at the thought of her martyred expression.

"Paper, sir?" The paper boy held one out.

Alf shook his head. "No cash."

"You want an old edition?" He lifted a sheet from a pile behind him. "No charge. With the new headline coming up so suddenly, these ones are going back to pulp."

"Well, alright then," said Alf. At worst, they could use it to light the stove or in the privy. He accepted the paper and walked away before he glanced at the front page.

A cry of "Oi!" from a steam carriage halted Alf's steps before he stepped out in front of it. Yikes! If being distracted by Rich got him run over, that would really take the biscuit.

Alf ducked his head as the driver hurled curses, then he returned his attention to the newspaper headline.

KING MICHAEL PLEDGES LARGE REWARD FOR DISCOVERY OF NEW DIAMOND MINES

Wow. He skimmed the article. It mentioned an obscenely large reward to any individual or team that could locate a new source of diamonds. There was a snide editorial comment about the reward attracting gamblers and crooks.

Who would have believed it? Rich was telling the truth after all. Alf grinned. If they were recruiting more secret agents, he might have a chance at a job. And if they offered him one on the spot, he could even go home with good news for Mum. His smile widened. Though he'd have to keep his mouth shut about the exact nature of his new employment. Tucking the paper under one arm, he walked on.

His footsteps took him to Parlay Square. He didn't often come here because it was where the really posh nobs lived. Paved footpaths criss-crossed the central lawn, and a gardener weeded flowerbeds.

Finding the right house, Alf walked up the side path to the servants' entrance. Statues of cherubs watched him disapprovingly through badly trimmed bushes. A curtain twitched in the front window.

When he knocked at the door, flecks of paint fell off its surface. Not quite what he'd expected.

The door opened a crack. "Yes?" came a woman's voice.

Alf snatched off his cap. "Are you Sally?"

"I am–Oh! It's Alphonse Wilson, isn't it?"

"Yes?" He blinked at the gap in the door. The voice was vaguely familiar, and less snooty than he'd expected for a toff's house staff. "But I'm just here to deliver a message."

"Don't you remember me?" The door swung wide with a creak. "Come on in, no point letting the cold into the house."

Alf gaped at the figure before him. Her schoolgirl pigtails were gone, or at least covered by the mob cap, and the faded black dress hid any grazed knees. But the amused dimples and long dark lashes brought back memories of passing notes in class. And trading boiled sweets. And imaginative dreams. His knuckles whitened as he gripped his cap tighter. "You're Sally Rosely!"

Her throaty chuckle made the hairs on his arms stand on end. "You noticed! You did ask for me, after all."

His face grew warm. "Well, I couldn't see you through the door, and..." Sally's quick tongue was one reason he'd not attempted to stay in touch. And after she'd gone off to work for some nob, he'd said farewell to thoughts of further friendship. "You've worked *here* since leaving school?" Did that mean she was Rich's assistant?

"Pretty much. Been with the family for fifteen years now." As he limped in, she glanced down. "Have you hurt your leg?"

He shifted his weight on to his good leg and cleared his throat. "Industrial accident."

"Oh, I'm sorry." She peered at his bruised face then pointed to a stool by an enormous granite-topped table. "Perch yourself there. Tea's brewing."

Alf did as he was told while she shut the door. The scent of baking bread made his mouth water, and his head swam in the kitchen's warmth. "Might there be a slice of bread?" He shut his mouth. Not the best way to impress her.

She folded her arms reproachfully. "It's for the master's breakfast."

"Ah. I don't think he'll be wanting breakfast. He's in jail."

"*What?*" Sally stared at him. "The house was empty when I arrived, but I assumed he'd gone to the bank."

Alf gulped. Had he fallen for a trick, and landed himself in it with Sally? "He sure *sounded* convincing. Tall, thin, Calesian-looking guy, pointy nose. Balding, though from his face he's barely twenty. And he..." He tried to put on a nobby accent. "*...tawks laike thies?*"

She tittered, then covered her mouth with a hand. "Sorry. Sounds exactly like I'd describe him. Though he's a tad older–just ten years younger than us. You'd better tell me everything." Without asking, she poured a mug of tea, adding a dash of milk and two sugars. She remembered how he liked it!

"Well, I'd had a spot of trouble..." Slurping his tea, Alf shared the brief information he'd received. Rich's clandestine mission had gone wrong. Hence, he'd been arrested for breaking and entering. "... So you're to tell anyone who asks that he was called away on urgent family business. He plans to do his time under the false name, and he hopes you can manage without him for a while."

Sally's jaw dropped. "*He told you he was a secret agent?*"

"Oh, wasn't I supposed to mention that? I'd assumed you knew, but this whole business is confusing."

A clockwork timer dinged. Grabbing an oven glove, she opened the range door and pulled out a baking tray. When she turned round again, her lips were pursed. "The master hasn't thought this out very well. Him and his bright ideas."

"Sorry, I'm just the messenger. Didn't even know if it was a pack of lies. Does Rich really sit on the Council of Lords as well as his secret agent stuff?"

"I'm just a maid and in no position to comment about secret business. He's certainly a lord. Not that he acts like one, mind. He's taken to eating cabbage and dripping for his supper, along with this bread." On seeing Alf's longing glance at the bread that was now cooling on a rack, she sliced and buttered a piece and handed it to him. "His heart's in the right place, but the chances he takes... I have a bad feeling about this."

"How come?" Alf mumbled with a full mouth. The butter melting into the warm bread was heaven.

"He's always been able to talk his way out of trouble, but jail is a completely different matter. Especially if he's using a secret identity. Even he acknowledges that, since he sent you here. We need to do something."

"Hey, hey!" There she went, automatically taking charge. Now that Alf was an adult, he wasn't going to dance to her tune. "What's this 'we' business? I just said I'd deliver a message! I'm not sticking my neck out further for no reason." Sally obviously knew more than she was letting on, but they probably had rules on what she was allowed to say. Not wanting to beg her for a job, he shut his mouth.

"Listen, Alf. I've had a nosy at the paperwork he brings home from council meetings." She winked. "He makes sure us working folk have a voice. His parents were the same."

"Were?"

"They went away three years ago and haven't contacted the master since. Good people. They even paid for me to get extra schooling." She sliced more bread for him.

"Three years?" This piece was topped with strawberry jam. He licked a blob off his finger, its tart sweetness making his tastebuds sing.

"So... things have been difficult."

"I can imagine." Alf eyed Sally's anxious face and the grey hairs peeking out from under her cap. She'd smiled when he arrived, and he felt guilty for bringing bad news. "But still—"

The bang of a door knocker sounded from the front.

Sally gasped. "The tax collectors! And Rich not here!"

What was the big deal? "Can't you just tell them to come back some other time?"

She shook her head. "Did that yesterday. I can't put them off for a whole month. They'll go and seek an order or something–Oh Alf, I could lose my job!"

That did it. Helping her seemed like something he'd regret less than not helping her, especially if he wanted to see her again. "Can I help?"

She gazed up at the ceiling and clenched her fists before turning to him with wide eyes. "Yes. Yes, you can. Upstairs. Second bedroom on the left. Change into something nobby. I'll keep them occupied, give them tea and so on. You pretend you're leasing the place for the month."

Alf gaped. This sounded completely mad. But what if it was a secret agent test?

"Got it?" demanded Sally.

"Uh, yeah. Change. Nobby. Lease." That was renting for posh folks, wasn't it?

"Go!" She dragged him out of the kitchen and shoved him towards a flight of stairs. The knock came again, and she hurried towards the door as Alf hobbled up the steps, muttering, "Second on the left."

◊ ◊ ◊

Rich was woken at some ungodly hour by the clang of cell doors. The other prisoners were being released, Alf among their number.

The night guard paused by his door and gave him a nasty grin. "Not you, mate. Inspector Castor is looking forward to your interview."

Rich shrugged. No point in giving the man more ammunition. "Any chance of breakfast while I wait for him?" When the guard snorted, he added, "Subsection thirteen of the 'Humane Treatment of Prisoners Act'—"

"Where'd you learn that? I've not seen you in here before."

Damn. But soon afterwards, a breakfast tray was shoved under his cell door. The watery porridge wasn't much worse than that in his own household, though he did miss the bread that Sally baked every day.

Hopefully Alf would keep his word, but trusting him was a gamble. However, even if he told the police, they wouldn't seek to disturb Lord Hayes based on a ridiculous story from an uneducated labourer.

Rich considered the scenarios. Of paramount importance was maintaining his working-class identity, rather than implicating the Hayes name in petty crime. At worst, he'd be found guilty of conspiring with that other gang of thieves, and he'd end up doing time. Perhaps optimism wasn't warranted, but he had hopes of Sally's quick wits. Even if Alf didn't contact her, she'd come up with some plausible excuse for the tax collectors.

After the day guard removed the breakfast tray, footsteps sounded on the stairs. A gaunt man in a fur-trimmed trench coat walked into the room, followed by a clerk. It seemed that Inspector Castor had arrived. Rich stood.

Castor surveyed the room. "No other prisoners?"

"No, sir," said the clerk. "All drunk and disorderly, so we released them earlier."

"Saves money if we don't have to feed them." Wearing a thin smile, he strolled over to the cells. He was nearly as tall as Rich. "And this is the culprit."

"Suspect." Rich eyed Castor's wispy beard. Thinning

hair was one thing, but at least a man could shave rather than dangling a rat's tail from his chin.

An eyebrow rose. "Hardly any difference when caught red-handed." He snapped a finger, and the clerk hurried over with a chair. He sat down and pulled out a notebook. "I'm Inspector Castor. You are... Henry Duggins. Last night you were apprehended in a private household by a security automaton. Are you going to claim you wandered in by accident?"

"No." Rich licked his lips. "I had planned to burgle the place. But believe me, I picked it because the door was open. Once inside, I found another team at work. I didn't touch any valuables."

"A likely story." Castor's lip curled. "And I suppose you'll say you had no idea there was a kidnapping going on right under your nose?"

"A kidnapping?" With the room closing in on him, Rich gripped the rusty bars. "I knew nothing about that, honest!"

A messenger clattered down the stairs and handed the clerk a paper.

The clerk cleared his throat. "Sir? Our telegram reached Chief Inspector Kirby. He's returning from his holiday to deal with the case."

Kirby! Rich's hands trembled. The man had previously visited Rich's house, generally for discussions about policy with his father. He'd even addressed the Council of Lords a couple of times. No way would he fail to recognise the prisoner.

Castor glowered. "I'm perfectly capable of handling this myself."

"Chief Inspector Kirby insisted. Leave everything, keep the prisoner here, and he'll handle it on his return. He's chartering an airship to minimise delay."

With a wave of his hand, Castor dismissed the others and stood. "Well, Duggins, it seems you have a small reprieve. You'd better think up a good story for the Chief Inspector."

While Castor departed, Rich kept his chin up despite his roiling gut. Some reprieve. No longer burglary but kidnapping. Even if the victim's family paid the ransom, that wouldn't get Rich out of jail. And with his messenger gone, where could he find help?

Alf tugged at his tweedy sleeves, then readjusted the strangling cravat around his neck. At least the trousers fastened, although he'd had to fold up the legs. His own honest togs lay strewn atop an enormous four-poster bed.

He scowled at himself in the mirror, wincing as his split lip twinged. Nothing more for it. Sally was keeping the visitors downstairs occupied, and she was relying on his help. He set his shoulders back and raised his chin. Time to impersonate a nob.

His leg still wasn't powered up since the winder was at home, so he limped down the stairs. Not wanting to trip on the ragged carpet, he kept a careful grip on the banister. If he fell and ripped the trousers, displaying his arse to all, it probably wouldn't create a good impression.

In the wood-panelled entrance hall, a hat stand held two bowler hats. Voices sounded from a door that was ajar. His feet scuffed on the floorboards, and he shuffled into a room far bigger than his whole flat.

Blimey! Alf gaped at the velvet curtains and massive fireplace before Sally's cough brought him back to his senses.

She bobbed him a curtsey. "Good morning, sir!"

Grinning nervously at her demure expression, he waved a hand. "Be at ease, my good woman." Was that how toffs spoke? He looked at the two men perched on nearby shabby armchairs, each holding a cup of tea. "And who might these fellas be?"

The older visitor set his teacup on an inlaid side table and tugged his ample white beard. "I'm Mr Farlow from the Tax Office, and this is my colleague, Mr Mont. Lord Hayes is due to make his quarterly patriotic contribution." He glanced at Sally. "But I gather he's not here."

"That's right," said Sally. "After you came yesterday, a messenger told me he'd been called away on urgent family business." She wrung her hands. "You know his parents have been absent for three years? If they made contact again, I wouldn't be surprised that the young master rushed off. So that the house wouldn't remain unoccupied, he arranged for, Mr, uh, Smith here to rent the house for the month."

The younger visitor–Mont–ran a hand through oiled wavy hair, his nose twitching. "And are you of noble blood, Mr... Smith?"

With the jacket collar scratching the back of his neck, Alf stuck his nose in the air. "Of course I am"–Sally shook her head frantically–"not! I'm not."

Mont gave him a sceptical look. "So, lacking a town house of your own, you've opted to rent this one from Lord Hayes. I take it you've recently arrived in Ironfort?"

With concern deepening his facial wrinkles, Farlow added, "I can't help noticing you've been injured. I do hope local ruffians haven't spoiled your visit. Rest assured, the Ironfort police force are determined in their pursuit of crime."

Yikes! Alf glanced at Sally's carefully neutral face. Of course she couldn't help him. He'd need to create an explanation himself. What was topical? "I'm a self-made man, I am. Heard of an interest in diamonds and thought it was worth checking things out for myself." He forced a laugh, waving at his sore lip. "As for this, it was my own fault. Fancied a bout of fisticuffs. Sally here was kind enough to direct me to a local club. But I'm not as fit as I used to be."

"Diamonds? Interesting." Farlow sipped his tea. "And you also injured your leg boxing? Reputable clubs shouldn't permit attacks below–"

"It's nothing, honest!" Would they insist on looking at his leg? "Besides, you shoulda seen the other bloke after I gave him a right good–"

"The lease was all quite a rush," blurted Sally. "I wasn't able to remind Lord Hayes about his contribution before he left. No forwarding address, I'm afraid. Surely Mr Smith here isn't liable?"

Alf felt a bit of bluster was warranted, especially where money was involved. He glared at the wall, which held a row of portraits that looked like Rich. "That's right! I rented this house in good faith, and I certainly didn't expect to be met with a tax bill."

"Understandable," said Farlow. "It's a considerable sum of money. No doubt you'd rather spend your hard-earned cash on something else."

The amount he mentioned made Alf's eyes water. And Rich was supposed to pay that four times a year? "Too bloody right! Got plenty of other things I want to buy. I'm glad I'm not a noble."

"Clearly you're not," murmured Mont. He stood. "But

thank you for clearing up the matter. When Lord Hayes returns, I'm sure he'll meet his obligations."

While Sally showed the tax collectors out, Alf slumped on one of the chairs. His head spun. Had he gone completely bonkers?

Sally returned and perched on the other chair with a grin. "We did it! That's got them off our backs for a bit."

At the sight of her dimples, Alf cheered up. They were worth the effort. "Do you remember covering up for Ellis and Katie when they snuck on board that ship one night, and it set sail?"

"Oh, I do! Though come to think of it, Ellis said he'd pay me back and he never did."

"Hey, they never paid me back either. And *I* was the one who got soaked getting them back to shore. At your suggestion, as I remember."

"Well, it worked." Her smile faded. "If only matters were so straightforward this time. I need to visit the jail and find out what's really going on."

"But it's not really your responsibility to sort out, is it?" He couldn't imagine sticking his nose into his old foreman's problems. Surely personal service wasn't so different? It wasn't as if servants were family. "If things get really bad, you could find a job somewhere else?"

"I've been with the family since I was a junior maid." She raised her chin. "His parents treated me like I was— They were good to me. I'm not deserting them now."

He scowled. What did she see in Rich? "You sound grateful to be running around, doing stuff for him."

"I am!" She met his glare then deflated. "Anyway, it's not so easy to find another job."

"Tell me about it. I got laid off a couple of days ago."

"Oh, I'm sorry! No wonder you're so grumpy."

"Grumpy? You're one to talk–" Alf shut his mouth. Better get out before he provoked an argument and blew his chances of seeing her again. Difficult though she could be, he'd never met anyone else like her. He glanced at the staircase. Obviously he couldn't have a quick nap before he left. "Well, I'll just go and put my regular togs on and be off. Good luck."

Sally opened her mouth, looking mulish, then paused. "Thanks for your help. Er... where are you living these days?"

Alf's heart leapt. He hadn't ruined his chances with her! Though she wouldn't be impressed with his flat. He provided his address, muttering, "Pop in sometime. But I don't know how much longer we'll be there. We'll get kicked out if I can't pay the rent."

Chapter 6

Rich paced his cell, wearing the dingy tiled flooring down further. He studied his grimy hands with distaste. No doubt the rest of him was equally unimpressive. Other than the guard's hourly checks, he was alone. His stomach quivered although, he couldn't say whether it was hunger or nerves. The lunchtime tray hadn't yet arrived.

The suspicion of kidnapping was bad enough, but Kirby's arrival would be a disaster. He would recognise Rich, and then the game would be up.

Closing his eyes, Rich pressed his forehead against the rough brick wall. With his thoughts darting like a clockwork mouse, he indulged in far-fetched scenarios. Maybe the ransom demand would stipulate release of any kidnappers. *Sure.* Or Kirby would prioritise some other case. *Hmm.* Not quite so unlikely, given political tensions and the potential for fraud over diamonds. Kirby's absence would allow Rich to plead guilty and serve his time as Duggins. Poor Sally. If his message didn't get through, she might think he'd vanished like his parents.

His shoulders slumped at the thought of failing Mother and Father. Before they'd left, they made him promise to hold the family seat on the Council of Lords. For a moment, he clenched his jaw in resentment. So why couldn't they have left him an allowance to maintain the house? He'd been *forced* into unconventional means.

Admittedly, his forays into burglary had given him an illicit thrill. Initial, tentative experiments with lock picks had sparked a compulsion to use them in earnest. Anyway, what other source of money was there? While nobles might invest, or direct, or be consulted for advice, they didn't actually *work* for pay. That distinguished them from the lower classes, along with their better education. Any paid menial employment would require a false persona: an unpalatable combination of tedium and risk.

Two sets of footsteps sounded on the stairs. Rich tensed. When Sally followed a weasel-faced guard into the room, he puffed out a breath of relief. After all those worries, Alf had kept his promise. It was a pleasant surprise that Sally had decided to visit. He'd better think of some reward for her loyalty.

The guard inspected Rich before addressing Sally. "Early twenties, like a beanpole and balding, just like you said. So is he yer brother, Miss Duggins?"

"Yes." She stepped up to the bars. "I'm glad I thought to ask here after he didn't come home last night. It's so much better than finding him in the hospital or morgue."

"Sally, am I glad to see you!" Rich resisted the temptation to run a hand through his hair. *Balding indeed.*

She removed her bonnet and unbuttoned her cape, revealing a thoroughly respectable blue gingham dress. "What trouble are you in now, Rich?"

"Rich?" The guard frowned, stroking his unshaven jaw. "You said your name was Henry."

Sally's gaze flicked between Rich and the guard, and she gulped. Obviously she was new to the game of misdirection.

"Oh, it is!" said Rich. "But they call me 'Rich' because I'm always broke."

"Well? Where were you?" Voice shrill, she waved a finger at him.

Rich couldn't bamboozle the eavesdropping constable the way he had Alf, and Sally was unlikely to believe him either. He could only tell the truth. "I was on a burglary job, but turns out another gang was hitting the same house. I'd no idea they were kidnapping someone, honest!" He held up his hands. "You know me, wouldn't hurt a fly."

"Of course you wouldn't–" Sally blinked. "Hang on, kidnapping?"

The guard grinned. "Yeah, it was all over the newspaper. Professor Bergrim-Hoyt is a juicy target."

"*Professor Bergrim-Hoyt?*" Rich clung to the bars for support, hating how his voice came out in a squeak.

"Mark my words," said the guard, "this'll be a hanging offence."

"But..." Spots danced in front of Rich's eyes, and his head swam.

Sally whispered, "Hanging?" She swayed.

The guard grabbed Inspector Castor's chair and assisted Sally to sit. "Sorry, I should have worded that better."

She gazed at her boots. "This is quite a shock."

"Obviously *you* weren't involved, miss. I can tell by your reaction." He patted her shoulder. "They teach us how to read people."

Rich nearly snorted. That certainly wasn't in the police training curriculum.

"How clever." Fanning herself with her bonnet, Sally licked her lips. "I wonder... would you mind *very* much fetching me a glass of water?"

"Regulations say–"

"Please?" Her eyelids fluttered. "I'm feeling rather faint."

"Well, alright. Since you're such a delicate little thing." With a final pat on her arm, he walked away, calling, "Don't worry, I'll be back before you know it."

As soon as the guard's hasty footsteps ascended the stairs, Sally glared at Rich. "Idiot, what kind of story was that?"

Rich gaped. "It's true!"

"Couldn't you have made up something more convincing? Like, you noticed something suspicious, and so–"

"I had lock picks in my pocket!"

Fists clenched, she stood. Within a split second, her hand slipped through the bars to grab Rich's ear. He yelped as she dragged his head down to her level and back to his teenage exploits.

"I've had enough of your feckless ways," she snarled. "You remember the last time I did this, don't you? When you climbed out the window?"

"Uh, yes?" He'd been thirteen, and Sally had caught him late one night. She'd never mentioned it again. What had got into her now? "Look, I really didn't–"

"Miss?" came the guard's strained voice. He hovered awkwardly behind her with a glass. "Would you mind stepping away from the prisoner? Please?"

Sally's vice-like grip loosened, and Rich straightened up, massaging his abused ear.

She offered the guard a tense smile and accepted the glass. "Sorry, lost my temper there. You know how kid brothers are, always sneaking out the window and whatnot. They never learn responsibility. What happens now?"

"We're holding him until Chief Inspector Kirby returns to the city."

"I see. Henry got himself into trouble, and he can get

himself back out."

A cold lump of betrayal landed in Rich's stomach. "But, Sally—"

She threw the contents of the glass into his face. As he spluttered, she handed the empty glass back to the guard. "Thank you for the water."

Sopping wet and in a state of disbelief, Rich watched his hope walk away.

Alf lay in bed, gazing up at the blotched ceiling. On arriving home mid-morning, he'd walked into a confrontation between the landlord's agent and Mum. He'd stalled the agent's demands by claiming he'd stayed overnight at the factory after a break-in attempt. Once the agent left, Mum exclaimed in relief at Alf's reappearance and fussed over his battered face. She then gushed about some special project Gwen had been recruited for until he pleaded the need to rest and retreated to his room.

A knock at the door broke the tedium of pretending he was asleep. Mum's slippered feet shuffled past. The door creaked, and voices murmured.

"Alf, you awake?" Mum called. "Visitor for you. A young lady." Her voice was speculative.

Sally? "Just a minute," he called. After swinging himself upright, he reached for his cane with a scowl. The prosthesis was in the sitting room. He hadn't expected anyone would ever visit him at home. Well, if Sally was revolted by his missing leg, better to find out now. Hopping out of the bedroom, he paused in the doorway.

Seated at Gwen's desk, Sally glanced at his empty trouser leg and gave him a tense smile. "It was sheer luck bumping into Alf earlier, Mrs Wilson. I recognised him immediately, even though it's been years. I bet you have some stories to tell."

Mum chuckled while he sat beside her on the sofa. "That I do, but maybe when he's not around. Would you like a cuppa?"

"Not right now, I'm afraid. I was hoping Alf might be able to help me."

"Of course he will!" Mum looked at him expectantly. "You being old friends and all. Well, as long as it doesn't take too much time. He got a promotion at work, you know."

"Did he?" Sally beamed. "He's certainly been busy today. I guess being laid off opened up new opportunities." At Mum's indrawn breath, her face froze. "I mean, he's the sort of bloke who if he *was* laid off–"

"Laid off?" Mum screeched, her glare boring a hole in Alf's head. "You told Sally you were laid off? What happened about that promotion?"

Alf shrank away from her, his stomach churning. Her appalled expression knocked thoughts of fibbing right out of his head. He mumbled, "Uh, no promotion. I lost my job a couple of days ago."

"And just *when* were you going to tell me this, Alphonse Wilson?"

He hunched his shoulders and gazed at the floor, wishing he could sink into the sofa. "I didn't want to worry you."

"And you hoped I'd never find out?" Mum's lips flattened. "I can't stand being lied to. So where did you spend last night?" She raised a gnarled hand. "Actually, I don't want to know. You don't need to make up even more tales."

Sally chewed her lip, but there was a thoughtful gleam in her eye. Her chair creaked as she shifted her weight.

Mum glanced over at her and blew out a breath. "Never mind. I'm sure we can cope. Gwen's new project is bringing in a bit of money, and she's even getting her bed and board. See? Now she's found her calling, things are working out for her."

"That's good." Alf clenched his jaw. Things were embarrassing enough without his kid sister showing him up.

"No need to worry yourself." She sighed again. "I can go back to full-time at the laundry. I'm sure my back will hold up. I might even get some overtime..."

Sally coughed. "I can't promise anything, but I could ask around and see if there's any casual work. Or maybe laundry opportunities. The other domestic staff in Parlay Square sometimes need extra hands."

"Parlay Square!" Mum's face brightened. "But where are my manners? You've come here seeking help, and here's me wittering on about Alf's lost job. Of course, it was a shock to hear that he deliberately–"

"What *is* the problem?" asked Alf.

"My *brother* is in a spot of trouble." Sally looked at Mum.

"Oh, don't mind me." Mum levered herself up from the sofa. "I'll just go and... tidy up the kitchen."

After she left the room, Alf caught Sally's eye. She pressed her hand to her lips as if she were trying to hide a smile. His shoulders slumped. Things were more straightforward without the secrecy, but now he'd made himself look bad in front of both Sally and Mum.

"Sorry," mouthed Sally, her face growing serious. She glanced at his prosthesis, which was propped against the wall. "Do you feel up to a walk?"

"Sure, once I recharge my leg and put it on." Getting out of the flat for a bit seemed like a good idea. Plus, he was curious what Sally was after.

He braced the prosthesis on his thigh, fitted the winding handle and cranked it. His early attempts had given him blisters, but now his hands bore calluses in the right places.

While the clockwork mechanism whirred, Sally chatted about Rich's family. His parents had ensured their servants were well educated. Because Rich had modest habits and didn't entertain, the household staff–Sally excepted–had moved to other positions with his blessing.

Alf disconnected the handle. "Doesn't sound too bad for you."

"There's enough for me to do there, and it's an interesting position."

"I guess." Did secret agents' servants assist them on missions, or did they just keep the house tidy and cover up for their bosses? Alf rolled up his trouser leg while Sally politely averted her face. No doubt she didn't want to see his scars, never mind his hairy thigh. Still, the false leg was an impressive thing compared to the old wooden ones, all stainless steel components and gleaming articulated joints. The only mundane aspect was the work shoe covering the metal foot.

Leg attached and functional, he stood and stamped his feet a few times. After a couple of tumbles when the attachment mechanism failed, he'd learned to make that extra check. "Shall we go?"

"Make sure you invite Sally for supper," came Mum's voice from the kitchen as they left the flat. "It'll be nice to have a new face around the place."

Alf's face grew hot while Sally stifled a giggle.

He followed Sally up the stairs, trying not to stare at the way her skirts swished around her ankles. At street level, she hooked her arm in his.

He cleared his throat. "Where are we heading?"

"Nowhere in particular, but I don't want to be overheard."

"Towards the docks, then." Old habit made it his default destination, and the noise from the water and factories would cover up their speech. Thinking like a secret agent wasn't so difficult.

As they strolled through the market district, she brought him up to date with her visit to the prison. "With the kidnap victim being so important, the police said it was a hanging offence."

"I bet! Think of the advantage to Calesia." The afternoon headline caught his eye:

HUGE REWARD OFFERED FOR INFORMATION ON SCIENTIST'S WHEREABOUTS

He pointed. "Can't Rich claim that reward?"

Sally's dimples briefly visited her cheeks. "Don't forget, he's already a suspect. He'd have to prove he wasn't in on it in the first place, as well as finding out where she is now."

"Are you *sure* he didn't do it?"

Dropping his arm, she glared. "Of course he didn't! He's a lord!"

"Well, obviously," muttered Alf. "Automatically above all suspicion."

"I don't know why you're so against him." She huffed. "Anyway, if he wanted the professor out of the way, or to hand her over to someone else, he could just set up a meeting and have henchmen grab her. Why break into her house at night?"

Alf held his hands up. "You're right. And I guess secret

agents have their own way of doing things."

"What? Oh, yes..." She rubbed her forehead. "But the other problem is the Chief Inspector is coming back."

"And?"

"He knows my master and his parents. If Kirby recognises him, it'll cause all kinds of complications. Either Rich is hanged for a kidnapping he didn't do, or his, ah, secret agent cover will be ruined." Taking his arm again, Sally ambled on. At a fork in the road, she picked the route that would take them past the college district rather than the middle-class residences.

He glanced in the direction of the engineering college where Gwen was studying. And earning more than him, right now. Alf certainly wouldn't mind a shot at the reward, and he felt sorry for Sally's distress, but the whole business sounded way above his head. "And why do you think *I* can help? Surely Rich has secret contacts of his own."

"He never mentioned any. I wondered if you knew someone from your old factory who, ah, might have the skills to help someone leave prison?"

The thought of arranging a jailbreak made Alf sweat, yet here was Sally chatting about it as if it was an everyday task. Maybe it was, for her. He strove to keep his voice even. "Sorry, no. Even if I did, I've no idea where to find them now. Nearly all of us got laid off. A couple of my old team are still there, but busy enough guarding the gates." He paused. Time to be more assertive. "Plus, this is a big favour you're asking. If I help, it ought to be a proper job. For pay."

"Job?" Her eyes widened, and then they walked on in silence for a block. "I'm not in a position to offer you a job. But I can offer you something else."

"You can?" At her scowl, he dropped his smirk. "I mean, what?"

"You live in a poky damp flat."

"Thanks for drawing that to my attention." Now he remembered why he'd never asked the snarky pigtailed teenage Sally on a date. One reason, anyway.

"You're unemployed, and your rent's running out. How about you and your family move into Parlay Square for real?"

"What?" Alf gaped. "Us, living in a nobby house? With those huge beds?" That four-poster had been so tempting.

"It's not as nobby as you think. And I'm talking about you using the servants' quarters downstairs, so don't you go getting ideas."

Thinking this over, Alf kept pace with Sally as they approached the T-junction with the main road that ran parallel to the docks. Mum wheezed a lot, and her joints were always aching. Sorting out proper beds for her and Gwen would be a big achievement and help reinstate him in Mum's good books.

"In fact," Sally continued, "that would allow me to move in again too, and save me paying for a boarding house."

"How come?" What was the point of servants' quarters if the servants didn't live there?

"It's only me and the master now. Didn't seem right for us to be living in the same house. By ourselves, so to say."

Quite right too. Who knew what nobs got up to behind closed doors? But might *Alf* soon be sleeping under the same roof as Sally? Despite the chill breeze, a light sweat broke out on his brow. At the T-junction, he turned left, away from his old factory. "Sounds like a great idea if you can pull it off. But won't Rich mind?"

"Since he'll owe you, he'll have to like it. I'll tell him that."

Alf chuckled at the idea of Rich being bossed around. "I'm sure you will. One condition, though. You stay out of trouble. Even if I end up in jail alongside Rich, you take care of Mum and Gwen, right?"

"Right. But we need to act before tomorrow."

"Break him out of prison tonight?" Alf belatedly looked around, but nobody was paying attention. Water slapped against a pier. The rumble of machinery sounded from behind high walls, along with shouts from an angry foreman. "How?"

"I don't know. At first, I thought of the cell window, but the bars look too strong to break. How about getting the constables drunk? There's good quality brandy in the house."

Alf mused. Going in through the front door of the police station seemed risky, especially as he wanted to keep Sally uninvolved. Someone was bound to raise the alarm. Rich's cell was on the back wall, away from the door and suspicious eyes. If Rich could escape via that window, the street-level railing shouldn't be a problem.

Wheels crunched. Something thudded into the wall, which juddered. Alf dragged Sally away as a loose brick fell.

"You idiot!" roared an unseen voice. "Did your granny teach you how to drive?"

"I have an idea," said Alf. In for a penny, in for a crown.

Chapter 7

Rich shoved his empty dinner tray through the door slot and inspected the bars. Although they were strong, there was plenty of space to slide his hands through, and the corroded lock was laughably primitive. His pockets contained only a few coins and a grubby handkerchief. If he'd had his lock picks, escaping the cell would be a piece of cake. Though he'd then have the problem of fleeing through the staffed area upstairs.

He stood and inspected the window opposite, beyond which a heavy smog swirled. The aperture was far too small for an exit, even if he could remove the bars. When he patted the adjacent brick wall, a fragment of mortar became dislodged. He crumbled it between his fingers. Given time—say a century—he could probably dig his way out.

Raucous shouts echoed down the stairwell. Damn. Tonight's drunks were starting to arrive, and he still hadn't come up with a workable plan. It would add insult to injury if he were also deprived of sleep.

Scents of cheap beer and vomit permeated the air as the stumbling bodies were assigned to cells. On the plus side, Rich was spared any company in his. One privilege of being a special prisoner.

Job done, the night guard glanced through Rich's door.

"Thicker than usual tonight," said Rich.

"Huh?"

"The smog, I mean."

The guard grunted and left.

Rich settled on his bunk, but the off-key singing and snoring made it impossible to sleep. He touched his ear and winced as it stung. Finally, he'd reached the limits of Sally's tolerance. Perhaps he'd erred by not confiding in her, but how could he? It would have placed them both in an untenable situation.

Just as he became used to the drunken noises, the cough and splutter of a steam-powered engine sounded outside. Great, now someone was starting nocturnal construction work. Maybe because this wasn't a residential area? He squeezed his eyes shut.

In between the engine's rhythmic chugs, a metallic clank sounded from his window grille. He groaned, then his eyes flew open as the clank came again. Could he bribe the machine operator to deliver his apologies to Sally? He slid off his bed and padded towards the window.

Outside, at street level, on the other side of the railings stood a trousered pair of legs. Tilting his head, Rich made out a flat cap silhouetted against a street lamp. Behind the lamp was a hulking crane arm, from which dangled a chain.

Rich's eyes widened, and hope surged in his chest. He whispered, "Alf?"

"Yeah." Alf leaned over the railings and swung the chain towards Rich's window. "Here. Break the bars. Quickly! Patrolling cops."

Rich caught the chain, which rattled as he pulled it through the bars. "But–"

Alf had moved off.

Rich glowered at the hook on the end of the chain. Why couldn't the window have been bigger? Bars or not, he couldn't fit through that opening.

The engine's chug grew rhythmic, and the metal links

quivered in his hand.

What could he do with the chain? As the crane squealed, his gaze fell on the cell door with its weak hinges and ancient lock. That was it! With a strong enough pull from the crane, the door would give way. Rich would have to take his chances with the guard or guards upstairs. If luck was with him, a bar might detach and yield a makeshift weapon.

He skidded to the cell door and wrapped the chain around the bars, securing it with the hook. He then retreated to the outer wall with his arms protectively around his face. Better be poised for action.

After he passed the chain to Rich, Alf returned to the crane and patted the familiar dashboard, inhaling the scent of steam tinged with oil. The engine belched nicely, although its copious smoke made his eyes water. This old model wasn't as efficient as newer ones. On the plus side, nor did it need a security key.

It should take Rich only a few seconds to fasten the chain to the bars. Time to work the controls. Alf squinted towards the dim light coming from the prison window, muttered through a brief calculation, and set the best angle and force of pull.

He soothed his conscience by telling himself the attempt shouldn't do much damage. Snapped window bars would be easy to repair. It was fortunate the guards were stationed upstairs at ground level rather than in the basement prison, so they probably wouldn't hear anything. It certainly wasn't *his* problem if the police complained afterwards to whoever had left the crane standing here.

Still, it was as well to be cautious. With the crane set up,

Alf slid out of the cab, pressed the starter button and stumped around the corner, taking care not to trip on stray pieces of building rubble. He hugged the wall, listening for the tell-tale plink of bars breaking.

Rich held his breath. The chain grew taut. The bars creaked.

With a thunderous crash, the entire door slammed inwards in a shower of bricks and mortar. Twisted metal screeched across the floor.

Rich dived to the side. The mass of bars and concrete hurtled past him. Its impact with the outer wall made his head ring.

Ow, ow, ow! Cowering with his hands over his head, he flinched while fragments rained down on him. Brick dust caught in his throat, and he gagged.

When he opened his eyes again, he gaped at a vaguely door-sized hole in the outer wall and a pile of debris outside. "Hell's teeth," he breathed.

"Cor blimey!" The gaping drunkard across the way rubbed his eyes. "That's it, I'm not touching another drop."

"Oi!" came the guard's roar from the stairwell.

Rich scrambled through the gap. The former door lay propped against the wall, and he used it as an impromptu ladder to reach street level.

"This way!" came a voice.

Rich ran.

A dreadful shriek assaulted Alf's ears, followed by scraping and then a thud. At a resounding crash, he flinched before peeking around the corner. A cloud of dust expanded from the prison, adding to the haze from the smog. His chest tightened. What had the nobby twit done?

The smog and dust cloud made it difficult to see. Rich's gangly outline staggered closer, coughing and hacking. An alarm bell clanged from the other side of the station.

Tempting though it was to abandon Rich, Alf had promised Sally his help. Reluctantly, he called, "This way."

Rich hurried towards him then kept walking at a brisk, long-legged pace that left Alf struggling to keep up.

"Thanks, I guess." Rich brushed grit and dust from his dark clothing. "Although I wouldn't have minded a *little* more subtlety than bringing down the wall."

Alf's fists shook with outrage. Bloody toff! "I only meant to pull the bars out! Why did *you* have to destroy the wall?"

"Pulling the bars wouldn't have helped. I couldn't have fitted–"

A shrill whistle sounded from ahead, and a constable approached at a run.

Wishing the smog was thicker, Alf looked around for somewhere to hide. Of all the people to get caught with–

Rich threw an arm about his shoulders and bellowed, "When I'm on the dock... my girl shows up in a frock... but once we leave the mess... we'll take off–"

"Gerroff!" Alf shoved at Rich. Had prison driven him mad?

"Out of the way!" the policeman shouted, not even glancing at them.

Dragging Alf to the side, Rich bawled, "... and that's why my girl is the best!"

Alf winced, then he sagged with relief at the lack of an encore. "That was close."

"Tell me about it. Anyway, I really am grateful you got

me out."

Clenching his fists, Alf shrugged Rich's filthy arm off his shoulder and started walking towards Parlay Square. "I'm not doing this out of the goodness of my heart. You owe me."

"Oh, yes, sure. I can't pay you immediately–"

"Your house."

"What?" Rich stopped and peered at him, his eyebrows shooting up. "I'm not giving you my house!"

"That's not what I meant. My rent runs out in a few days. Sally said me, Mum and my sister Gwen could stay in your house."

"Aha!" With a skip, Rich resumed his walk. "I should have known she'd come through after all. When she's on a mission, who am I to gainsay her? She's pretty forceful, isn't she?"

"Forceful?" She really bossed Rich around? "Er, maybe with them that deserves it. She told the tax collectors I'm living there. Said you'd leased the place to me for the month."

Rich chuckled. "What an audacious plan!"

The admiration in Rich's voice annoyed Alf for some reason, even though the memory of that visit made him squirm. "You should be glad of her quick thinking."

"Oh, I am, I am. Let's go tell her I'm out."

"You mean, I got you out," muttered Alf.

"What?"

"Nothing. Uh... Do you have a key?"

Rich stopped short then slapped his forehead. "Of course not. It'll be in a police station drawer. And won't they have fun trying to find out where it fits? I suppose Sally isn't there this late?"

"No, she said she was heading back to her boarding house."

"Ugh, and her landlady's one of those purse-lipped nosy types," said Rich. "Well, that's put paid to the idea of going home. Any suggestions, Alf? Short for Alfred, I take it?"

Alf glowered. "No. Alphonse." It was a grand name for a humble worker, but Mum liked fancy names. Most people didn't know his sister's full name was Guinevere, taken from some soppy romance book. "I suppose we'd better go to my flat." And if Rich turned his nose up at the place, he could bally well take his chances on the street.

"Absolutely capital. And then we can come up with a plan to clear my–"

"Hey! I've caused enough trouble with your jailbreak. I'm only staying in your house because it's good for Mum and Gwen. Otherwise, you're on your own from now on. You can take your secret agent job and stuff it!"

"Hmm." Rich kicked a pebble, which went skittering into a side road. "As you wish. Let nobody say I recruit unwilling allies."

"Good." Alf's relief was mixed with offence that Rich dropped the idea of his involvement so quickly. Was he such a bad prospect? "Reward money or not, this business is far too risky, and I've a family to support."

"Quite understandable, old boy. Oh, did you say *reward money*?"

By the time they arrived home, the clock was striking two. Alf's key rattled in the lock, and he gestured to Rich to enter quietly.

"Is that you back, Alf?" came Mum's voice from the kitchen.

Alf winced as he lit a candle. He'd hoped to postpone an

explanation till morning, in the hope of thinking up a story by then. "Sorry, Mum. Didn't mean to wake you. I've, uh, got company."

"Oh, did you bring Sally home? It's a bit soon for that, isn't it?"

He tried to ignore Rich's smirk. "No! It's... the problem Sally came to see me about earlier."

Massaging her back, Mum shuffled in. She wore a housecoat, and her hair was in curlers. "Oh! It's a man!"

Rich clicked his heels together, then he took Mum's hand and bowed over it as if he weren't covered in grime and dust. "Delighted to meet you, Mrs Wilson. I'm Richard, Lord Hayes." His voice dropped. "I'm on a secret mission to investigate Professor Bergrim-Hoyt's kidnapping."

Alf's mouth dropped open. The cheek of him, behaving like that with Mum! Though he *was* investigating nobs, and the professor fell into that category, so he wasn't exactly lying. Nor had Sally contradicted his claims. Maybe there was even more going on than Alf had appreciated. Anyway, whatever Rich's motivations, Alf was now able to help his family.

Mum went pink. "Lord Hayes! What an honour!" Her free hand went to her curlers. "I'll just, er, put the kettle on, shall I?"

Still holding Mrs Wilson's hand, Rich smiled at her flustered expression. "I'm very grateful to Alf for his help, and my apologies for disturbing your sleep. A cup of tea would be lovely." It couldn't be worse than Mrs Madeley's. He shook his head sadly. "I had a little misunderstanding with the authorities. An unfortunate hazard of clandestine work. It rather ties my hands when I need to find the kidnapped professor *and* prove my own innocence."

She went even pinker with excitement. "To think of my boy helping a lord, and a secret agent, at that! It's just like in *Inspector Grimley's Casebook*. When I have the chance, I love reading the customer copies at the laundry."

Releasing her work-roughened fingers, he tried not to laugh at her reference to the popular serial. "I'm afraid the reality isn't quite that exciting. No rooftop chases or last-minute rescues. Just careful and quiet work."

"You're being modest. I bet King Michael himself has good things to say about you."

Rich didn't dare look at Alf's glower. "I'm sorry to disappoint you, but I don't report to the king."

"Oh." Mrs Wilson's face fell.

Obviously, rumours of the king's heavy drinking and erratic behaviour hadn't reached these common folk. Might as well give her something to enjoy. Most of the lords weren't household names, but the head of the council should be well known. "I report to Lord Pettigrew."

"Ah well, that's nearly as good as telling the king." She elbowed Alf. "Isn't it? You should be glad of this opportunity."

"Yeah," grunted Alf.

"And such good timing!" She beamed. "You see, Alf's out of work, so he'll have plenty of time to help you. I was so disappointed when he lost his job, especially as he tried to cover it up, bad boy that he is, but it's as if fate–"

"Mum!" Alf's face was scarlet.

"It's just as well you're keeping an eye on him," she continued. "What would you like him to do?"

No wonder poor Alf looked so harried. Rich had better smooth things over. "Your son will be indispensable, and I hope the arrangement will suit you as well. I need to create the impression I've left the city. Alf has kindly agreed to move into my house for the duration. To lend verisimilitude to our ploy, he suggested that you and your daughter—Gwen, is it?—also take up residence. The house is in Parlay Square."

She clutched her chest. "Parlay Square? Well, never in my wildest dreams..."

"I'm afraid it would be the servants' quarters, but I hope they will be to your satisfaction."

"Ooh, I'm sure they will be! But where will you be stay—residing, Lord Hayes?"

Good point. Damn. There weren't many options. Best to work with what he had. "I wonder if you'd mind my using this apartment for the moment."

"*Here?*" Her hand flew to her lips, and she mumbled, "It's not what you're used to. Wouldn't you rather stay at one of your clubs?"

"I'm afraid I can't. That's where certain parties would seek me out. Nobody would suspect me of living here." Rich glanced at the rickety desk and sagging couch. With luck, there would be no fleas.

Alf regarded his boots. "Rent's due. A florin a week."

Was that all? Discerning fleas wouldn't bother visiting here. Rich pulled two florins from his pocket and handed them to Mrs Wilson. "Here you are."

She beamed at the coins. "You must have been sent by an angel, Lord Hayes. Oh, but will you be here by yourself? Who's going to do for you?"

"I'll manage." Surely it wouldn't be too taxing to cope without servants.

"No." She drew herself up to her full height, which was

about his mid-chest. "It wouldn't be right. I'll stay on here for a while and keep the place tidy for you. Anyway, Gwen's away right now. I don't want her coming back to find you here by yourself, no offence."

"Couldn't you send a message?" asked Rich.

Mrs Wilson shook her head. "The college said she wasn't to be disturbed until her project's finished. And she did so well getting that sponsorship after Alf couldn't arrange–"

"Mum!" Alf scowled at Rich. "And there's no reason to get her all exercised about the fact you're stopping here."

"Now, Alf, Gwen has a better head on her shoulders than you give her credit for. There's no need to be jealous of her success–"

"I'm not jealous!" Alf's jaw clenched.

It didn't look as if Rich had much choice. He might as well give in gracefully. And if he were honest, he wouldn't mind the company. He'd never lived in an empty house before. "I'm afraid I don't have any spare clothing. Maybe Alf could take a message to Sally, and she could send some over."

"Oh, clothing's easy. We've a pile of unclaimed garments at the laundry." Screwing up her face, she studied him. "Yep, Calesians–especially holiday visitors–don't always come back for their stuff. I'll bring back some in your size. What do you want?"

"Something similar to what I'm wearing, please. And..." He thought about where he might gather information. "Would you happen to have a set of tennis whites?"

Chapter 8

Alf strolled along the street, his borrowed trousers tugging with each step. Sally had insisted he be seen around town, to support their ruse regarding the Parlay Square house. It made sense to allay neighbours' suspicions about Rich's absence, but he wished the person keeping up the deception didn't have to be *him.* His top hat kept threatening to fall off, and his bright red cravat screamed for attention. On the plus side, pedestrians politely stepped out of his way, and a chestnut seller had given him a curtsey! This was something he might get used to, even if he felt like a fake.

His grip on the carved silver-topped cane tightened as he neared the police station. Two constables stood at the entrance. What if they remembered him as the drunkard they'd jailed overnight? Sally was confident nobody would recognise him, but how could she be so sure? Trying to keep his steps leisurely, he let his route take him round the back.

The wall that had been damaged by Rich's escape came into view. Boards had been laid across the defect. The gap continued into an impressive vertical crack reaching the main floor above the basement prison. That crane he'd used had been removed.

Alf stopped and stared at the damage before studying two men who also inspected the area. One was a builder, going by his dusty overalls, monocle and the pencil tucked behind his ear. The other was a snooty-looking man in a fur-trimmed trench coat. A silver whistle dangled around his neck, which would make him one of the plain-clothes detectives: someone to be extra wary of.

The builder shook his head. “I’m as keen on the repairs as you are. But I’m short of help, what with all the army recruitment. So it’ll take a bit longer than usual. Fortunately, the rest of the building is safe to occupy.”

“Simply unacceptable, Norton.” The policeman sniffed. “While you’re dawdling, the draft in my office makes it impossible to work.”

A constable approached–the one who had released Alf.

Oh, no! It was too late to sidle off since that would look more suspicious than staying. Alf pulled the cravat over his chin.

After walking past Alf, the constable held up a paper. “Inspector Castor? Telegram from Chief Inspector Kirby. High winds have prevented his airship from taking off. He’s decided to travel by road, so he’ll be delayed by a few days.”

“What a shame.” Castor smiled. “I’d better press on with the investigation. It’s an ill wind that blows no good, eh?”

“Sorry, sir?”

“Nothing. I want the wall repaired before Kirby’s return. Mustn’t give him more reason to criticise.”

Norton’s shoulders slumped. “Me and the boy will get started right away, and I’ll put up a recruitment notice. Even unskilled hands would help us do the work quicker. But I’m doubtful whether we’ll get any decent applicants.”

“Offer a bonus, man!” snapped Castor.

“Yes, sir.” He unrolled a paper and started to write a sign.

The two policemen headed in the direction of the station entrance. Castor gave Alf a polite nod on the way past. “Quite shocking. It appears the working classes do not, in fact, have much of a work ethic."

Alf scowled behind his cravat before realising Castor hadn't meant *him.* He grunted a non-committal reply to Castor's disappearing back.

A bonus? Better hang around and see what the job offered. He strolled a little further, then paused at a newspaper stand when the headline caught his eye:

MIDNIGHT JAILBREAK

An artist's sketch of the prisoner graced the front page. It looked vaguely like Rich although maybe a bit older. There were no eyewitness accounts of an accomplice. Phew!

Alf retraced his steps and read the builder's notice. His eyebrows rose at the money offered. What an opportunity!

Obviously, he couldn't ask Norton about the job while dressed up like a toff. He'd need to change into real clothes and return here. And he'd better do it quickly, before word got out.

He'd got three strides up the street when a voice called, "Mr Smith? Mr Smith!"

Blimey, someone was calling his fake name. He turned slowly, dreading what he would see. Argh, that tax chap with the white beard stood a few steps away, a folded umbrella tucked under his arm.

Alf raised his chin. "Yes? Mr..."

"Farlow. It's a pleasure to meet you again, and in a less formal setting. I hope you've settled into your new residence. I remember your mentioning an interest in the diamond trade. I've recently been made aware of an opportunity..."

"Oh?" Alf's good leg quivered as if wanting to flee. What if the constable came back out and recognised him on a second glance?

"Unfortunately, my privileged position doesn't allow me to make use of it. However, I have a friend..."

"That's good." Gah, it would be the height of frustration if that job went to someone else because this Farlow wanted to chat. He chewed his lip.

Farlow raised an eyebrow. "Oh, don't worry. As gentlemen, we would naturally keep the arrangement quiet so as not to cause a stampede..."

"Naturally." When a hefty one-eyed chap stopped and spoke to Norton, Alf's breath hissed in. But Norton shook his head. Phew!

"So, Mr Smith." Farlow smiled faintly. "Might you be interested? You just have to say the word, and I'll arrange the necessary introductions. Discreetly, of course. You're a man of the world, and you know how these things work."

"Uh, I'll think about it," muttered Alf. "But I really must go now." He stomped off as quickly as he could, not daring to look behind himself.

On opening the front door at Parlay Square, the aroma of pea soup and warm bread met Alf's nose. His mouth watered.

"Nearly ready," called Sally from the kitchen.

"Great!" Alf rushed up the stairs to the bedroom where the nobby clothes were kept. He threw his togs on the floor and hastily wound up his false leg. Then he scrambled into his proper clothes and returned to the kitchen, where Sally tossed a piece of bread at him.

"Yum!" He snatched it. Still warm from the oven. This was the life.

Ladling out the soup, she raised an eyebrow. "Someone's in a hurry."

"Found some work," he mumbled through his mouthful of buttered bread. "But it might have gone by the time I get back."

With a smile, she joined him at the table. "It's a shame Rich couldn't convince you to help him further. You're so good at seizing opportunities."

"I can do that without being a secret agent." Scraping his bowl clean, he dared a wink. "But I'd better be off again."

On his arrival at the police station, his heart sank. Norton was already talking to another couple of prospective assistants. One was a small boy while the other was a muscular man with a walking stick.

"You lookin' for help?" asked Alf breathlessly.

"Yeah," said the Norton. He looked Alf up and down and then frowned at the man with the stick. "You able-bodied? Got the use of all your arms and legs?"

Alf was so glad he'd taken time to wind up his leg. "That's right."

"Good. I'll need you to carry materials, including up and down ladders."

"Not a problem." Alf crossed his fingers that his false leg wouldn't let him down.

Norton waved away the other two hopefuls. "What do I call you? And how come you're not signing up?"

"I'm Alf." What could he say, since Norton was insisting on able-bodied men? "Uh... and I'm a pacifist."

Norton sneered. "I suppose that's lucky for me, but you should be ashamed of yourself."

Suppressing his instinctive glower, Alf looked down. "Sorry."

"Get to work."

The sun had set when Alf tottered back to Parlay Square, his arms and back aching. His leg had run out of power, but since he'd dropped a brick on his foot, it served as a reasonable excuse for his uneven gait.

Sally let him in the side door. When he showed her his earnings, she said, "I don't need to ask if your day went well."

"It certainly did. Though I'd forgotten how tiring manual work is, compared to driving machines..." He brightened at the sight of dinner. Considering the fact Rich wasn't here, Sally was being remarkably generous with the food.

"Where were you working? I forgot to ask."

Alf loosened his collar, not sure whether to be amused or embarrassed. "The police station. Repairing the damage from the spy's escape."

"Oh, that's fantastic!" Sally beamed. "What did you find out about the kidnapping?"

"Kidnapping?" Alf swallowed. How silly. Of course the police station was a source of information. "Nothing yet, but I'm going back tomorrow."

"Keep your eyes and ears open."

"Of course I will. That's why I went for that job." Surely, if he happened to overhear something, he could mention it to Sally without counting himself as involved? He basked in the approval of her smile.

"I'll have the port and a sharp cheese," Rich told the butler before settling into his wing-back chair. At the Solitude Club, each member had his own nook. It reduced embarrassment if patrons who were enemies could pretend to ignore each other. The club's guarantee of complete discretion was laudably consistently applied. In wealthier times, his father had paid for permanent membership, so he needn't be concerned about unpaid bills here.

Rich was glad to remain below notice today. He'd entered via the back door with its blank-faced doorman. Officially, that door was used by patrons who had engaged in sport and didn't want to be seen arriving dishevelled. Hence the tennis gear, although a closer inspection would reveal it was ironed and beautifully clean. Mrs Wilson was obviously proud of her work.

The *Ironfort Guardian*'s front page featured an account of Rich's escape last night. The reporter speculated that the captive was a plant who had deliberately got himself jailed so he could spy on Lesser Grenia's boys in blue. Rich shook his head. As if mouldering in a cell would yield useful strategic information. If there were any clues to be had, club gossip was the best place to start.

When a shadow fell across the page, Rich looked up. His automatic smile froze on his lips. The head of the council himself!

"What ho, Hayes!" The speaker's black moustache was topped by a bulbous red nose. "Fancy running into you. We missed you yesterday."

"I had some personal business to attend to." Waving the speaker to the opposite chair, Rich leaned back, trying to appear relaxed. "How's business, Pettigrew?"

"Absolutely capital, lad, other than the usual issues." Pettigrew ran a hand through his luxuriant mane of hair. Rich was convinced it was a wig. "We mainly discussed the shortage of diamonds. Though with old Ina Bergrim-Hoyt being kidnapped, I'm not sure how much further her technology can be pushed, especially that wireless transmission project. It's not as if anyone else could replicate her methods."

"It was certainly a shock to hear the kidnapping," murmured Rich.

"*About* the kidnapping, you mean."

"Oh, yes. Do they have any suspects?"

"Not yet, according to this morning's report. Hopefully things will move quicker once Kirby returns. King Michael's increased the reward for any information. Not a peep out of the usual informers. And there's been no unusual activity among the Calesian community."

"It's reassuring that we don't expect pitched battles on the streets," said Rich. He wasn't the only citizen with Calesian roots. Migration of Calesians to Lesser Grenia–and the converse–had unsurprisingly slowed over the last few years. It had been judged prudent to monitor incomers more closely. There had been no major trouble. If anything, in comparison to native Lesser Grenians, recent arrivals from Calesia were more law-abiding and industrious: displaying no interest in alcohol, and rarely being hauled up in court.

"No news from across the border, either. According to our diplomats, it's business as usual at Shambito's military school."

"Definitely a relief." Calesia's size and population made her a serious military threat, but her equipment and technological knowledge was no more advanced than Lesser Grenia's.

Pettigrew continued. "I'm surprised they bothered springing the chap who was caught. He was surely a very minor link in a well-organised chain."

"Maybe he had information they needed?" Rich nodded as the waiter set out a selection of cheese and crackers before pouring a glass of port.

"Could be. Anyway, you'll have seen the sketches pinned up all over the place. If he's still in the city, he won't dare poke his nose into a public place." Pettigrew leaned forward and peered at Rich's face, then he squinted at the newspaper Rich held. "Though I don't think much of the artist, or the police description. It looks like you!"

Flapping a sweaty hand in front of his face, Rich laughed weakly. "Come on! You know where my parents came from. Surely you don't have the common prejudice that all Calesians look the same?"

Pettigrew stroked his waxed moustache. "Of course not. But your wispy hair is just like in the drawing. Most Calesians crop their hair."

He eyed the cheese knife. "How d'you know that?"

Pettigrew snorted. "They don't wear those fur hats *all* the time. The other day, when the new ambassador doffed his, I noticed he was nearly bald."

Rich resisted the temptation to feel his own hair, instead sipping his port. The voices he'd overheard in the Bergrim-Hoyts' house had sounded local. "If it wasn't the Calesians, who else might have kidnapped the professor?"

"Competitors, such as those who make engines powered by coal and wood? Or even others who want to use diamond technology? Maybe they're torturing her to give up her secrets."

The port turned to vinegar on his palate. This wasn't a game, after all. "Perhaps they're blackmailing her husband?"

"Well... he has a finger in lots of pies. Naturally, he has trade contacts all over the place, including Calesia. My main concern is that they might pressure him if he joins us on the council."

"Has that been agreed?"

"No. In fact, he just withdrew his application. Too many other issues on his plate, I suppose."

After they exchanged some more small talk, Pettigrew headed for the dining room. Rich savoured the last of his port then quietly wrapped the cheese and crackers in his napkin. Mrs Wilson might enjoy it once he arrived back at Alf's flat.

Chapter 9

Alf's shoulders ached as he balanced on the scaffolding, and his prosthetic leg twitched. It had been a long morning so far. He'd begun by passing materials and tools to Norton while the apprentice ran other errands. Now he was mixing mortar in small amounts, and his fingers were freezing off.

The vertical crack they were filling meandered close to a window. Castor's voice had floated through the gap earlier, bemoaning a lack of competent note-takers.

Now, furniture scraped inside. Castor said, "Show Mr Bergrim-Hoyt in."

What did the victim's husband look like? Following a half-hearted stir of the bucket, Alf rose from his crouch.

"Problem?" asked Norton.

"Need to stretch a bit." While bending from side to side–it wasn't entirely a pretext–Alf peered through the window.

Castor was seated at an oak desk, his back to Alf. Opposite him sat a gaunt man with wavy white hair and bags under his eyes.

Poor chap. Alf returned to his stirring. Unfortunately, the noise he and Norton were making meant he couldn't hear the interview clearly. Plus, the scaffolding creaked any time either of them moved. At least they weren't too high, and Norton wasn't the chatty type. So far, he'd restricted himself to curt orders and reprimands.

"Separate bedrooms? How come?" Castor's voice had deepened with full, rolling syllables. Did he think he was delivering a speech?

Alf frowned at the indistinct reply. Getting only Castor's side of the conversation was unlikely to be helpful, although he didn't really want to hear about the couple's sleeping habits.

"I see." Castor chuckled. "I won't ask which of you snores. How did you become aware of the intruders? What? How alarming. I suppose a knife to the throat is only to be expected from such criminal types."

Foul cigar smoke drifted out through the wall, making Alf sniff. Were detectives really allowed to smoke at work? He rubbed his nose, smearing it with grime. Gah!

"My constables found your downstairs security automaton holding one of the kidnappers. Here's the artist's sketch of the prisoner. Was he the one who tied you up? Oh, really? Despite this one's Calesian looks, his accent was Lesser Grenian. I interrogated him myself. A local collaborator, no doubt."

At a bout of coughing from inside, Alf winced.

"Odd how they stole your wife's papers but not your own. Ah, I see. Mr Bergrim-Hoyt, I am jealous. I barely merit a lockable desk drawer here, never mind an entire industrial storage vault. I don't have any further questions for the moment. Let us know if a ransom note arrives."

The scaffolding wobbled under Alf's feet.

"Bugger!" Norton made a grab, but the spirit level slipped out of his hand. "Alf, fetch it."

"Right away." Alf clambered down the scaffolding and retrieved the instrument. After returning it to Norton, he peeked through the window again and nearly yelped.

Castor glowered at him from the other side of the glass. He was standing, hands behind his back, dictating notes to a clerk.

Alf hastily tugged his forelock and sank to his knees, hopefully out of sight. His false leg squeaked.

"Did you knock something else off?" grumbled Norton.

"No," said Alf. An anxious glance at his trouser leg confirmed the prosthesis was still covered. Phew!

"Item found at scene," declared Castor. "Half-full bottle of liquid. Chemists identified it as an anaesthetic of foreign make."

Norton rapped his trowel on the planking. "Keep mixing!"

"Sorry." How did secret agents manage to spy while pretending to do something else? He picked up the stirring rod and prodded the gloop in the mortar bucket.

"Neighbours observed a steam carriage parked in a driveway of an unoccupied house," said Castor.

"Alf, stop wool-gathering and hand me a Size Three trowel!"

Alf passed the item over. For a few minutes, he busied himself aiding Norton.

"Stand up straight when you report!" Castor's voice came through the crack. "Did you get anything from the spy's belongings?"

"An old set of lock picks, likely obtained in Ironfort," came an unfamiliar male voice. "The key is obviously high quality and custom-made. We asked the locksmiths to check their records. It belongs to a house in Parlay Square."

"I see. Hmm, Lord Hayes' house? I'd better go over there and pay my respects. Hand me that etiquette book, will you? And get a boy to polish my good shoes."

Oh, no! What to do? If Rich was connected with the crime, Alf might come under scrutiny too. He'd have to warn Sally—Damn! And that would mean quitting this job. But better a lost temporary job than getting arrested again.

He replaced the stirring rod in the bucket and swallowed. "Mr Norton?"

"What?"

"Remember I dropped that brick on my foot yesterday?"

"Yeah?"

Alf screwed up his face. "My foot's hurting worse today. I can feel it swelling in my shoe. Mighta broken it."

Norton glowered. "That was your own stupid fault. Don't think you're entitled to compen—"

"No! Just that, I don't think I can keep on working today." Alf squirmed. It wasn't *completely* a lie, but would Norton notice him radiating guilt?

The builder huffed and grudgingly said, "I'll give you a half-day's pay. Now bugger off, and let me find another assistant."

"Thank you!" Alf accepted his wages with a mix of regret and relief. He made sure to limp until he was out of Norton's sight before hurrying away.

On arrival back at Parlay Square, he barged through the side door of the kitchen where the scent of pork roast met him.

Seated at the kitchen table, Sally looked up in surprise. The newspaper was open in front of her at an article about the jailbreak.

"We're expecting a visitor." Alf caught his breath. "You know the police confiscated Rich's key? They've worked out it's for here."

She pursed her lips. "You better get changed. Oh, wait."

"Huh?"

Grabbing a tea towel, she marched up to him and scrubbed his nose. "Can't have you all dressed up with a dirty face."

"Uh, thanks." Cheeks flaming, he fled upstairs.

After putting on his nobby suit, Alf returned to the sitting room where he'd met with the tax collectors. The front door knocker banged.

"Looking nice and smart, just in time." Sally winked from the hallway.

Alf cleared his throat and tugged his cravat while she spoke with the visitor. By the time she led Castor in, he had sunk into an old leather armchair, an empty brandy glass by his side. He hadn't felt bold enough to pour some.

"Visitor for you, sir," said Sally.

"Plonk yourself there." Alf waved Castor to the opposite seat while Sally stationed herself by the door.

Castor wore a serious expression and sat rigidly upright. "Mr Smith–"

"That's me," said Alf.

"–my name's Inspector Castor. I understand you are leasing this house for the month. I have some grave news."

"What's the matter?" Alf glanced down at his hands. Cripes, they were filthy! He shoved them in his pockets before Castor could notice.

"You'll be aware of Professor Bergrim-Hoyt's kidnapping?"

"Yes, read it in the paper. What of it?"

"We caught a Calesian spy." Castor lowered his voice. "However, the spy escaped. The newspapers are having a field day."

"No! What is the world coming to?"

Castor stood and paced in front of the fireplace. "A desperate business. They literally broke him out by destroying the prison wall. Do I recollect seeing you at the station–"

Alf's blood chilled. "Uh..."

"Yes, you walked past yesterday morning, didn't you? When we were inspecting the damage."

Phew! "That's right. But what's all this to do with me?"

"We've been examining the spy's belongings. And they include"–Castor pulled a key out of his pocket–"the key of this house! It's a custom-made key, which is how we traced it here."

"How strange," said Alf, sweat trickling down his back.

"With your agreement, I'd like to try the key. The locksmith said it should fit the kitchen door."

"Shall I do that, sir?" Sally asked.

"I need to try it myself–"

"But the kitchen's a mess! The master would be horrified if I let you in there before cleaning up." She flourished a duster. "Or at least, if you could wait while I make the place presentable..."

At the sight of Castor's scowl, Alf gulped. He'd no idea what Sally was planning, so how could he help? "I've discovered that Sally's very house proud. Maybe just a couple of minutes, so we don't distress her?"

Castor folded his arms and huffed. "Two minutes only, so we don't waste even more time debating the issue."

"Thank you!" Sally darted out of the room, duster held aloft.

Without her presence, Alf shrank under Castor's silent attention. He'd grown accustomed to following her cues. "I hope your investigation is yielding fruit otherwise? I'm, uh, full of admiration for your determination."

"Oh, thank you." Castor glanced at the mirror above

the fireplace and straightened his bowler hat before starting to pace. "The prisoner's escape suggests he had a local accomplice. None of my patrolling constables noticed any Calesians in the vicinity during that time window."

"Wow." Alf licked his lips. Castor's fidgeting was getting on his nerves. "It's shocking how my fellow Lesser Grenians might betray their country for money."

"While we're waiting..." Castor pulled a paper from his pocket and held it out to Alf. "Here's a colour sketch of the spy. Has anyone resembling this man approached the house?"

Still seated with his hands tucked away, Alf studied the drawing then raised his head. "Definitely not. We'll be sure to keep an eye out–"

He gasped. Over Castor's shoulder, the portrait of Rich's father regarded the room. Other than a goatee beard, his resemblance to the artist's sketch made the hairs on the back of Alf's neck rise.

Bugger! If Castor spent any longer walking around, he was bound to notice that face. Better get him out of the room and slowly lead him to the kitchen. Hopefully Sally would have finished whatever she was doing.

"You're right to be worried." Castor put the sketch away. "I warn you, he's dangerous."

Alf nodded vigorously. "Yes, he certainly looks like a nasty type. More than ever, I'm convinced you're the man to bring him in. Let's go and try this key."

"About time too." Castor strode out of the sitting room before Alf could even stand.

Yikes! "Wait!"

"Don't be concerned, Mr Smith." Castor's voice sounded from the servant's hallway. "Once I've checked the lock, I'll be on my way and leave you in peace."

Cursing under his breath, Alf struggled out of the enveloping armchair and stumbled after him. On entering the kitchen, he winced.

Duster in hand, Sally lingered beside Castor at the external door. The detective studied the lock before inserting the key. It turned smoothly. He opened the door and stepped out into the light drizzle.

While he inspected the door from outside, Sally sent Alf a reproachful glance. His shoulders sagged. But what else could he have done?

Castor stepped back inside with a frown. "Good to have confirmation. But there are fresh scratches around the lock. On the *inside* only."

"Sorry, sir." Sally waved the duster. "I was cleaning it for you. Must have been some grit caught in the cloth that I didn't notice."

Stomach trembling, Alf forced a chuckle. "See? Sally's very house proud."

"Ye-es." Castor's gaze dropped to an open toolbox lurking under the table, and then he shook his head. "So, I have confirmed the provenance of the key the kidnapper was carrying. The locksmith cut six keys in total. You have one, Mr Smith. Your maid here has one, Lord Hayes has one, and I notice a spare hanging on the hook. Where are the others?"

"The master's parents each had a set." Sally chewed her lip. "So this key must have belonged to one of them."

Castor's gaze bored into her face. "And just how would the spy have obtained a key from them? One might think you had something to do with—"

"Bandits!" Eyes and mouth wide, Sally threw her hands up in the air, almost knocking Castor's hat off. As he retreated, she continued, "The master's poor parents went travelling, and they never returned. We don't know what fate befell them. What if someone stole their keys and decided to kidnap the master too? What will I say when he returns? Deary deary me!"

Alf didn't dare watch Sally any longer. Her overacting in school plays had always sent him into fits of laughter. He focussed on the rain outside and said in a quivering voice, "When I leased this property, I didn't expect to be dragged into a criminal investigation. Especially one involving a pair of vanished nobles."

Castor subsided. "I'm sure it's nothing to do with you, Mr Smith. But the whole matter is odd, especially with Lord Hayes' sudden absence. I need to take Sally down to the station for–"

"Oh, don't," blurted Alf. At Castor's suspicious expression, he added, "I'll be left without a maid if you arrest her. She's obviously not your escaped prisoner, and I'm renting her along with the house." *Did I really say that?* Trying to ignore Sally's outraged gasp, he forged on. "Can't you at least give me a day or two to find a replacement?"

Castor huffed. "Can you guarantee she won't leave this house until I interrogate her? Gentleman to gentleman?"

Oh, crap. That meant she'd be sleeping here tonight rather than going back to her boarding house. Alf's heart jittered. What if he inadvertently offended her again? "Yes, I guarantee it."

"In that case..." Replacing the key in his pocket, Castor stepped outside. "I shall bid you good day. I'll warn my constables to keep a close watch."

Alf held his breath while Sally closed and locked the door.

“Oh, Alf.” She sighed.

“Sorry. Me and my big mouth.” He’d never live *that* comment down.

“Couldn’t you have delayed him a bit longer?”

“Oh. But he showed me a sketch of Rich, and...”

After he explained about the portrait, she pursed her lips. “Well, can’t be helped now. I’m stuck in the house, and Castor’s suspicious of me. For all we know, he might decide to let himself in again.”

“At least he’s not suspicious of *me*.” Alf’s gaze dropped. “Well, not quite so much. Time to find Rich and warn him Castor’s making connections. I guess I’d better keep wearing this suit.” He regarded his nobby togs with disgust. What would the neighbours say when he arrived home looking like this?

Rich sauntered down the street towards Parlay Square, his tennis whites packaged under his arm. Today, he’d changed into something nondescript before leaving the club. At the thought of the meagre information he’d gleaned, he shook his head: plenty of speculation about the culprits, but still nothing solid to work with. It was a pity Alf had been disinclined to involve himself beyond maintaining a presence in Rich’s house. Even an unpolished labourer could have been an extra set of eyes and legs. However, there was no point in pressuring the man.

On entering the square, Rich paused to look around. After just a couple of nights in a damp basement flat, the grand old mansions seemed ostentatious, although the lure of the beds inside was palpable. A constable made his rounds, nodding politely at a nanny pushing a perambulator.

Rich had run out of options for more assistance. Cheese, no matter how fine, could hardly persuade Mrs Wilson to do his spying for him, nor would she have access to anything useful. He briefly grinned at the thought of her face if he asked for her help—*Inspector Grimley's helpers come from all walks of life!*—then he pushed the idea out of his mind. It would be imprudent to look up too many old friends since word might spread that he was still in Ironfort, and then the tax collectors would also be on his tail. Nothing for it, his best bet was to go home—to his own home—and see if Sally might make enquiries on his behalf.

"What are you doing here?" came a disgruntled voice.

Rich halted. *Alf.* What a stroke of luck. On closer scrutiny, the fellow wore out-of-fashion clothing that must have been left in that old wardrobe. "And a good afternoon to you too."

Alf shook a silver-topped cane, his posture tense. "Look, you shouldn't be wandering around. The coppers—"

Truncheon in hand, the constable strolled up. "Is this fellow bothering you, sir? I'm afraid even this area sometimes attracts unsavoury characters."

Rich opened his mouth to demur, then he realised the policeman was addressing Alf.

"No." Alf made a sour face. "He's just leaving. I told him this ain't a good place for him to be, not if he knows what's good for him."

"My sentiments exactly, sir. But you'd better be careful when speaking to these types." The constable stood shoulder-to-shoulder with Alf and frowned up at Rich. "Ironfort's police remain vigilant about anything suspicious."

"I guess I'll be on my way then." Seething inside, Rich bowed politely.

That had torn it. They couldn't even exchange a few more words. The constable would be watching out for him, and no doubt take him in for loitering if he returned. He'd seen it happen before. He couldn't afford to land back in jail. Castor had been bad enough, but once Kirby arrived...

One thing at a time. Might as well drop his borrowed clothing back at Alf's flat, along with the cheese and crackers. Rich walked from the grand houses of Parlay Square through the more modest residential district, then past the market district to the working-class area. The scent of brine hung in the misty air, and a breeze from the industrial area followed him. Every so often, a whiff of cheese reached his nostrils.

By the time he arrived in Alf's street, there was a light drizzle. He held his package so the food wouldn't get wet, peering at the building numbers. He descended the steps to Alf's basement flat, and heaved a sigh of relief as he shouldered open the communal external door.

Footsteps descended behind him. Habitual politeness prompted him to hold the door open for a couple of equally damp chaps in the usual working-class outfit of woollen jackets and flat caps. One had a bottle protruding from his pocket. Rich's nose wrinkled at the acrid odour which overpowered even the cheese. Workers' moonshine was nothing like his club's port. A pity he'd had no way of bringing some back.

"Thanks, mate," said one wheezily, blowing into his hands.

"You're welcome." Finding Alf's door, Rich fumbled with the key in the lock, but before he could turn it, the door swung open.

"Oh, come in and get dry. I was worried you'd get

caught in the rain." Mrs Wilson peered past him. "Who are your friends?"

"Friends?"

A heavy weight struck his shoulder. He staggered forwards and tripped, dropping his parcel.

As he fell, he glimpsed the two men barging into the flat. One slapped a wet cloth over his face.

Rich's eyes stung with the chemical vapour. What the– Trying to suffocate him? He grabbed for his assailant's hand, but sudden lethargy weighed him down.

"Get your hands off me!" came a shriek.

His thoughts grew hazy...

Chapter 10

After winding up his leg and changing back into nondescript comfy clothing, Alf slurped his tea in the kitchen. “That copper was watching us, though at least Castor wasn’t around. All I could tell Rich was that being out and about was risky, which he knew already. He must have seen the posters up all over town.”

“Never mind.” Sally patted his hand, which he didn’t mind at all, then went back to sorting a pile of keys. “It was a stroke of luck you had the chance to say something. I know you don’t think he should be showing his face in public, but how’s he going to investigate the kidnapping if he stays hidden in your flat?”

“I guess you’re right.”

Sally frowned at the keys. “If I’d been more on the ball, I could have distracted Castor and switched the key—messing with the lock was never going to work—but his visit caught me on the hop. Do you reckon Rich will be back at your flat now?”

“I hope so. If Mum’s there as well, I can check how she’s getting on.”

She gave him a sympathetic smile. “I guess you’ve not lived away from home before. Do you miss her and Gwen?”

Unwilling to admit that the distance was a relief, he snorted. “It’s weird to think Gwen’s spent longer away than I have. Though that’s only because they’re paying for her to live in. She’s probably working all hours of the day and night. I hope the other students aren’t luring her into hijinks."

"I don't remember her. Is there a big age gap?"

"She'd have been a toddler when we finished school. She's a bit like you. Doesn't take any nonsense, though between you and me, you're smarter than she is." Sally's blush sent warmth through his chest. "One month she wants to be a chef, and the next she fancies carpentry. Now she wants to be an engineer! I'm worried about this project she's working on. Power sources or something."

"Experimental technology?" Sally grimaced. "I'd be pretty scared too."

He waved a hand. "That's not the problem. The other students are nobby types, and they pick on her, and she's not a natural in the first place. When she messes up her experiments, they don't let her forget it. Once she graduates—I hope she gets that far—she can get a well-paid job, but she has to put up with them in the meantime." He put his mug down. "No time like the present. I'll be back for supper."

"It's pork and mash tonight. If you pick up an oxtail at the market, I'll make a stew tomorrow."

"Sounds great." Rich must be mad to exist on cabbage and dripping, when Sally clearly revelled in cooking. Mum and Gwen would be in for a real treat when they moved in.

Alf joined the stream of workers heading home. He might be jostled and cursed at, but the anonymity of his working clothes was a comfort in some ways. Plus, his cap and jacket withstood the drizzle better than those fancy clothes.

Still, he was wet through when he squelched his way down the steps to the building and through the communal front door. An odd smell lingered in the hallway, like a combination of mouldy cheese and cleaning fluid.

The key seemed to be sticking until he realised the door was unlocked. He scowled. Rich must have forgotten. Couldn't the irresponsible fop do anything without servants tidying up after him? Mum wouldn't be pleased if anything had gone missing.

Alf swung the door open and took a single step inside. The stench of cheese intensified. He stared at the floor in disbelief.

Rich lay groaning on the tatty carpet, amid toppled furniture and Gwen's books. He cracked open an eye: the other was swollen shut in a bruised face. "Alf?"

As Alf started to kneel beside him, Rich grabbed his sleeve. "Alf! They took your mother!"

"What?" Mouth open, Alf scanned the room for Mum, hoping his ears had deceived him.

"Two chaps pushed their way in. They overcame us with some–Ah! I smelled that stuff when they kidnapped Professor Bergrim-Hoyt."

"But why'd they take Mum?" Alf's stomach plummeted. She couldn't be gone. Any moment now, and she'd come through from the kitchen, snickering over how they'd wound him up.

"The bigger one with the hoarse voice said I was to confess to the police. Say that I'm a kidnapper and that Professor Bergrim-Hoyt's been taken out of the country. Otherwise"–he swallowed–"I wouldn't see my mother again. They must have thought I was you!"

"But how come–Those posters!" Alf fought down the urge to slap Rich's hand off his arm. "They must have bloody spotted you! Why did you have to go out–"

"Yes, I suspect they followed me." Releasing Alf, Rich eased himself on to the sofa and clutched his head. "Look,

I'm really sorry about causing trouble. I'll go hand myself in. I'll demand an interview with Kirby. He knows who I am. Even if he doesn't trust or believe me, he can arrange–"

Footsteps scuffed outside. An envelope slid under the door, and the footsteps moved away, their owner whistling a cheerful tune.

Alf picked up the envelope and frowned. It was addressed to Mum, in Gwen's clumsy scrawl. He stuck it in a pocket. "Kirby's not back yet. That's why I came here. I overheard some stuff from Inspector Castor..."

While Alf updated him, Rich carefully patted his black eye and ribs. "Hmm. Do you think Mr Bergrim-Hoyt knows more than he told the good inspector?"

"I don't know as I'd have told him all I knew either." If even Alf found Castor a pompous git, what might a gentleman like Mr Bergrim-Hoyt think?

"I've never spoken with him. Pity."

"Mr Bergrim-Hoyt? Funny. I worked for him, kinda." At Rich's enquiring look, Alf continued, "He bought the factory, and then most of us got laid off. It's a skeleton crew there now. Mainly for security, with the other stuff done by programmed machines. He's done okay for himself, not that it's doing anyone else any good. Other factories have already gone bust. Why does so-called progress lead to–"

"I don't understand why the kidnappers are making the effort to force me into a false confession."

Alf had a daft thought. "Unless they're really still in the city? I mean, they must have taken Mum somewhere local?"

"Seems an odd way of causing misdirection. But you could be right. And..." Rich winced. "I occasionally sit in court. Kidnappings are far less common than, er, killings. It's reassuring that they used a drug, as if they're trying not to harm anyone."

Mum *had* to be alright, didn't she? "But *you're* injured."

Rich waved dismissively. "My black eye? I fell face first into your pile of books there. Had far worse while boxing. I'm not saying there's *no* danger, but they could have done far worse than take your Mum away."

Fine words. *Rich* wasn't the one who'd been kidnapped. If he confessed and got clapped in jail, it would serve him right. But would that really get Mum back? *Inspector Grimley's Casebook* was full of kidnappings gone wrong, and real life didn't guarantee a happy ending. If Rich was detained—again—that would leave Alf and Sally on their own. It was a galling truth that a lord could achieve more, simply by virtue of his position, no matter how much effort Alf was willing to make. And what would he tell Gwen? That reminded him... He opened the letter, and a coin rolled into his hand. A crown!

Guess what, Mum! There's an extension to Mr Bergrim-Hoyt's hush-hush project. It'll last around a month. Huge bonus, so I'm paying a boy to sneak this out to you. It'll really put Alf's nose out of joint that I'm earning more than him! Love, Gwen.

Rich peered over his shoulder. "Bergrim-Hoyt again? And a secret project? Sounds like his wife isn't the only one of interest. What if the Calesians are putting pressure on him through her? Maybe it's him they're really after—No, that wouldn't work. They could have kidnapped both at the same time."

"I don't like Gwen being involved as well." Alf's gaze dropped to his boots. She might be an irritating pest at times, but it was only right he look after his sister. "How about we speak to Mr Bergrim-Hoyt about you seeing the kidnapping?"

"Yes, perhaps he'll have some suggestions since the police didn't believe I was a witness. It seems likely that whoever has his wife also has your mother, maybe in the same place."

Alf shoved the letter back in his pocket, carefully tucking the coin away. "And while we're there, I'll also tell him I'm not happy about Gwen."

"That's the spirit! Though I've just realised a problem," said Rich. "Those goons may be watching the Bergrim-Hoyts' house. If they see me visiting, they'll know I'm not doing what they want. You'll need to speak with him on your own."

"And what if he doesn't believe me?"

"You'll just have to convince him."

Chapter 11

Hands in his pockets, Rich slouched along the pavement while Alf preceded him towards the Bergrim-Hoyts' house. It lay en route to the police station, so any observers shouldn't get too suspicious. It wouldn't do to endanger Mrs Wilson any further. Assuming Alf was successful in speaking with Bergrim-Hoyt, they would have to play it by ear after that. It was frustrating to take a back seat over such a delicate matter: with his lack of polish, Alf was likely to blunder into trouble.

Admittedly, it was Rich who had his face on posters all over town as a suspect in the kidnapping. For caution's sake, he wrapped the scarf more snugly around his face, wincing as he touched a bruise.

While Alf strode up the Bergrim-Hoyt's garden path, Rich paused to study a poster. Reassuringly, repeated soaking by rain had rendered it barely legible. He turned his attention to the house.

Hmm. Unlike the neighbouring properties, the Bergrim-Hoyt's chimney didn't belch smoke. Was the house empty? No, the side door opened briefly and Alf spoke to someone. Maybe they had a diamond-powered furnace too? Professor Bergrim-Hoyt was certainly productive with her inventions.

Alf retraced his steps, a scowl on his face. Rich started ambling further down the pavement. Uneven footsteps scuffed behind him.

"He's at work," muttered Alf as he passed. "My old factory. Hopefully I can persuade the gate guards to let me in. I know them from before. That job would have been ideal for me, but..."

Fortunately for Rich, Alf continued to walk towards the police station. Rich tagged along behind, pausing to gape at mansions as if he were a country bumpkin. Nobody sinister was obviously dogging his steps: at least, he and Alf were the worst-dressed men on the street. When one lady and her parcel-laden maid crossed the street to avoid them, Rich responded with a courtly bow, grinning at her confused frown.

Alf came to a T-junction and turned right. Although foot traffic remained light, horse-drawn carts passed up and down. Rich eyed a steam-powered carriage with suspicion, but it was larger than the one he'd seen on the night of the kidnap.

On the other side of the facing street was a high brick wall, behind which lay the various factories at the docks. He strolled along and also turned right, just in time to see Alf cross the street and head for an opening in the wall.

A pair of gatehouses stood opposite each other. Alf halted at one. The guard stepped out and shook Alf's hand, patting him on the back. Alf pointed at his bad leg, then waved a hand dismissively.

This looked promising. Rich ambled closer then halted. His breath caught as he took in the guard's appearance. Damn! That stocky build and rounded chin: he was one of Mrs Wilson's kidnappers. That tore it. What was he doing here? Was Bergrim-Hoyt behind his wife's kidnapping? Or some employee forming a plot?

Rich stared, barely aware of draft horses and crates obscuring his view. The guard beckoned his colleague over from the other gatehouse. The smaller guard had a nervous energy about him that Rich also recognised. He would bet his last crown that both guards had been behind the kidnappings.

Alf pointed to a small brick building with windows that was dwarfed by its warehouse neighbours. The larger guard shook his head and walked further into the compound, beckoning Alf to follow.

No! Rich scuttled across the street, dodging carts with irate drivers. Then he paused. If he tried to intervene, the kidnappers might do something desperate. All he could do was watch helplessly as the three men walked past the closest warehouse, leaving the gatehouses unmanned.

Well, that was a small opportunity. Rich sidled through the gateway. A scrape of gravel sounded to his left, and he twitched. An unmanned trolley heaped with rubble tipped its load into a skip. Other heavy lifting machinery was parked close to the wall. None of the machines had the glowing eyes of security automata, and there was no sign of other people. Rich's shoulders relaxed.

As Alf and his escorts moved round a corner, Rich straightened up. No point acting as if he didn't belong here. Hands in his pockets, he strolled after them, pausing as he reached the end of the building. His eyes widened.

Alf staggered against the larger man, the smaller one returning a familiar bottle to his pocket. They were drugging him too!

Rich's fists clenched, but then his injured ribs twinged. His odds in a fight would be poor. These were two well-prepared criminals on their home ground.

He plastered himself against a wall while the two men dragged the unresisting Alf into a single-storey building near a side wall. That was a slight relief: much better than flinging him into the sea. It might offer Rich a chance to rescue him and, with luck, the other two captives. If only he'd had his lock picks.

By the time the two guards exited a few minutes later, Rich was shivering from a mixture of cold and nerves. He crouched in the alcove of a padlocked door, holding his breath until the crunch of their footsteps diminished. A quick peek confirmed they were heading back to the gatehouse. Then he crept over to the building where Alf was being held.

Its walls were of corrugated iron rather than brick, and it had a simple wooden door. More like a shed than a prison. A neatly painted sign on the door said: *AUTHORISED PERSONNEL ONLY.* Rich turned the handle. To his surprise, the door opened smoothly.

He stepped inside, and his eyebrows rose.

The outer shell of the building served to conceal an enormous vault. The door in front of him was heavy, metal and included a lock with blinking lights. Etched into the lock was a logo: a diamond containing the initials "AB".

Rich pressed his ear to the door and then cursed under his breath. There was no tell-tale clockwork vibration. Presumably another diamond-powered device. His lock picks would have been of no use.

He rubbed his forehead with a grimy hand. Breaking Alf out would be impossible. But neither could he abandon the man. Even without the lure of the reward, it wouldn't be right to leave Alf and his mother at the mercy of the kidnappers.

Where could he find help? Who had heavy equipment and the skills to use it? Or at least the authority to order–

Damn! The police did, of course. Rich would need to talk them into opening the vault, either through an order or brute force. An illicit hobby wasn't worth anyone's life. If Richard, Lord Hayes, had to confess his history of crimes, so be it. His honour would allow no less.

Alf blinked up at the ceiling, a lump digging into his back. What a strange dream he'd had. "Sally?"

"You're awake!" Someone wiped his forehead with a damp cloth.

Mum! She was *here*? He levered himself upright and peered at her anxious face, hoping she hadn't heard him. Although her laundry uniform was creased and grubby, she seemed unharmed. He sagged with relief. "Are you alright?"

She straightened up from kneeling on the floor beside him. Multicoloured rugs were strewn underfoot. "Yes, yes, but I didn't even have a chance to pack a change of clothes before they brought me here."

"They?" His memory prodded him. "*Gorman and Brooks* kidnapped you?"

"They didn't bother introducing themselves," came a clipped female voice.

Dim light came from a glass bulb in the ceiling. In a corner of the windowless room stood an elderly woman with a sour expression and folded arms. She wore a high-necked cotton nightdress and her grey hair was messily braided, but her fingers glittered with jewellery.

Alf gaped. "Professor Bergrim-Hoyt? You really haven't left the country!"

"Indeed I have not, young man! And once I get my hands on–"

"But why did your husband put you here?"

"*Husband?* Impossible!" Her nostrils flared.

"Oh." Alf's brow creased. "Maybe I got confused. When I arrived at the factory, I told Gorman I wanted to speak to your husband about you..."

While he told his story, he stood and stretched, although the room was a bit cramped for pacing. Professor Bergrim-Hoyt took a seat on an embroidered ottoman beside Mum.

"... So you see," Alf concluded, "it's too much of a coincidence that we've ended up here, plus Gwen's special project. Does that make sense, Professor Bergrim-Hoyt?"

"Oh, call me Ina," she said impatiently. "It's short for Angelina. Your story makes no sense at all. I know people gossip about Leo's Calesian connections, but he's a man of business. Besides..." She regarded her hands and mumbled, "We've been married for forty years. He *can't* have been plotting against me."

"If you say so." Alf eyed the ottoman. Certainly no room for *him* to sit as well. After moving a covered pail to the side, he rolled up one of the rugs into a makeshift seat and carefully perched on it.

"Well." Ina looked up again. "Leaving the issue of Leo aside, I suppose your two guard friends didn't want witnesses. But they told Rich—Lord Hayes—to confess?"

"They didn't know Rich's name, but they also knew he didn't kidnap you. Because it was them all along. Throw the dogs off the scent or something?"

"Possibly. We need more data. Which means we need to get out."

"Really?" As if he hadn't figured that. "But how? Rich might have seen them put me here, but he doesn't know about you two. We can't rely on him."

"Lord Hayes is a fine gentleman," said Mum with a fond smile. "I'm sure he'll come up with something."

Alf decided to ignore that. He stood up and shuffled around the cramped enclosure, running his hands along the walls. The sturdy plate metal was bolted together, not that he had any tools. "What kinda room is this?"

"This is a secure vault." Ina pursed her lips. "I use a similar one to store my more dangerous inventions. As you can see, this one's full of handmade silk rugs."

Crikey! Alf's eyes widened in horror. Each of his steps was causing a week's worth of damage. Placing his feet more carefully, he reached the door. It was hinged to open outwards. "It's locked, obviously. And heavier than a regular door."

Ina nodded at Mum. "Delia noticed a control pad when she arrived, which will operate the door. No doubt they're also using one of my diamond-powered locks. I have the patent on those." She waggled her fingers. "An irony I'm wearing these rings, but I have nothing for the gems to power. If Leo ordered the kidnapping–not that I'm saying he did–he would of course know not to give me anything to work with."

Alf glanced around for more clues. Waxed paper testified to sandwich deliveries. "They'll feed us, right?"

"They did," said Mum. "The last one was ham and pickle. That reminds me, when did *you* last eat–"

"These vaults aren't designed to house people. Every hour, they open the door for ventilation." Ina scowled. "Day and night, although that's better than suffocating. But they only set the door mechanism to open by a few inches. You can't rush them when they come."

"Hmm." Alf ran his hand across the door. There was a small central hole. He stuck his finger inside and felt a sheared-off edge. "What's this?"

Ina sighed. "There would have been an emergency exit handle there, but they've removed it."

"How does the handle work?"

"Simply by pulling it." She eyed him sardonically. "Even an old besom like myself could manage it. But we have nothing to grip it with."

Bugger. Forcing their way outside seemed impossible.

Chapter 12

Rich massaged his bruised cheek, trying to ease its throbbing. The immediate challenge was leaving the factory compound since the guards had returned to their posts. Not only was Rich an intruder, they would recognise him. The lack of employees that had aided Rich's unobserved entry now threatened to hamper his exit. At least there was plenty of equipment to hide behind, and dusk was approaching.

The walls were around fifteen feet high: too far to climb without help. A lope around the perimeter confirmed that there was only one entrance, other than the opening to the dockside loading area. He had no desire to take a swim.

Remembering how Alf rescued him from the prison, Rich inspected one of the silent machines. If a rough labourer could operate one, surely he could... He hissed in annoyance. His gentleman's education hadn't covered this, and–unlike locks–he'd had no reason to learn how they worked. If he attempted to rescue the prisoners using this unfamiliar technology, he might make things worse.

The trolley was still shifting rubble into a row of skips, moving rather slowly. He paced alongside it, inspecting the controls. There was a labelled on/off switch, but no obvious steering mechanism. Rather, there was a row of buttons with lights that flashed intermittently.

Well, perhaps he could turn it into a distraction. He mashed some buttons at random then skipped out of the way. Would it speed up or change direction?

The machine completely ignored him. How disappointing. He looked again.

Ah, there was a "manual override" lever. Pulling it, he repeated the previous performance. Gratifyingly, the machine lurched to one side. He ducked to avoid a shower of gravel. A whining noise filled the air.

With a grin, Rich slipped in between two enormous skips while a hoarse voice shouted, "Gorman! Autoload's gone haywire!"

Running footsteps crossed the yard, accompanied by the crunch of stone. Rich peeked out from his hiding place to see the machine accelerate through the opening in the wall that led to the dockside.

Oops. He winced at the almighty splash.

"Fuck!" came a tenor voice. "Mr B. will kill us! This is your fault, Brooks."

"Mine? I never touched it." Brooks' growl came from the other side of Rich's skip. "Them dratted machines have a mind of their own."

"Yeah, dumb minds too. Wilson wouldn't have crashed."

"Why'd he have to show up just then?"

"How should I know? Better do the rounds and check the prisoners. Tonight, I'll ask the boss what to do with them."

"Uh, you don't mean–"

"Quit yer fretting. He'll probably just want them moved. With three of them, the air'll grow stale quicker."

Both men's footsteps moved off.

Three? That must be Alf, his mother and Professor Bergrim-Hoyt. Surely they weren't kidnapping other people too.

Rich crept away from the skips, around the other buildings and out into the street. Once he was out of line of sight of the gatehouse, he leaned against a rough brick wall and took a long, shuddering breath. Phew!

Now for his next port of call. Hurrying would attract undue attention, especially if someone misidentified him as a fanatical Calesian on the rampage. He ambled away from the water and towards the police station.

A frown creased Rich's forehead while he walked and considered. Even though he'd resigned himself to revealing his true identity, summoning help wouldn't be straightforward. If he marched into the station with his story, they might well throw him into a cell to await Kirby's return.

Given Brooks' mention of "stale air," Rich couldn't afford such a delay. Not when it put lives at risk. He needed to be more daring.

As he rounded the final corner, the scent of cigar smoke reached his nostrils. He stopped behind a skip of rubble, suppressing a nervous chuckle at the rusty lock that lay on top.

Two men stood outside the police station, talking in low voices. Castor wore his trench coat with the fur trim, while the other man's woollen overcoat protected his bulk from the chill. Kirby had arrived.

Rich chewed his lip. Was that a good thing or not? Even though an appeal to Kirby might be successful, it might still cause too long a delay. The chief inspector believed in doing things by the book.

However, if Rich could catch the man by himself, there might be some scope for negotiation. He crossed his fingers that Castor would depart and leave Kirby alone.

"I bumped into Mr Bergrim-Hoyt at the coach station," came Kirby's confident rumble. "He was rather agitated when he told me of your interview. Did you really interrogate him about their sleeping arrangements?"

"Yes? It was necessary to establish—"

"I didn't want to embarrass you in front of the clerk, but you need to be more tactful if you want that promotion. It was bad enough that kidnapper escaped on your watch."

Castor's posture was stiff. "I'm sorry about that," he mumbled.

"Additionally, our budget can't support extra patrols, just on the off-chance they notice the spy. I was horrified to find the station barely manned. What if we have an emergency? From now on, you're not to interfere with the duty rota. Understood?"

"Yes, sir."

"Good. I still have hopes for you." With a nod, Kirby re-entered the police station.

Castor took another puff of his cigar. "Patronising bastard."

Damn. Not the policeman Rich would have picked. But time was running out, and he had to work with what he was offered. He poked his head around the skip. "Psst."

Castor looked round suspiciously. "Who's there?"

"Henry Duggins, remember me? I wanna turn the kidnappers in. Come along with me, and I'll give them to you."

"You think you can lure me into a trap?" He reached towards his waist, but no truncheon hung from his belt.

"Nah, why would we wanna? You're not valuable like the prof." Stepping out from cover, Rich waved a hand at the scaffolding. "Else we'd have made sure you were inside when we pulled down the wall."

Castor's face hardened, and he tapped ash from the end of his cigar. "You don't sound like you're trying to be helpful."

Timing would be everything. As his boxing trainer had taught him, he balanced lightly on his feet before speaking. "You caught me bang to rights, guv."

With one sweep of his arm, Rich snatched Castor's cigar. He took a quick puff. The end was still glowing when he leaned forwards and stubbed it out on Castor's precious fur collar. An odour of burning hair overpowered the cigar smoke.

Castor snarled. A vein on his temple bulged. "Why, you–"

Rich stepped back, grinning. "Yeah?"

The policeman grabbed his whistle and blew it.

Yes! With the shrill alert in his ears, Rich ran. A quick glance confirmed Castor half a block behind him. A stocky figure jogged out of the station. Kirby. Damn, showing up with two policemen, no matter how senior, wouldn't be enough. Rich changed direction and dodged a pile of rubbish. He'd need a circuitous route to collect more pursuers.

Castor's whistle blew again. Answering whistles sounded from all around. While rounding a corner, Rich's foot skidded on some vile substance, and he slammed into the wall. Ow!

Rubbing his shoulder, Rich staggered on. His feet pounded the pavement, and blood rushed in his ears.

There! The docks factory walls lay ahead. He ran into the street, head whipping around.

Damn! He'd misjudged. His destination was two factories further up, and police were running down the road towards him from that direction. These efforts were yielding *too* much success.

With no other choice, Rich ran through the gateway

straight ahead. The salt-rich air seared his heaving chest while he scanned his surroundings.

This compound was in disrepair. Skeletons of warehouses stood around him, along with ancient machinery leaning drunkenly against the walls.

"Now we've got him!" came a shout.

What to do, what to do? Jumping into the water would be no good.

Walls! While a dozen police flooded into the area, Rich scrambled up the framework of a hoist. Flecks of rust fell off as he moved. He jumped the short distance to the top of the wall and landed in a crouch, ribs aching. The wall was a foot wide, and mortar crumbled in his trembling fingers. Heart racing, he stood and squinted. His destination wasn't far.

"A mere two factories up," he muttered, "where I have to run along the top of a wall with a congregation of coppers chasing me. Most excellent."

He chanced a downward look and gulped. On both sides of the wall, pale faces gaped up at him. Pacing up and down the street, Castor shook a fist.

"He'll smash his skull in if he falls!" called a cadet, his voice cracking.

"Don't remind me." Rich took a wobbly pace, arms outstretched. Nobody was foolhardy enough to follow him up here.

One foot at a time. Don't think about the drop.

He shuffled along the uneven surface, dislodging pieces of grit. An occasional stone pinged off and, going by the curses, on to a pursuer on the street.

"Don't let him escape," shouted Castor. Did he think Rich was going to fly away?

When he reached the border with the next factory, he paused and wiped his sweating brow. Most of the massed policemen–including Castor and Kirby–were on the street side. A few enterprising constables ran ahead and through the next entrance with its decrepit brick archway.

"Not that one, boys," Rich muttered, resuming his careful walk.

When he reached the archway, he eased his weight on to its thinnest point, holding his breath. The structure quivered. *No!* With an awkward scramble, he landed lying on the other side. Nauseous, he clung to the bricks as if his life depended on them. Maybe it did.

Stuff dignity. He'd crawl the rest of the way. Should have thought of that in the first place. Pushing himself up on all fours, he winced as the irregular surface dug into his palms and knees. Next time–*ha!*–he'd bring a pair of gloves.

At the junction with Alf's factory, he paused to double-check his route. The police milled in the street to his left. His destination lay at the back of the compound, near the dockside and close to this wall leading off to the right.

Turning along the side wall, he levered himself upright. It wouldn't do to lose his pursuers now. Arms again outstretched, he set one foot in front of the other. From the exclamations behind him, the police had arrived at the compound's entrance.

"What the bugger's going on?" came a distant hoarse complaint.

Brooks. Grinning, Rich shouted, "It's a security alert! An unauthorised intruder. Better come and see." Unless Bergrim-Hoyt himself appeared, one of the gate guards would need to open the security door. Surely the police wouldn't let them slink off now.

Testing each move with painful care, Rich stepped along the wall until he arrived as close to the vault as he could manage.

He folded his arms and waited. Some two dozen policemen streamed towards him. Kirby and Castor's plain clothes stood out among the regulation uniforms and capes.

"That's the boss' vault," came Brooks' voice.

Locating the two guards in the crowd, Rich pointed at them. "Those men are the kidnappers. They've stashed their victims inside."

Gorman held up his hands. "Dunno what he means. 'Sides, only the boss has the key. We can't open it."

Gah, what now? Even without the "stale air" concern, Rich didn't want to spend the night on this wall. He re-examined the vault. It was a mere four feet away, its flat roof of corrugated iron a few feet below him. Jumping from here would be no problem.

Bending his legs slightly, he called, "Then come and get me!"

He sprang forwards, thrusting himself away from the wall. His impact with the vault's roof drove the air from his lungs, and he sprawled flat. Argh, it sloped! *You idiot!* He scrambled for purchase on the ridged surface. Legs inelegantly flailing, he slid towards the edge.

If he could just his foot into a gutter or something—

Hands grabbed his ankles.

"There are people inside!" he yelled as his pursuers dragged him down.

Chapter 13

Leaning against the vault door, Alf squirmed. Normally he'd relish being somewhere warm, but this little room was a bit *too* cosy. And maybe it was his imagination, but the air felt stuffier than it had before.

Still seated on the ottoman, Mum and Ina paid him no attention. How he wished he could ignore them as well.

Mum patted Ina's shoulder. "When Alf's father was courting me, he spent a day's pay on champagne for my birthday, even though he had no head for drink. Still, he was never the practical type–was run over by a dray before we could get married."

Alf growled under his breath. Did Mum *have* to tell that story again?

"Leo and I were finalists in a design contest," said Ina. "He invited me out for drinks the evening before the practical. I saw through *that* ruse, but I treated us both to dinner with the prize money."

"How sweet!" Mum sighed. "But you never had any children?"

"No." Ina chuckled. "Though it wasn't for lack of trying. Over all the years of our marriage, I've had no complaints about his performance in..."

Would they notice if he stuck his fingers in his ears? Alf started to pace again, so it didn't seem like he was deliberately listening in. His trailing foot caught on a heaped-up rug. He stumbled, then lifted his bad leg over the obstacle.

Mum looked up as if she'd just remembered his presence. “Careful! I guess we’ve been here a while if your leg has run down.”

“Yeah. I didn’t have time to wind it up properly earlier.”

Ina stood up with a frown. “You have a prosthetic leg? Clockwork?”

“What of it?” Alf said defensively.

“Wonderful!” To his amazement, she knelt beside him and yanked up his trouser leg.

“Hey!” He steadied himself against the wall, trying not to fall on top of her.

As if it were the most natural thing in the world to paw complete strangers, she inspected the tiny connections and stainless steel joints. “This is based on the Gibbons Responder, isn’t it?”

“Uh, dunno. Is it a big deal?”

“Of course it’s a big deal,” she said impatiently, straightening up. “Although these limbs are clockwork, they can also be powered by diamonds.” With her thumbnail, she prised open a gleaming cover and handed it to him. The palm-sized plate bore a diamond logo. She poked a finger into the prosthesis’ cavity and rooted around. “Yes, the holder’s there. I insisted that all newer models have that functionality.”

“And that means...” Alf shrugged at Mum, who looked equally confused.

“It means your leg can generate an electrical field.” Ina pulled off one of her rings and waved it at him. “These aren’t just decorative. They’re cut to standard device-powering size.”

Alf scratched his head. To him, one shiny rock looked much like another. Not that he’d ever seen one up close. “You’ll use my leg to power the door?”

"No." She screwed up her face. "How can I put this simply? The door controls are partly magnetic. Electricity will enhance the magnet's pull. And we can then trigger the emergency exit mechanism."

"Oh. So you can do something with your ring and my leg that'll make the door open."

"Exactly!"

"Well, let's get started. Move up, Mum." Alf sat and detached his leg.

As soon as his leg was off, the professor sat cross-legged on the floor with it laid across her knees. Alf tried not to stare. She was more limber than he'd expected for someone her age. He hadn't thought of her as getting much exercise, but perhaps her husband–*don't think about that!*

Mum yawned. "It's kind of warm in here. What else has been going on?"

Ina squinted at the leg and muttered something in jargon. While she worked, Alf started to fill Mum in on his last few days, but he stopped when she slumped against the wall with a snore. He made a face. His adventures hadn't been *that* boring, had they? But at least it meant she wasn't interrogating him about Sally.

His eyelids drooped. Maybe Mum had the right idea with her nap. The stress of the day was catching up with him. When a thump on the roof was followed by scrabbling noises, he gazed blearily upwards. Surely the building wasn't going to collapse? He wasn't sure he cared.

Ina shoved his false leg under a pillow. "Throw a blanket over yourself! We don't want anyone to suspect."

He dragged a floral-patterned rug across his lap. Lifting it took all his energy. He leaned his head against the wall and closed his eyes.

◊ ◊ ◊

The jumble of people surrounding Rich made it difficult to pick anyone out, even with his height. As the policemen handcuffed him, he looked around frantically, trying to catch his breath. "There are people inside. They'll suffocate. You need to open the door. Kirby!"

Castor pushed his way to the front of the crowd. "I don't know what you're playing at, Duggins, but you're being put away for a long, long time."

"Tell the guards to open the door. Brooks! Gorman!" Rich's voice shook with a mixture of frustration and terror.

Gorman leaned against the vault wall and shrugged.

Standing beside him, Brooks said hoarsely, "I've no idea what he's talking about."

"This is a vault," Rich insisted. "And there are people inside."

Castor swung open the door. "Well, it's certainly a vault."

"Sure it is." Gorman glared at Rich, no doubt recognising him on a closer look. "Boss has lots of valuables. But he's the only one who can get in. Special code on the lock."

Rich ground his teeth. "I saw you kidnap Alf and put him in here, and you also kidnapped Professor Bergrim-Hoyt."

"Never met the woman. Though we work for 'er hubby, of course." Brooks tapped his temple and winked at Castor. "Maybe this fella's touched?"

"Nonsense," said Rich. "I recognise your voices from when you were inside her house."

"You're completely making that up." Castor fingered his singed collar and frowned. "Mr Bergrim-Hoyt said they sounded foreign. These chaps are as local as they come."

"Bergrim-Hoyt was lying to you." Rich pulled against his captors' arms. "He was in on it from the start. Kirby!"

The crowd parted, and Kirby stepped forwards. He peered at Rich, then blinked. "Why, you're–"

"Sir, we've caught one of the kidnappers!" Castor stuck his chest out.

Kirby gave him a curt nod. "So I see. But perhaps we should deal with this in private."

Rich could have screamed. "Open the door first!"

"Ah, *now* I see your ploy." Castor's smug expression made Rich want to head-butt him. "You set this up so you can steal Mr Bergrim-Hoyt's business secrets. He told me he stores them in a vault."

Gah! Would the man not let things alone? He was worse than a terrier with a rat.

"Maybe not." Kirby frowned. "He might have taken them with him. I did see him at the coach station, after all. Castor, I don't think we should discuss this business in full earshot of, well, everybody. Let's take the prisoner back to the station."

"Don't you think it odd," said Rich, desperately changing tack, "that the man goes on a trip while his wife's missing?"

"He might have something there, sir." Castor looked at Kirby with hope. "If Mr Bergrim-Hoyt was handing over a ransom, we could have arranged to follow him. I should have interrogated him further."

This wasn't getting the door open, not with the guard's claim they had no access. How could he throw suspicion on them? "What about Alf Wilson? Suffocating inside?"

Brooks looked uncomfortable. "Suffocating? What–"

Gorman elbowed his workmate. "He's nothing to do

with this."

"Yes, he is." Rich nodded at Gorman. "There's that bottle in his pocket. The one you used to render him unconscious."

"Away with yer!" With a forced smile, Gorman patted his jacket. "Just a little something to keep the chill out."

"Castor, open it and have a sniff. I'm sure it'll convince you." Rich strained towards Gorman, but the policemen still held him fast.

Castor huffed. "A seasoned criminal like you should know we don't just randomly search innocent–"

Rich sagged into his captors' arms. They instinctively caught his weight as he shot his foot forwards, catching Gorman on the hip. Long legs had their uses.

The policemen forced Rich to his knees as Gorman grabbed for his pocket. But the bottle slipped out and clanked on the ground. The stopper popped off. A harsh smoky odour filled the air.

Hunched under the policemen's weighty grasp, Rich called, "That's no booze."

"Why, you..." Flapping a hand in front of his face, Gorman staggered and slid towards the ground. He took a couple of policemen with him.

Brooks leapt out of the way and gaped at Rich.

"Brooks," said Rich rapidly, jerking his chin at the vault. "If anyone inside dies, it'll be a hanging offence. Alf was your buddy, right?"

Kirby rubbed his forehead and asked Castor, "Who's this 'Alf' he keeps talking about?"

"He got tangled up in the kidnapping," said Rich before Castor could reply. "He used to work with Brooks."

"But the boss–"

"Your boss has gone away." Rich glanced at Kirby. "The Chief Inspector saw him leave. He's not around to make decisions for you. And with Gorman unconscious as well, the responsibility's purely on your shoulders. If you choose right, you can save three lives. If you choose wrong... accessory to murder and treachery will be just the start of your charges."

"Uh..." Brooks' shoulders sagged, and then he stepped into the doorway. "Yeah. We were only doing what Mr B. told us."

Kirby and Castor followed him. A series of beeps came from inside the shed, and then the whir of motors. Rich breathed raggedly, straining his ears. Had he been in time?

"Cor blimey," came Castor's voice. "Look at 'em, laid out like–"

"Castor!" Kirby growled.

"Are they alive?" Rich croaked.

In the silence, he started to tremble.

Kirby reappeared. "Yes, they are."

Chapter 14

Propped up in a hospital bed, Alf squirmed as the thin cotton gown slipped off his shoulders. His chest was nearly as pale as the sheets. He self-consciously tucked the blanket around his neck, but then his foot stuck out the other end. The privacy of a single room didn't preserve his dignity against the visitor in the chair beside him.

Sally fiddled with the ribbons on the bonnet she held. "Rich was just in time."

"Good for him, I guess." He grimaced. All the nurses kept gabbing about how lucky Alf was to have been rescued by such a hero. He didn't *want* to be grateful to Rich, especially as it was Rich who'd dragged him into trouble in the first place.

"Alf, you nearly all suffocated! It took a whole day for you to regain your wits."

"I know. I just feel too washed out to care much." Even Sally's company was a burden. He just wanted to sleep again, now that matron had reassured him about his fellow captives. Mum was busy gossiping in the women's ward. The professor was also there. Although she was fully awake, the effects of her longer captivity hadn't worn off: she refused to let go of Alf's prosthesis. "I'm glad we survived. And that Rich brought the coppers."

"Just imagine, the chief inspector chasing him!" Tying the ribbons into a bow, Sally shook her head. "Though he's always had a knack of making up tales and provoking folk. More often than not, it led him into trouble when he was a boy. His parents—Well. They didn't spend much time with him, although they made sure he had a good education. Tutors and so on."

"Figures." Now that he thought about it, Alf could imagine toffs paying for their children's upbringing rather than doing it themselves. "I can't believe Gorman and Brooks were in on it. I was jealous when they got kept on, with so many of us being laid off. But I guess Mr Bergrim-Hoyt picked them, special-like."

"Chief Inspector Kirby questioned them himself. He and Rich are speaking to the Council of Lords today."

Alf puffed out his cheeks. "Hmph."

"Aren't you curious to know the details?"

"To be honest, I'd rather forget about the whole thing. I'd be happy if I never saw any of that lot again." At her downcast expression, he added grudgingly, "Uh, apart from Rich. He's not so bad. And you, of course."

"Thanks!"

"Hey, I'm no smooth talker like he is. But I mean it."

"Your straight talking is part of your appeal." She grinned suddenly. "And you're now a man of means!"

"How come?" He gaped. "Oh, the reward money?"

"It's being split equally between you and Rich. It's enough to support you for a long time. You could move somewhere a lot nicer, even buy a little house..." She chewed her lip. "And Rich can pay the tax collectors."

Alf took her hand, feeling pleased when she blushed. "Mum's been on at me to find a nice girl... I wonder—"

She slipped her hand out of his and gripped her bonnet. "Hold your horses. I've too much on my plate to be courting."

He blinked. "How come?" Surely all that kidnapping

palaver was now finished?

"Before Rich's parents left, they told me to watch out for him." She raised her chin. "I promised. And he's not out of trouble yet."

"Oh." Alf slumped. She'd been with that family for nearly half her life, far longer than he'd known her. Of course she'd need to reassure herself about the outcome. As a minor consolation, the reward money didn't seem to be a factor. "Might there be some hope in future?"

"Maybe. Can't say." Her pursed lips signalled the end of the matter.

"Damn." Alf clenched his jaw before he made things worse. Probably something to do with Rich's secret agent business.

She tipped her head to the side. "What'll you do with the money?"

Alf scratched his head. A house and leisurely retirement was tempting, but then he'd be no better than the toffs he despised. Though after seeing some of Rich's situation, he was less sure that toffs had a completely easy life. "First, I'll buy Gwen all the clothes and books she needs. She's behind in her coursework. Then she can catch up with her classmates, though I bet they'll still pick on her."

"She's lucky you take an interest."

"She complains I'm too protective. But I know what's good for her." At a knock on the door, he continued, "I can't wait to see her face."

In stepped the messenger boy Alf had sent up to the college. His face was red, and he was breathless. "I ran all around the whole building lookin' fer yer sis."

Alf frowned as the door closed behind the boy. "Wouldn't she come back with you?"

"I couldn't find her! But she left a note fer ye on her desk." He handed over a paper.

Haha, Alf, you were wrong! I'm doing even better than I said in my note to Mum. Mr Bergrim-Hoyt told me more about his project–he says I have a special aptitude. And Shambito is a better place for me to learn. He'll escort me there personally! We were going to travel by air, but the weather isn't good, so we need to take the fast coach instead. By the time you get this note, we'll be on our way. You can't stop me, so there!

Alf's pulse rushed in his ears. He bolted fully upright, ignoring the linen that crumpled at his waist. "Shambito?" His voice cracked.

Sally looked at him enquiringly. "That's the capital of Calesia."

"I know that! Just 'cos I didn't get your fancy education... Sorry, it's bad news." The note was dated two days ago. He crumpled the paper. "Can you find out where my clothes are? I need to visit the coach station."

Sitting in the front row of the circular Council chamber, Rich tugged uncomfortably at his cravat. He'd last worn this formal suit three years ago, when being transferred his father's title. Now he stood to lose that same position. Even if his parents were no longer among the living, the thought of their disappointment lay heavy in his chest. *Focus.* What could he do to salvage the situation?

Today, two dozen lords graced the wooden benches: more than usually attended. Chief Inspector Kirby was at the podium taking questions, and then it would be Rich's turn to give his statement. He'd resolved to be completely truthful, but part of him hoped they'd overlook certain aspects of his evidence. It didn't help that his peers kept staring at his still-bruised face.

"So," said Pettigrew, stroking his waxed moustache, "Mr Bergrim-Hoyt only specified that his wife was to be kidnapped and the plans stolen? Not that Mrs Wilson and her son also be taken captive?"

"That's what I gathered." Kirby's bass voice was less assured than usual. Even an experienced policeman might find the Council intimidating. "In the absence of further instructions from Mr Bergrim-Hoyt, it seems the kidnappers attempted some misdirection of their own."

Pettigrew sniffed. "I suppose desperate criminals are more than capable of low cunning. Did they know why they were to kidnap the professor?"

"No. Their instructions were to keep her safely out of the way and make sure she was unharmed. Mr Brooks was more forthcoming than Mr Gorman–of course they were interrogated separately–but both men volunteered that they were awaiting further instructions from Mr Bergrim-Hoyt. Instructions that never came, apparently."

One of the lords with investments in airships cleared his throat. "It seems most likely that Bergrim-Hoyt is in league with the Calesians, but why take them his wife's papers and not the lady herself? For ease of transport?"

Pressing clammy palms together, Rich took long, slow breaths. Think about Bergrim-Hoyt's mysterious motives. Papers were certainly more portable than unwilling captives. But if he truly wanted his wife unharmed, why abduct her in the first place?

"This is assuming our prisoners told the truth, which I

think likely. They have the look of hired muscle." Kirby's expression was dour. "Professor Bergrim-Hoyt was most insistent we must have been mistaken, and that her husband is completely innocent. I can't agree with her that it's a set-up. We found more of that anaesthetic liquid in his warehouse."

"Maybe he's auctioning the plans?" suggested Pettigrew. "What steps have been taken to find him?"

"I have people enquiring at the airport, docks and coach stations. If he's travelling any distance, it's unlikely he'd use a steam carriage."

That made sense. Conventional horse-drawn carriages were less prone to complicated breakdown, and they needed no special fuel.

"Thank you, Chief Inspector Kirby," said Pettigrew. "You may sit down. Now, as to the kidnap itself, we have an eyewitness account."

So soon? Rich had hoped Kirby's statement might go on for longer. Taking a deep breath, Rich stood. Surprised murmurs filled the auditorium as he approached the podium. When he ascended its three steps, his legs quivered as if he were climbing a mountain.

"Richard Hayes," announced Pettigrew, "happened to be in the Bergrim-Hoyt house at the time of the kidnapping. Tell us what happened."

Rich lifted his scribbled notes in a shaking hand. He might never be known as "Lord" Hayes again, but he would face his future with dignity. "My Lords, I entered the house through a side door which was open. My intention was to pilfer valuables. But while I was there..."

Pausing once to sip some water, he delivered his statement. He didn't dare meet anyone's eye. His audience did him the courtesy of remaining silent, other than a gentle snore from the longest-standing lord.

With a dry throat, Rich concluded, "... but a security automaton apprehended me."

"I'm sure you have questions," Pettigrew said to the lords.

"The information about the two kidnappers seems clear enough," said the florid-faced Lord Angus, who enjoyed port and was lousy at cards. "And consistent with what they confessed."

Rich's shoulders relaxed.

"But how many other houses has Hayes burgled? And how much has he stolen?" Angus scowled. "Is he also a *card sharp*?"

"Of course not!" Rich burst out. Damn. It was funny how being addressed only by one's surname could still make clear one's title or lack of it. "Just because I confess to burglary..."

Kirby stood. "With respect, My Lords, this is not a court of law."

Sweat trickled down Rich's neck. Would Kirby insist on a public trial?

"We know." Pettigrew inclined his head. "The issue for this council is that Hayes has engaged in behaviour inappropriate to a noble. There must be compensation, and we must agree on Hayes' future status. After that, perhaps a trial would be superfluous."

Kirby subsided. "I suppose a trial would be an expense on the public purse."

And it would make the lords look fallible, thought Rich sourly. However, he might be spared the humiliation of his criminal record being spread via the tabloids.

After some debate, while Rich shuffled uncomfortably from foot to foot, Pettigrew nodded at him. "You will of course compensate your victims. We could arrange that discreetly. It seems the reward money from rescuing Professor Bergrim-Hoyt will cover that adequately."

"Of course, sir." Rich's heart sank, and the words stuck in his throat. "It's the least I can do to make amends." He'd be lucky to see any of the reward. How was he going to pay the tax collectors now?

"And we now need to consider your position in this Council and make a recommendation to the king. You might as well sit down. We may be some time."

Rich sat. If he were stripped of his title, he'd also give up the house. No more taxes. That was only a minor consolation.

Chapter 15

Alf's teeth rattled while hooves clopped on the cobbles. Did toffs really prefer this to walking? It was his first cab ride ever, and he hadn't realised the journey would be so bumpy. Even worse, he was at risk of sliding off his seat and embarrassing himself further in front of Sally. He gripped his borrowed crutches and braced them against the opposite wall.

Sally gave him an encouraging smile. "Not far now."

"I wish the professor had given me my leg back." Despite Alf's pleas, the old biddy had stubbornly retained the prosthesis. It was all very well for her to witter about enhancements, but he wanted his property! Speaking of which... "Uh, thanks for forking out for this. Once I get the reward money–"

"It's no problem." She waggled her fingers dismissively. "Just pay me back when you can."

Alf hunched his shoulders. First Sally turned him down, and then she spent extravagantly on his behalf. Obviously he'd never understand women. Never mind that: the priority was finding Gwen, not romantic aspirations.

"Here's the coach station," called the cabbie.

While Sally paid the driver, Alf eased himself out of the carriage. Wobbling slightly–it had been ages since he used crutches outside–he looked around. Workers harnessed coaches and helped passengers with their baggage while clerks wandered around logging packages. The scent of horses and dust made him sneeze.

"Right, let's go." With a steadying hand on his elbow, she led him towards a wooden building with a part-closed door. "Coachmaster's office is this way."

They stopped by the door. Voices came from inside. When the conversation paused, Sally spoke. "Hello?"

"Why, if it isn't Sally Rosely!" called a melodious baritone voice. "Haven't seen you for weeks. Just give us a couple of minutes..."

"We'll be right outside," she replied, and then murmured to Alf, "Coachmaster Ralph has been here forever. He knows everyone."

"If you say so." Alf leaned against the building wall, wondering at Sally's ease with so many classes of folk. Domestic service wasn't the slavery he'd previously imagined. Or perhaps it was her *unofficial* work that provided her with such confidence?

"... Nothing like the two days by airship," said the coachmaster. "But it's far safer in bad weather. Is that all, Inspector Castor?"

Making a sour face, Sally mouthed, "Oops."

Alf nearly groaned. Of course he would be here.

"Yes, I have what I need from you." Castor's voice was as curt as always. A chair scraped on wooden floorboards. "Send word if you remember anything else."

When the inspector stepped out of the office, Alf's grip tightened on his crutches. He met the inspector's glare with one of his own. "Good morning, Inspector Castor."

Castor's upper lip twitched. "Oh. It's you. Smith, Wilson, whoever you are. Turning up like a bad penny."

"That's us," said Sally cheerfully. "I see Chief Inspector Kirby is keeping you busy."

He stroked the fur-trimmed collar of his trench coat, his

thumb rubbing at a singe mark. "The chief inspector trusts me implicitly. Now if you'll excuse me, I have people to interview." With that, he stalked off towards the stables.

"Sally! Come in, come in." A bewhiskered man in a patched waistcoat beckoned them. "You'll be a breath of fresh air..." As they entered, he rounded the table, hand extended. "Who's your friend?"

"I'm Alf Wilson." Alf extricated himself from the meaty handshake. "You run coaches to Shambito?"

"Why, yes. Are you two eloping?" As Alf's jaw dropped, he laughed. "I guess not. What can I do for you?"

"Alf's sister is missing," said Sally, tugging him to sit beside her. "We think she might have headed towards Shambito. Perhaps in the company of Mr Bergrim-Hoyt."

The coachmaster tugged his moustache. "Odd, that's who that policeman was asking about too."

"Was he?" Alf frowned. "I don't suppose he mentioned my sister, did he? Her name's Gwen."

"No. Let me check for her as well." He flicked through a notebook. "Mr Bergrim-Hoyt did board our weekly coach to Shambito two days ago. Also on the coach were three regular commercial travellers, a holidaying Calesian couple and... yes, a young woman. Name of Vera Wilson?"

"Her full name's Guinevere Wilson." She obviously wasn't hiding her identity, but did she really think "Vera" sounded posher than "Gwen"? That's what came of spending time with toffs. Alf wasn't going to start calling himself "Phonse," was he?

The coachmaster confirmed the weekly coach schedule. The journey normally took two days to cross Lesser Grenia's northern border into Calesia, and then another twelve days after that. The coach stopped overnight at various towns along the way.

Sally chewed a fingernail. "They'll be across the border already."

A lump of unease in Alf's throat made him swallow. Things got complicated in foreign countries. Would the Calesians assume Gwen was Mr Bergrim-Hoyt's bit on the side? Even if not, would diplomats from either country care about a runaway working-class girl? No doubt the Council of Lords would throw their efforts into pursuing the kidnapper, but Gwen might be abandoned in the process. Alf's head hurt, and the walls felt like they were closing in on him.

"Thanks. I'd better tell Inspector Castor about that note." Gripping his crutches firmly, he levered himself up and swung outside while Sally exchanged a few last words with the coachmaster.

Should he head towards the stables, or maybe wait by the entrance? Surely Castor hadn't left already. As he hesitated, the policeman strode round a corner, glowering at the muck on his polished boots.

It was now or never. Alf took a deep breath. "Inspector Castor?"

Lip curling, the inspector looked him up and down. "What?"

"Uh, sorry about misleading you the other day." He swallowed as Sally silently joined him. "You see, Lord Hayes wanted us to help him. It's difficult to refuse a toff. Like, they're so much higher up, and we can't really say no, and... my sister's missing!"

Castor's brows drew together. "Lord Hayes is holding your sister hostage?"

"No, no." Sally squeezed Alf's arm. "But while Lord

Hayes was, er, acting oddly, she got mixed up with Mr Bergrim-Hoyt's plans."

"Did she, now?"

Alf glowered. "My sister's a good girl. Mr Bergrim-Hoyt filled her head with tales, and she's gone off with him, thinking she'll become a great inventor."

"So you see," said Sally, "Alf has a personal concern in the matter. Plus, we felt bad about behaving towards you the way we did. We'd like to help you with some information."

"What kind of information?"

"My sister left me a note..."

After Alf explained, Castor sniffed. "I suppose the information is helpful. I'll visit the Council of Lords and update them."

Sally bobbed a curtsey. "Would you mind if we came too?"

"What for?" Castor frowned. "I can't imagine they'd admit–"

"It's a useful extra clue you picked up, that Mr Bergrim-Hoyt isn't travelling by himself," said Sally. "I bet Chief Inspector Kirby wouldn't have thought of it. And Alf can provide more details if they want."

"Well, when you put it like that..."

"We'll stay well out of the way," said Alf. If it got Gwen back, he'd be happy for Castor to grab all the glory.

Once again, Rich stood on the platform in front of the Council of Lords. Despite his galloping heart, he kept his head high and gazed around the audience as if he were here for amusement. Kirby sat on the front bench while the lords were scattered around their habitual positions. Angus threw him a look of contempt, no doubt still convinced his card losses were Rich's fault.

With a heavy sigh, Pettigrew planted himself on the other side of the podium. His face bore a grave expression. "A damn shame, young Hayes, but we can't let your crimes go unpunished."

Rich flinched slightly, but he kept his chin up. "I understand, Lord Pettigrew."

"It's a sorry way to end this meeting, but we might as well get it over with. We're not cruel men. You will be permitted to retain your country property, but—"

The chamber door creaked open, and the usher called, "Begging your pardon, My Lords. Inspector Castor brings new and urgent information."

A reprieve, or some new horror? Rich clasped sweating hands behind his back as Castor strode in. Behind him, Alf swung in on crutches with Sally holding his arm. What in the blazes had brought the pair here?

Pettigrew frowned. "I take it this is important?"

"It is, Your Lordship." Castor approached the podium and halted at the foot of its steps. "We have discovered the direction of Mr Bergrim-Hoyt's flight."

"And Gwen's," muttered Alf while the usher pointed him to Angus' bench.

What? Bergrim-Hoyt had absconded with *Alf's sister*?

"Go on, man," said Pettigrew.

"He took a coach to Shambito. They loaded three trunks. Since he's a gentleman who usually travels with only one, presumably he doesn't plan to return. Alternatively, he is transporting items that we, uh, might rather he didn't transport."

"I see. Kirby, what do you think? Can Mr Bergrim-Hoyt

be apprehended openly?" Pettigrew's gaze rested on Rich. "Or are less official measures required?"

Rich nodded back politely. Damn. No chance of Pettigrew forgetting him in the excitement.

Kirby stood and stroked his beard. "We do have a reciprocal policing arrangement with Calesia. And we are not at war. Yet."

True enough. If the fragile peace continued, moving to Calesia might even provide an opportunity for a fresh start.

"So," said Pettigrew, "they should cooperate if we wish to investigate a crime carried out on our soil."

"Officially, at least," said Kirby. "We have aided their investigators in the recent past. Law is enforced by their military–they do not have a separate police force."

"And we have a crime to investigate. Two crimes, even. The kidnapping of Professor Bergrim-Hoyt, and the stealing of her plans."

"Don't forget kidnapping me and Mum," called Alf from his seat. He didn't seem to notice his card-playing neighbour's glower.

Kirby nodded at Alf. "Strictly speaking, Mr Gorman and Mr Brooks decided of their own volition to kidnap Mrs Wilson and yourself. They kidnapped Professor Bergrim-Hoyt and stole the plans on Mr Bergrim-Hoyt's orders. So that's the only charge we can directly lay on him."

"Damn." Alf thumped his crutch on the floor.

"It seems clear enough," said Pettigrew, moustache twitching. "We will send a police representative to Shambito to investigate and apprehend Mr Bergrim-Hoyt. The major charge will be of kidnapping, but we'll want to also retrieve the stolen plans. The Calesians are duty-bound to aid us." He gave a thin smile. "Of course, they may have *copied* the plans by that point, but they and we will politely not mention that. Chief Inspector Kirby, will you go?"

Rich crossed his fingers that Kirby would decline. It looked like he mightn't insist on a trial, but if Castor were left in charge–

"I think not," said Kirby. "It's certainly a crucial matter. But sending the chief of police in person might lend too much significance to the investigation. Plus, if something goes wrong–diplomatically speaking–it's better to have an element of distance."

Pettigrew chuckled. "You'd make a damn fine politician, Kirby. So, whoever goes will bear the brunt of any Calesian displeasure?"

"Exactly. That said, success in the mission would be a considerable accomplishment, and viewed favourably when it comes to promotions. Castor!"

Castor's head jerked round. "Yes, sir?"

"You fit the bill, assuming you're willing to travel to Calesia."

Castor's mouth dropped open. Then he licked his lips and squared his shoulders. "Yes, I'm willing."

"Don't let us down," said Kirby. "Or if you do, try not to make a big mess."

Rich suppressed a smirk. Kirby was obviously using Castor to distance himself from the inevitable repercussions.

"That's all very well," said Pettigrew, "but Inspector Castor may need some help negotiating the... higher echelons of Calesian society. We'd prefer not to provoke a diplomatic incident."

Castor gulped. "N-no, sir."

Pettigrew nodded at Rich. "I suggest that Mr Hayes accompany Inspector Castor. For the time being, he can remain 'Lord' Hayes, which should help smooth over some aspects of the investigation."

Work with Castor? Rich's cravat constricted his neck, and his pulse rushed in his ears. "But why me?"

"You have a unique familiarity with the situation, and it's only fair you contribute to the success of the mission. Plus, your Calesian appearance may, ah, open doors that might normally remain closed."

"Really?" Rich stared. Was Pettigrew suggesting clandestine action?

"Only if you agree. In view of the urgency, disciplinary action against you will need to be delayed until your return. I suppose we might take your performance into consideration when we reconvene regarding your actions."

Damn. He bowed to Pettigrew. "In that case, I would be honoured to help."

"Good," said Pettigrew. "We'll take care of your town house during your absence. You can hand your keys in before you depart."

"Of course." No doubt if he absconded, the council would sell it to cover the taxes. "And on my return?"

"We'll see, lad."

"Thank you for this opportunity." Rich bowed again. Perhaps he would avoid dragging the Hayes name into disrepute, after all. But only if he got this mission right. Looking at Castor's truculent expression, he didn't feel so confident of that.

Chapter 16

Alf shifted uncomfortably on the hard wooden bench while the Council of Lords debated. They wittered on about the diplomatic implications of asking Calesia for help. And the need to apprehend their quarry with all dispatch. And the need to retrieve those blooming plans. But not a single mention of his sister!

After the police dragged Mr Bergrim-Hoyt home, would Gwen be abandoned on the streets? How would she cope? Where would she go? If she couldn't find a hot meal and a roof over her head, would she have to–

He could stand it no longer. Shrugging off Sally's hand on his arm, he levered himself to his foot and clutched the bench for balance. "And what about my sister?"

The lord who'd been talking about paperwork–bloke with a ruddy face and huge moustache–paused with his mouth open. Then he said, "What about her?"

They'd forgotten about her already! Alf brandished his crutch. "She's travelling with Mr Bergrim-Hoyt, is what! Who knows what he might do to her?"

The lord glanced at Castor. "So we're after a conspirator too?"

Alf's eyes bulged. "No! She's nothing to do with the kidnap. She didn't steal those plans, either. That sneaky toff tricked her into going along with him. Told her he wants her help with his project."

The lord sighed. "I see, Mr Wilson. How old is your sister?"

"Nineteen."

"I'm afraid in that case, the default assumption would be that she went with him willingly, albeit ignorant of his crimes. There's no reason for direct police involvement."

"Alf!" whispered Sally, tugging at his sleeve. "Sit down. This isn't the place for it."

"But she's my sister! Who's going to look after her if I don't? She's never been out of Ironfort." Admittedly, neither had he.

Sally huffed. "As Lord Pettigrew says, she's an adult. She can make her own decisions."

"But what if they're the wrong decisions?" Alf's guts writhed inside his belly.

Lord Pettigrew coughed. "Then she'll be at liberty to deal with the consequences. We have to leave her to it, as your young lady says."

"What bloody use are you lot then?" Alf's voice echoed around the hall. Rich's appalled gape brought him back to his senses. "Uh, sorry, sir." He sat. *My young lady?* A glance at Sally showed her with a hand over her mouth, although her eyes sparkled. He should have kept his big mouth shut.

Chief Inspector Kirby looked at Alf thoughtfully. "We can't officially investigate Miss Wilson's departure. But perhaps Mr Wilson could travel with Inspector Castor and Mr–Lord Hayes as a private individual. After all, he is an aggrieved party for a number of reasons."

"Me?" Alf's voice cracked. "Go all the way to Calesia?"

Rich raised an eyebrow. "Gwen did. Don't worry, I'll watch out for her."

"That's 'Miss Wilson' to *you*, Lord Hayes." Alf clenched his fists. He'd better fetch Gwen himself. It was bad enough to have Mum singing Rich's praises: it would be unbearable if Gwen joined in the chorus. "Alright, then. We've got four days before the weekly coach–"

"We need to get you there quicker than that." Lord Pettigrew stroked his moustache. "If you take the airship at the start of next week, you should arrive in Shambito three days before the coach does. That will give you ample preparation time for the journey, and you'll still arrive ahead of Mr Bergrim-Hoyt."

"I'll telegraph the Calesian security department so they know to expect you," said Chief Inspector Kirby.

"I'd rather you sent a letter," said Pettigrew. "Call me an old fuddy-duddy, but if Bergrim-Hoyt is working with some other party, I'm concerned about a telegram being intercepted. Send a brief note on the airship leaving tonight. I'll write a formal introductory letter for Castor to present on his arrival."

Alf groaned. To think his biggest concern this morning had been whether Sally glimpsed his bare chest. "What have I done?"

"You've gone and volunteered to travel to Calesia, is what you've done." Sally's voice was tart. "Better make the trip worth while."

Rich was still Lord Hayes! He wanted to laugh with relief at his temporarily averted disaster. Alf stood with bulging eyes and gaping mouth while the lords discussed acceptable expenses for the Calesian trip. Conversely, Castor stood with his chest puffed out, legs quivering as if he wanted to spring into action immediately.

Sally wore an irritated expression. When Rich caught her eye, she mouthed something incomprehensible. Probably just as well. She wasn't like any other domestic servant

Rich had ever met. Going by the number of times she'd lectured him, she'd spent so long in the Hayes household that she'd forgotten who was in charge.

Pettigrew drew the meeting to a close. As the council members started to disperse, he said, "I'd like a final word with Kirby, Castor and Hayes. And we'd better include Mr Wilson."

The council filed out. In order to let the card-playing Angus depart, Alf and Sally slid out of their seats. Rich and the others joined them in the aisle.

Sally bobbed a curtsey. "Would you mind if I stay too, sir? Alf isn't quite ready to be out on his own."

"That's fine," said Pettigrew. "As long as you don't gossip."

"Sally's very discreet," murmured Rich.

Pettigrew surveyed the emptied room then nodded. "This mission is purely a police investigation, with Mr Wilson accompanying you as a concerned party. Is that clear?"

Everyone indicated their understanding.

"You must not do anything to destabilise our current relationship with Calesia. No references to war. Don't even mention the word 'weapon'."

If only Rich had nicked those plans when he saw them, they wouldn't have fallen into enemy hands. How ironic. He said, "Presumably we think the stolen plans are of military use?"

"Yes," said Kirby. "Professor Bergrim-Hoyt said she'd been designing an explosive device. Incidentally, she also wished to set out in pursuit of her husband. I discouraged that idea."

"Good. It's far too dangerous," said Pettigrew. "Things are tricky enough without guarding her as well. Our acknowledged priority is to capture Mr Bergrim-Hoyt and return him to Ironfort to face justice. Retrieving the stolen plans is of lesser importance."

Castor's brow wrinkled. "But isn't–"

"That's our official stance." Pettigrew smiled faintly. "However, Castor, your real priority is to recover the stolen plans. Or to ensure their destruction. Though of course, we don't want Mr Bergrim-Hoyt to get away with his crimes."

Alf paled, his gaze darting around his companions. "You're not talking about *assassinating* him, are you?"

"What?" Pettigrew's moustache bristled. "Of course not!"

"Oh, that's a relief." Alf's cheeks coloured, and he mumbled, "Mum must have filled my head with too many stories from *Inspector Grimley's Casebook*. And, well, I got confused with all Rich–Lord Hayes' secret agent stuff."

"Secret agent?"

"Sure. He said he reported to you, and that you sent him..." At Pettigrew's uncomprehending stare, Alf's mouth dropped open. He pointed a trembling finger at Rich. "What? You bloody imposter! You lied about that *as well?* You got me scarpering around, breaking you out of jail and lying to the police, all under false pretences?"

Throat closing up, Rich loosened his collar. He peeked at Pettigrew's stony expression. Maybe his title wasn't so secure. "Er, sorry, Alf. I was desperate."

Sally's lips twitched. "You certainly were."

Pettigrew sighed heavily. "This is all very interesting, but a needless distraction. Castor, are you clear on your priorities?"

"Yes, sir!" Castor stood rigidly at attention.

"Lord Hayes." Pettigrew's tone was icy. "Inspector Castor will be in charge. You are to facilitate his work in whatever way is necessary. No messing around. Understood?"

"Yes, sir," Rich managed through gritted teeth.

Kirby said, "Castor, this will be a career-defining mission. Don't disappoint me."

"And don't forget, Hayes," continued Pettigrew, "that your fate is intertwined with Inspector Castor's."

Great. Rich met Castor's glare. His title depended on aiding this promotion-seeking twerp.

In the women's ward of the hospital, Alf tried ineffectually to keep Mum calm. He wished Sally had been around to help, but she'd gone off on some errand.

"My little girl gone!" Mum bawled, wiping her face with the pillowcase.

"Don't worry, Mum," he said, shifting uncomfortably on his rickety chair. "I'm going to fetch her back, even if I have to argue with the Calesian king himself. Or whoever they have there."

"But how? You know nowt about the place."

Don't remind me. Despite the cement mixer of anxiety in his chest, he squared his shoulders. "I'll find a way. It'll be fine."

"Both of you in foreign parts! I'll be all by myself!" She wailed even louder, making the desk nurse grimace.

"Calm down, Mum. It's not the end of the world." He tried to smile reassuringly at their fascinated audience of bedbound old ladies. In between Mum's lamentations and the professor's curses in the opposite bay—she was doing something with Alf's leg—they were having a field day.

"He's a good son, he is," gasped a blue-lipped woman to the wizened crone beside her.

Before Alf had time to feel gratified, the crone said, "Just like my poor, dear boy. He got himself killed trying to douse a fire."

Mum's sniffles grew quiet while Alf regarded the floor.

Her eventual sigh was replete with the world-weariness of long-suffering mothers everywhere. "I suppose you know best, son. Don't worry about your old mum. I'm sure I can manage on my own. It'll be a nice change, being in the apartment all by myself..."

Alf groaned inwardly. "I've asked Sally to watch out for you, and she can help you move into Parlay Square. You needn't worry about your job, either, now that I'm getting reward money. Even if it doesn't come through before we leave next week, Sally can loan us some."

"Isn't she a gem!" Mum beamed. "I'd no idea it paid so well to work for the lords."

"It's nothing more than domestic slave–Oh." He cut off his automatic response. If Sally was so comfortable, even without any secret agent business, perhaps working for nobs wasn't as bad as he'd previously believed. "Actually, if all this palaver puts Gwen off engineering school, maybe she'd consider going into service? But please, Mum, don't nag Sally about finding her a job."

"I'll stay out of the way. She'll barely know I'm there. Anyway, she'll be too busy looking after Lord Hayes to keep an old woman company."

"No, she won't. He's going as well."

"Oh, what was I thinking? Of course he's needed on such an important mission!" She glanced at their audience. "But I can't believe what you said about him. About what he was doing in the professor's house. You must have misheard. It's a scurrilous rumour."

"No, he said it himself. I, uh, listened through the door while we were waiting to speak to the Council of Lords."

"Nonsense! Lord Hayes is a fine gentleman. Someone must be plotting against him." Mum tapped the side of her nose and winked. "Aha, he has to cover up the you-know-what stuff that he's doing, and he wouldn't allow the blame to fall on someone else. So of course he'd pretend–"

"Delia!" barked the professor, making him flinch. "Tell your boy to come here and see this!"

"Of course, Ina." Mum's voice held extra syrup. "On you go, Alf, and see what my new friend wants."

Alf swallowed his instinctive rebellious outburst against bossy women. No point offending the entire hospital ward. After patting Mum's hand, he hopped over to the professor's bed and stared. "What have you done?"

His false leg lay dismantled over the blanket. He squinted at the tiny springs, wires and plates. She'd bloody better put it back together again. A wheeled table beside the bed was stacked with strange tools which looked like they belonged in a laboratory.

Ina glowered at the mess. "It's perfectly feasible."

"What is?"

"I'll add some enhancements before you depart."

"But it's worked fine until now."

"Bah, where's your desire for improvement? I can make it *better*. I'll give it diamond power. Save you from winding it up."

"Oh, that's good." For a moment, he'd worried she might do something mad with it. "But aren't diamonds really expensive?"

She sniffed. "I have spares. But you must take care of it. And don't even think of taking a look inside when you don't know what you're doing."

"I wouldn't dare, ma'am."

"Once I'm out of hospital, I'll make the changes at my workshop." Her lip curled. "At least that Kirby chap hasn't banned me from there too. He assigned me a twenty-four-hour guard and told me not to leave the city. Damned inconvenient."

"If you say so." Alf swallowed. "May I have the leg back in the meantime? Please?"

"I suppose so." She pursed her lips as her hands sorted the disparate parts. "While I'm doing this, sit down and tell me about Gwen's studies. Delia told me she was quite the prodigy."

"She did?" He glanced at Mum's innocent grin and squirmed. Should he be honest about his concerns, or keep the family peace? "Er... Mum's very proud of her ambition."

"I see."

"I mean, I dunno much about this engineering stuff. I wouldn't like to say whether she's any good or not."

"Which course is she on?"

"From what she said..."

By the time Ina finished her interrogation about Gwen, Alf was gazing longingly at the adjacent empty bed. Who knew talking could be so exhausting?

"Hmm." She patted his now-intact prosthesis. "You may have this back for now, but bring it round to my lab at the engineering college before you leave for Calesia."

Alf swallowed his pride. She *was* doing him a favour, after all. "Thanks, I guess."

Shockingly, she winked. "You poor bugger. Your every thought broadcasts itself on your face."

Chapter 17

Brandy snifter in hand, Rich strolled towards the viewing area of the airport lounge. Glass clinked behind him as other travellers were offered pre-flight hospitality. The way things were going, this might be his last air trip ever. Better remember the moment.

A discarded copy of the *Ironfort Guardian* lay on a low table:

PROFESSOR BERGRIM-HOYT RESCUED!
KIDNAPPERS IN THE CLINK

Despite the *Guardian*'s usual lurid headlines, the article was long on speculation and short on facts. It stated that the rescuers had opted for anonymity because of the reward money, with only a passing mention that Mr Bergrim-Hoyt was unavailable for comment. Presumably Kirby and the Council of Lords had suppressed most of the details.

"Lord Hayes, fancy bumping into you here!" An Ironfort widow in a sombre velvet gown swayed towards him. On glancing at the paper, she pursed her lips. "A shocking business. I'm sure it was a foreign plot. You can't trust–"

Clearing his throat, Rich nodded pointedly at an approaching Calesian couple. The widow sniffed and glided away towards the bar.

The couple joined Rich by the window. The wife tightened a brightly embroidered shawl around her shoulders. "Trust the sun to come out on the day we leave. And for the whole trip, it's been nothing but rain and cold heads!"

"It'll be good to get home," said her husband as he offered her a steaming cup. Hot chocolate, by the aroma. He nodded at Rich. "I see you've gone native."

Rich blinked. "I beg your pardon?"

The man patted his fur hat then gestured towards Rich's bare head. "Your costume. You don't seem worried about the temperature of your brain."

"Oh." Rich swallowed. Wearing a hat indoors was unthinkable. Even his father hadn't, despite his Calesian origins. Superstitions didn't bolster a political career. "I'm an Ironfort man, through and through."

"Ah." The man bowed briefly. "Apologies, my mistake. Our customs must seem strange to you."

"Not at all. I wish you enjoyable travels." Rich focussed on the activities outside while the couple moved towards a padded leather sofa.

Their airship—the *Ascending Queen*—was being prepared. Heavy ropes attached to anchoring hooks kept the gondola on the ground. Its enormous helium-filled balloon shaded everything from the morning sun. Porters loaded trunks, comestibles and small crates of high-value goods for trade.

Rich hadn't travelled on an airship since his teenage years. His parents had stopped taking him on tour when he reached his majority five years ago, a couple of years before they disappeared. His early strenuous attempts to trace them gave way to disbelief, anger and then apathy. That had been around the time when Professor Bergrim-Hoyt announced her seminal discovery, and international tensions rose further.

Had they been caught up in some civil unrest? That would explain why he'd heard nothing since. Best not to dwell on it. Tipping his head back, he drained his glass.

"Lord Hayes," came a disapproving voice from behind him. "Drowning your anxiety again?"

Castor still wore that fur-trimmed trench coat, although he held his hat in one hand, a water glass in the other. He looked thoroughly out of place among the affluent business people and tourists who ambled around the area. Even Alf—wearing yet another of Father's old suits—blended in better, although he was noticeably following the canapé tray.

"Inspector Castor," Rich drawled. "Water? Isn't that unhealthy? Why don't you savour some good Ironfort brandy before we head into unknown territory?"

"Even after that Council of Lords meeting, I'm not convinced you take your responsibilities seriously." Castor glared. "This isn't a pleasure trip."

"We might as well enjoy the situation while we can. You, sir, are clearly a policeman, duty-bound to be serious. I, on the other hand, use suave elegance and refined conversation to fit in with my fellow nobles."

Rich beckoned Alf over. Wiping his mouth with the back of his hand, he walked towards them with no trace of a limp.

"Be that as it may," said Castor, "don't let your criminal impulses get the better of you. The Calesian judicial system is far harsher than ours."

"Touché." Rich raised his glass in a salute and allowed a passing waiter to top it up. "I'll be on my best behaviour. Though you're only bothered because you want that promotion."

Castor glowered. "It is my privilege and duty to uphold the law. And that includes observing *you* for signs of guilt."

"About what?" Typical policeman, suspecting everyone

of nefarious behaviour.

"For one, your parents' disappearance left you in an advantageous position."

Rich choked on his apple juice. "You seriously think I–"

"Blimey, it's enormous!" Alf gaped at the airship outside before blinking at Rich and Castor. "What're you chatting about?"

"We were just going over a few things." Castor's knuckles whitened on his glass. "Hayes, you remember my plan of action?"

"Yessir, Inspector Castor, I remember your plan of action. Sir." Rich smiled inwardly as Castor's jaw clenched. "Once we arrive in Shambito, you will enlist the help of the Security Office. First task will be to check when Bergrim-Hoyt's coach is due in. With or without local help, we will take him straight into custody when he arrives without, ah, anyone else gaining access to what he carries."

Alf jutted out his jaw. "And what of Gwen?"

"I'll watch out for her. Treat her like the precious treasure she is."

"That's what worries me," muttered Alf. "Her head's already full of grand ideas."

Castor said, "You can do as you wish, Wilson. Assuming your sister is still in Mr Bergrim-Hoyt's company, you might want to accompany myself and Hayes. But you're a private citizen on personal business and free to explore by yourself."

"By myself?" Alf's eyes were round. "I'll get lost! Uh, what's Shambito like?"

"Very impressive." Castor waved an expansive arm. "And lots of people, and buildings, and other things..."

Rich grinned. "You've not been there before, have you?"

Castor set his glass down with a clatter. "So? I read up about it. I've always lived in Ironfort."

"Oh." Alf's face fell. "Me too."

"Ladies and gentlemen, we shall be boarding shortly," announced a steward. The travellers started gathering their cases and parasols. One matron scooped up a yapping miniature poodle.

"Calesia is a huge country," said Rich. "Shambito is quite far north and much warmer than Lesser Grenia. Inspector Castor may find his coat too heavy, especially the fur collar. A coach would pass through a dozen sizeable towns to arrive there, as well as hill ranges and one mountain pass. I remember that journey from when I was small. Very bumpy in the mountains. After that, my parents opted to travel by airship."

"The governmental system is also different," muttered Castor.

"Indeed. Calesia has a Citizens' Assembly rather than a Council of Lords."

"What's that mean?" asked Alf.

How to summarise things simply? "Decisions of national importance are debated in public. They are then voted on by a randomly selected group of people. One hundred each time, I believe. Much larger than the Council of Lords. If you're selected, attendance is obligatory."

Alf's brow wrinkled. "So... rather than an elite few making the decisions, the population is sampled, but it's different people for each issue."

"You've been doing your reading, I see." For a labourer, Alf was better educated than Rich had expected.

"Had to help Gwen with her entrance exams," Alf muttered.

“Their laws are different from ours,” said Castor. “They have severe penalties for even minor infractions. Forced labour for public disorder, for example. You both need to watch your behaviour. I’ve already warned Lord Hayes to comport himself with decorum.”

Lips twitching, Alf fumbled with his cravat. “Sounds challenging.”

Rich opted to ignore his words and gave him a reassuring smile. “But we’ll behave ourselves, won’t we?”

The steward approached them. “Sirs? Time to board.”

Alf strolled around the polished deck of the airship, admiring the sunset and the way their shadow sped over the ground. Initial trepidation about being in the air had settled after a delicious three-course dinner and an even more delicious supper, which had ended with four types of cheese! Or should he say “lunch” and then “dinner”? No wonder nobs put on weight. At least Alf could easily work it off, and he felt like he’d got two normal legs again.

High-handed manner aside, Professor Bergrim-Hoyt was a marvel. When he’d thanked her for the power source and adjusting it so he could wear matching shoes, she scowled and warned him to treat it with the utmost care. It was her best invention yet, and she didn’t want some clumsy accident to ruin her work. The woman was a right fusspot—Alf wasn’t a child—but he’d promised he’d be careful. Maybe she didn’t trust him with the diamond. Or perhaps she had concerns about *Rich* stealing it? Alf grinned.

He lost his smile on glancing at his polished boots and the brown herringbone suit of worsted wool. It had hastily been adjusted by Rich’s tailor along with other garments from the previous Lord Hayes’ wardrobe. Alf was torn between resentment at a man who had so many clothes that he could leave them behind, and relief that the clothing allowed him to travel on the airship without being ridiculed for his outfit.

What would Gwen say when he turned up looking like this? Maybe she wouldn't recognise him! He tried to cheer himself up with thoughts of her amazement, but he couldn't completely suppress his worry over what trouble she might be in. It seemed like Bergrim-Hoyt valued her skills, and why take her all that way if he wanted to harm her? But he wasn't the only threat to her well-being.

"Lovely evening." Rich propped himself against the railing. He'd changed into a light jacket and hadn't bothered with a cravat. "Thinking hard?"

"What if Gwen's coach has trouble on the way? Bandits?" Hadn't Sally suggested that to Inspector Castor?

Rich chuckled. "Of course not. Remember, Calesia has *severe* penalties for breaking the law. The coach carries international passengers, and the Calesians will fervently want to avoid diplomatic incidents."

No bandits? Damn, Alf had been taken in as well. He clenched a fist. That had probably given Sally a right laugh. "But what if the coach crashes?"

"It's a possibility, but not that likely. The drivers are experienced. The roads are well maintained, and the coach route passes by towns each day, so help is at worst a few hours off. I think they even carry signal flares these days."

"Hmm." Something ahead caught his eye. He pointed. "What's that?"

Rich squinted. "Ah, another airship. Less elegant than this one, so it's Calesian. We crossed the border earlier–"

"We did?" Craning his neck, Alf studied the fields and

splotches of trees. "It looks just the same."

Rich snorted. "The border isn't a dotted line. And it's not like the countries are different colours like they are on the maps."

Alf shut his mouth. Not that he'd *really* believed that, but...

The seemingly oblivious Rich continued, "With Calesia being so large, it's no wonder they invest more in air travel than we do in Lesser Grenia. Even common, ah, *regular* workers travel by air."

"Wow." What an amazing country Calesia must be, where ordinary folks could use airships, and nobody thought anything of it.

Chapter 18

Rich leaned on the side rail, a faint smile on his face. In the mid-afternoon sun with the cloudless sky, Shambito's bright and cheerful vista was a far cry from the permanent haze over dirty old Ironfort. From this vantage, he could truly appreciate the architecture. The oft-imitated delicate central towers were surrounded by sprawling residential areas that expanded up the gentle valley slopes. As the airship descended towards the landing field, anticipation built up in his chest. Exploring this elegant city would be a new adventure.

The airport lay further from the city than the industrial district: any accidents with explosive fuels would cause less harm. If diamond power became commonplace, such incidents would become a thing of the past, although there was still the risk of mid-air collisions.

Castor paced up and down behind him, adjusting the belt on his trench coat. "Once we've dropped our trunks off at the embassy, we'd better visit the Security Office."

Did the man ever relax? Rich would rather take a stroll this evening before their mission started properly. "It's unlikely they'll be open so late. You should settle in, absorb the ambience while we're here."

"We don't have time to waste on frivolities."

"Stamping around and making demands won't help. That's why you have me to advise you on customs, so you don't inadvertently cause offence." Peering over the side, Rich pointed. "There's the army compound. Part of it, at least."

Castor gave a long, low whistle. "So large."

"Yes, it's grown since my last visit." The walled military compound dwarfed the industrial district which lay between the airport and the city. "Though perhaps my memory isn't so accurate."

Alf joined them, shading his eyes. "I see smoke over the factories. Manufacturers must be keeping busy. What do they make?"

"Your guess is as good as mine," Rich replied. Hopefully they weren't churning out weapons.

"What's the official reason for such a big army?" Castor asked.

Rich glanced round. The Calesian couple he'd previously spoken to were also on the viewing deck. He caught snatches of laughter and some reference to fresh mango. Otherwise, nobody was in earshot. "They've always trained here in the capital, but they maintain order in all outlying areas. The Council of Lords did ask the Calesian ambassador about the increase in recruitment. He explained it was due to concerns about civil unrest."

Alf laughed bitterly. "Just as well our unemployed boys had the opportunity to sign up too, eh?"

"Something like that," said Rich.

"Bloody diamond technology." Alf glanced at his leg. "Well, I suppose it has its benefits."

"True." Such progress had changed the relationship between the two countries. Calesia's desire to annex Lesser Grenia was a long-standing concern to the Council of Lords. After diamond technology was adopted, Calesia's efforts at persuasion had unsurprisingly increased. How ironic. A development that could aid Lesser Grenia's defence might prove the irresistible incentive for Calesia to finally declare war.

Castor was still peering at the ground. "What's that in the middle of the military area?"

Rich studied the army compound. Rows of rectangular dorm buildings lay along straight roads, with large empty spaces for training and exercises. In the centre stood a low-rise circular building. "I don't remember that from last time. It looks fairly new. We can ask at the embassy."

"We are preparing to land," a steward called through a loud-hailer. "Please make your way below."

After checking his trunk was locked, Rich inspected himself in the mirror. In anticipation of the heat, he wore a light silk top hat and a cambric frock-coat. He had advised the others to dress light. Hearing a curse through the wall, he knocked on Alf's part-opened cabin door. "Everything alright, Alf?"

"Just trying to tie this bloomin' cravat." Alf scowled at himself in the mirror. His grey cotton jacket had shiny patches on the elbows, but hopefully nobody would notice.

"Here." Suppressing a smile–Sally must have helped Alf previously–Rich demonstrated a simple knot that Alf could follow in his reflection. "But don't worry. We're going straight to the embassy, so you won't be on public display."

"That's a relief. I'm looking forward to solid ground again. At least the professor fixed my leg, or else I'd be staggering all over the place. Bad enough I stand out as foreign without also looking drunk."

Alf minded his feet while he descended the ramp and took his first steps on Calesian soil. Despite his words to Rich earlier, he didn't want to risk a stumble. Boots firmly planted—on paving stones identical to Ironfort's—he raised his chin and surveyed his surroundings.

Wow.

The landing area was heaving. Travellers flooded out of three small airships, which had a uniform blocky design rather than the curlicued elegance of the *Ascending Queen.* Alf's immediate grin of pride faded. No doubt the Lesser Grenian craft was outrageously expensive to maintain compared to her plain Calesian counterparts.

Heat radiated from the tarmac. Would it be rude to remove his bowler hat? But if he did, he'd feel even shorter than these natives who towered over him. The menfolk didn't wear fur hats here: their tanned, close-cropped scalps were bare under the bright sunshine.

Teams of handlers loaded cargo wagons in a hypnotic rhythm, occasionally calling directions to each other. Their muscular bare arms gleamed with sweat, but they wore heavy gloves and boots. Employers certainly took care of their staff. Not that Alf's factory had mistreated him, but better protective gear might have saved his leg.

"Stand aside!" blasted a voice in his ear.

He jumped. A yellow-clad man with a loud-hailer marched past him, followed by a forklift truck similar to one he used to drive. Steam chugged from its innards, adding to the oppressive humidity.

"Alf!" called Rich. He stood with Castor, who was fiddling with his coat.

Alf sighed. He wouldn't have minded nosing about the airport a bit longer. He'd never get such an opportunity again.

Rich hid a smile as he descended the ramp behind Castor.

The policeman's hair was plastered to his neck with sweat, where it wasn't hidden by his woollen bowler hat. He still wore his precious fur-trimmed trench coat: if he didn't heed Rich's warning, it would be no surprise if he fainted. Their fellow passengers on the *Ascending Queen* as well as other more local travellers wore light, flowing materials or patched overalls, depending on whether they were travelling for pleasure or work.

Alf had preceded them on to the airfield, and he gawped around him like a country bumpkin. Better keep an eye on the shorter man. It would be easy to lose him in the throng, especially if he wandered off in his distraction. Castor was tall for a Lesser Grenian, although he didn't match Rich's height. It wouldn't be so easy to shake *him* off, should Rich want to explore.

At the foot of the ramp stood a compact young man in a black linen suit. He bore a card that read: CASTOR AND PARTY.

Mopping his face with a handkerchief, Castor strutted up to him. "I'm Inspector Castor."

"Good afternoon, sir." Their welcomer's accent confirmed his Ironfort origins. "I'm Josiah Laurence, embassy attaché. Did you have a good journey?"

"Passable." Castor drew a cigar from the depths of his trench coat.

Before he could light it, Laurence urgently said, "Sir! Smoking is prohibited within the airport bounds. There's a fire risk with the aircraft fuel."

Rich grinned. "Dear me, Inspector Castor. Nearly committing a crime as your first action in Calesia. What would Chief Inspector Kirby say?"

Castor returned the cigar to his pocket with a glower.

Rich glanced around to see if Alf had noticed, but the labourer was staring at the luggage wagons with his mouth open.

Never mind. No doubt Castor would put his foot in it again. "While we're on introductions, I'm Richard, Lord Hayes. And the third gentleman in our party is Mr Alphonse Wilson. Alf!"

"Huh?" Alf's head jerked, and he trotted over to join them, his gaze darting all around. "There's so much going on."

"A pleasure, sirs." Laurence stared at Rich for a moment. "Are you familiar with Shambito, Lord Hayes?"

"I visited several years ago," said Rich. "There have been some changes, I see."

"Indeed." Laurence beckoned over a yellow-clad official with a clipboard. "Because the embassy is hosting you, there's no need to queue for the registration desk as the other travellers are doing."

Now that Laurence mentioned it, Rich noticed a slow flow of recent arrivals converging on a row of tables which were shaded by a light canopy. There, further yellow-clad men and women sat with stacks of papers. A line of soldiers armed with rifles stood behind them.

The official glanced at his notebook. "Good afternoon, Mr Laurence. Can your embassy guests please confirm their names and reason for travel?"

"Castor, Wilson and Hayes." Castor's eyebrows rose. "Do all travellers need to register, no matter their nationality?"

Uncapping his pen, the official said, "They do if they pass via transport stations. That would include airships, carriages and ships along the coast. It's helpful in measuring demand and deciding where to allocate resources. If people walk or ride, we don't record them."

"What about private steam carriages?" asked Alf. "Wouldn't they also be a demand on resources, even if they don't stop at stations?"

"You make a fair point." The official smiled tolerantly. "But our citizens generally do not indulge in private ownership of such extravagant vehicles. I gather that customs are different in Lesser Grenia."

"Oh." Frowning, Alf wiped sweat from his cheek.

The official logged their names and date of travel, and tutted when Castor explained they were pursuing a criminal. "Good luck," he said as he left.

Laurence then led them through the crowds to a tarmac area where rickshaws and other conveyances waited. Their horse-drawn carriage bore the Lesser Grenian colours, which made a sombre contrast to the almost garish patterns adorning its neighbours. The porters finished loading their trunks and grinned when the attaché tipped them.

Once the carriage was moving, Laurence handed some papers to Inspector Castor. "I took the liberty of arranging an appointment with the Security Office for tomorrow morning. I gather you have a few days to set your plans in place?"

"That's right." Rich eyed a market stall, where a trader and customer gesticulated with vigour. Hopefully the Bergrim-Hoyt business would be concluded speedily. After that, he could investigate Shambito for prospects that might suit an impoverished foreign gentleman. His gaze touched on a street sweeper. Surely *something* would offer itself?

"Is it far to the embassy?" Alf fiddled with his cravat. One end now dangled over his shoulder while the other was hopelessly crumpled.

"It'll take us about half an hour." Laurence raised his voice over the clopping of hooves. "It's nearly two hours on foot. Most Lesser Grenians don't like walking in this heat. Her Excellency is away for a few days, so you won't be dining with her tonight."

Castor studied the papers. "Perhaps a good thing. I need to familiarise myself with these."

As a whiff of manure seeped in through the window, Alf pressed his nose against the glass. "Is that the main coach station?"

"Yes," said Laurence. "The only one, in fact. With increasing airship travel–"

"Stop!" said Castor.

Laurence thumped the roof, and the carriage lurched to a halt. "What is it, sir?"

"Since we're passing, I'd better confirm the timings. Hayes, nip out and check when the coach from Ironfort is due to arrive."

Turning the door handle, Laurence said, "Shall I–"

"Don't bother, Laurence." Castor unbuttoned his trench coat and fanned his face. "Let my assistant do some work, for once."

Much annoyed at being reduced to minionhood, Rich complied. It was beneath him to make a scene. He'd left his top hat in the carriage, and sweat beaded his scalp as he stood in the queue. Sandal-wearing families with canvas bags stared at him. He shifted uncomfortably from foot to foot. Obviously blending in wasn't as straightforward as having a similar colouring and height. Once he reached the station clerk's desk, he confirmed the date that Bergrim-Hoyt's coach was due.

"We have three days," he said as he re-entered the coach, resisting the temptation to stand on Castor's foot. "If Bergrim-Hoyt slips through our grasp at the coach station—"

"And Gwen," muttered Alf.

"—and Miss Wilson, where might he head?"

After signalling for the coach to move on, Laurence considered. "There are various gentleman's clubs, and of course the Ironfort Society, where visitors and émigrés from Lesser Grenia mingle."

"We don't know who he's dealing with," said Rich, "but I'd be rather surprised if it were an independent party."

Laurence gave him a sharp look. "Indeed. You will be discreet?"

"Of course," said Castor. "I'll keep a close eye on these two, so they don't cause any trouble."

"A word of advice, sir."

"Yes?"

"Calesia has a more... egalitarian society than Lesser Grenia's. They're plain-speaking folk, mainly, and they don't like being ordered around. So maybe less overt hierarchy? Be careful how you address people, including your companions."

"No airs and graces, eh?" Rich winked at Castor.

"Is that so?" said Alf, suddenly looking very interested.

In his embassy bedroom, Alf dried himself with a huge fluffy towel. The enjoyment was a guilty pleasure, but that hadn't stopped him from luxuriating in the hot bath provided. Quite a change from a basin of lukewarm water. After putting his prosthesis back on, he donned a clean shirt, trousers and loafers. He placed his travel shoes outside his door for cleaning. They had a servant who polished shoes!

He stepped into the corridor and knocked on Rich's door.

"I'll be a few minutes!" a muffled voice called. "Just go ahead."

"See you there." Alf walked on, treading carefully on the polished hardwood floor.

Castor had beaten him to their private dining room. Like Alf, he wore an off-white linen shirt and faded cotton trousers. He stood by the window holding a glass of water, muttering to himself. "I have been sent by... I represent the Council of Lords–No. On behalf of the Lesser Grenian police service..."

Alf eyed the table, which bore three place settings with several pieces of cutlery he didn't recognise. He perched on an armchair and fingered its cloth-covered back. Even the furniture was different. Alf had grown up with plain wooden furniture, with occasional cushions for padding. Rich's house had overstuffed leather chairs. Here in Calesia, the lightly padded furniture was covered with bright embroidered fabric like the rugs in that factory vault where he'd been imprisoned. The locals wore clothing with similar patterns. He couldn't imagine wearing such garments himself: his modest height and stocky build would be drowned under all the details. Maybe the weird motifs were rude symbols, and everyone was having a good laugh.

Rich strolled in. His cream shirt had a light sheen to the material. Was that what silk looked like? "Evening, gents. I wonder what's for dinner."

Alf swallowed. "Is the food, like, foreign?" What if he got a tummy upset?

"We're in the embassy, which is like a little piece of Lesser Grenia. In fact, because Castor and I are on police business, we carry that national bubble around with us. We'll eat more or less familiar food, and the staff members are also our compatriots."

"Oh." Their shoes weren't being cleaned by a Calesian. He wasn't sure how he felt about that.

Castor eyed the cutlery with apprehension. "Is this going to be a *big* meal?"

Rich inspected the table. "Hmm, shellfish, consommé, an amuse-bouche, salad, main course, pudding, cheese and coffee with mignardises."

Castor's eyes bulged. "We're supposed to eat all that *tonight*?"

Rich chuckled. "Be glad there's only one main course. The portions will be modest. Come and sit down, so they can serve."

"But who does the washing up?" asked Alf.

"Not us." Taking a seat at the table, Rich beckoned to a servant hovering in the doorway. "We're ready."

The servant ascertained whether any of the three diners had particular food preferences. His rural burr made Alf feel a touch homesick as he followed Rich and Castor's lead and shook his head. What would it be like to uproot yourself and go to work in a different country? And with the risk of that country declaring war on your homeland. His stomach clenched. Had Gwen been so miserable at home that she was willing to take such a chance?

After declining the wine with a frown, Castor asked Rich, "Do you know what Bergrim-Hoyt looks like?"

"I've seen him speak to the Council of Lords, although I don't know him personally." Rich tasted the wine and held out his glass for more. "So yes, I'd recognise him."

"I've caught a glimpse of him too." Alf sipped his wine and made a face. Was this sour stuff something that nobs liked? Maybe Castor had the right idea, or maybe Alf should have asked for beer.

Rich asked, "Should we request local police backup?"

"Security force." Castor studied the prawns on his plate. "Really, Hayes, I thought I'd made it clear. To answer your question, no. I'd prefer to take him myself without local help."

"And have Alf standing by with a camera to record your heroic deed?" Rich grinned as he expertly peeled a prawn with a curved silver blade and popped it in his mouth.

"Hey, don't involve me," Alf muttered, selecting a fork that didn't look too fancy.

"Don't forget, I'm reporting back on your performance." Castor's glower changed to a wince as his prawn shell pinged on to the embroidered rug.

Cripes, if even Castor couldn't manage the cutlery, what chance did Alf have? After a few minutes of eating, he licked his fingers. This food wasn't familiar to *him*, but he'd certainly have it again. "What if Mr Bergrim-Hoyt makes a break for it?"

"Unlikely," said Castor. "He's an elderly gentleman. He won't do anything physical himself. And he'll be tired and sore after his two-week coach journey."

Alf's backside twinged at the memory of the brief cab ride he'd made with Sally. He regarded his shell-strewn plate, wishing he had some bread to mop up the sauce. Why did nobs have to eat so slowly? Did they have so much leisure time that–Oh. "Er... Mr Bergrim-Hoyt would be in a hurry, right?"

"Oh, yes," said Rich.

"And airships are faster than coaches?"

"Of course," said Castor. "That's why we came in one. We're lucky Bergrim-Hoyt was forced to use the coach because of the weather."

"But Calesia has airports all over the place." He waved a sticky hand around. "Could Mr Bergrim-Hoyt and Gwen transfer to an airship once they crossed the border and the weather improved?"

Rich choked. "Yegads, you're right! He could be here already!"

Castor scowled at Rich. "Why didn't you tell me?"

"I didn't know! You're the one who assumed–"

Couldn't they even have dinner without bickering? Alf cleared his throat. "How about we check at the airport?"

Rich asked the servant, "Is Mr Laurence around?"

"Yes, sir. I'll fetch him." The servant departed with the plates.

Laurence followed the soup tureen in, buttoning up his jacket. "Is there a problem?"

"Bergrim-Hoyt may have arrived by air." Castor pushed back his chair and stood. "I need to check at the airport. Don't trust Hayes to get it right."

Rich rolled his eyes then sipped delicately from his spoon.

"Might I suggest," said Laurence, "that I go instead? Tongues will wag if, no offence, a strange foreigner rushes to the airport to make enquiries about a well-known personage in the middle of the night."

Alf glanced at the window. Crikey, the sky was black. How long did these dinners take? He picked up his soup spoon. Soup should be thick and hearty, not this watery-looking stuff. Then his appetite waned. "Don't forget Gwen."

"That's an excellent point," said Rich. "Laurence, if you enquire about Miss Wilson instead, on behalf of Alf here, that might not seem so notable."

"I shall." With a brief bow, the attaché departed.

Castor resumed his seat. "Wilson?"

"Yeah?" What was it about coppers, that they prompted this feeling of guilt?

"Once we find them, I'll want to interrogate your sister."

Interrogate? "What in the blazes for?"

"She's supposed to be his assistant, isn't she? She might well have relevant information."

"*Now* the police take an interest in her?" Alf's grip tightened on his spoon. "After the council refused to help?"

"She's more likely to be honest than he is."

Was that supposed to make him feel better? "She's not a criminal, even if she's tangled up with one."

"To be fair to Inspector Castor, for once..." Rich winked. "The council *is* funding this entire trip, even yours. If Gwen can help, it would let us finish this mission more quickly."

Gazing into his soup bowl, Alf wished he'd paid more attention to the arrangements rather than being distracted by the journey. "What kinda questions do you want to ask?"

"Mr Bergrim-Hoyt's whereabouts."

That sounded simple enough, but why inflict Castor on her? He firmed his resolve. "If that's all you need, *I'll* ask her when I see her. No need for you to talk to her."

Rich laid his spoon down. "That might be a reasonable compromise. It's less obvious if Alf speaks to his sister rather than Castor chasing her around."

"It's not regular procedure." Castor frowned at his water glass. "And I don't trust you to give a straight answer–"

"Hey! Just 'cos I didn't grow up with–"

"–after you gave me the runaround already. Jailbreak, impersonation, colluding, for a start. Need I go on?"

"Uh, sorry." The policeman had a point. Alf's shoulders hunched, and he slurped his wine to wash away the bitterness of capitulation. The booze tasted better on a second go. "Fair enough, I suppose. Gwen says I'm too protective."

"That's understandable," said Rich. "She's your only sister."

"Yeah." He grasped at the chance to change the topic. "You not got any sisters?"

"No. I'm an only child." Rich's habitual smile faded. "Maybe I'm an orphan, now. I have no idea what happened to my parents."

With a sour expression, Castor set his spoon down.

"That's a shame," mumbled Alf. "After Gwen's dad passed on, at least she and Mum–"

"And now you have Sally." Rich winked.

Alf's ears heated, and he leaned back as the servant placed a tiny pastry before him. "Inspector Castor, do you have any family?"

"Me?" Castor's eyebrow rose. "My parents and younger brother live further down the coast. They run a tannery."

Rich smirked. "No wonder you wanted to move–"

"You not married?" Alf frowned at Rich. Castor might not be charming company, but did Rich have to make things worse?

The inspector's cheeks coloured. "I'm hopeful. But I need to get a promotion before I feel able to..."

"Inspector is a perfectly respectable position." For once,

Rich's tone wasn't teasing. "Your young lady must be of some status if you consider that too low."

"She is." Castor stabbed his pastry with a fork. "She gave me that trench coat you so despise. The one you damaged."

Rich's mouth dropped open. "Ah. Sorry about that."

In an attempt to break the tension, Alf waved at the servant like he'd seen Rich do previously. "Perhaps we could have the next course?"

By the time Laurence returned, Alf was finishing off the cheese. Rich slumped in an armchair with a glass of brandy while Castor moodily stared into his cold coffee.

Laurence's face was serious. "They arrived nearly a week ago."

Chapter 19

When they arrived at the Security Office the next morning, Rich was last to step out of the embassy coach. He tucked his ebony cane under one arm and retrieved his silk hat from the seat.

"Come along, Hayes." Castor strode along a path bordered with dwarf palm trees, Alf beside him. "Wilson, let me do the talking."

"We can hardly get a word in edgeways," muttered Rich. His feet crunched on the gravel as he followed them.

The Security Office was a square, two-storey building. Two soldiers in beige uniforms stood outside the double doors. One wore a blue silk sash, the other a green one. Laurence had explained the different colours indicated experience, and that in colder climates their fur hats bore corresponding coloured trim. Both had identical holstered pistols.

Fanning his face with his hat, Rich paused to admire the painfully clean granite walls. They looked thick enough to assure a cool interior. "What a well-maintained building. I'm sure it's less drafty than old Ironfort police station."

"What did I do to deserve you?" Castor straightened the collar of his regulation blue police jacket. At least he'd left his trench coat behind. He addressed the soldiers. "I'm Inspector Castor from Ironfort, with my assistant Hayes and one other party."

Tamping down his irritation–it was a fair blow–Rich smiled. "We're here to ensure that the great detective doesn't wander into trouble."

"You're expected," said the soldier with the green sash. "The desk clerk will help you."

"Will you not let up?" muttered Alf as they entered the building, their footsteps echoing on the tiled floor. "We're not here for your entertainment."

"It's an irresistible temptation!" On seeing Alf's morose face, Rich held out his hands. "But you're right. I'll desist. Anyway, getting a rise out of him is no challenge."

The receptionist showed them up worn stone steps and along a dim and pleasantly cool corridor. The soldiers they passed didn't stare, exactly, but Rich imagined their eyes boring into him with every step he took. When a black-sashed officer with a vicious scar on his temple marched past, the other soldiers snapped to attention.

The receptionist led them into a cramped office filled with box files. A round-faced, red-sashed officer looked up from his desk. "Ah, the party from Lesser Grenia. Welcome to our beautiful country. I'm Officer Moon. Please sit down. How may we cooperate with you?"

After they were seated on stackable rattan chairs, Castor launched into their official story while the officer studied his letter of introduction.

"I see." Moon set down the letter. "Kidnapping as well as theft? These are very serious accusations. Professor Bergrim-Hoyt is renowned even here. And Mr Bergrim-Hoyt has visited Calesia several times and arranged many mutually beneficial trades."

Castor nodded solemnly. "All true, I'm sorry to say. We have confessions from his henchmen."

Henchmen? That wasn't official language, surely. Maybe Castor read *Inspector Grimley's Casebook* in his free time.

"A dreadful thing. I assume they confessed before paying the ultimate penalty."

"Sorry?" Castor blinked. "They haven't yet gone to trial."

"Ah, I misunderstood. The pace of justice is rather quicker here." Moon stood abruptly. "I must consult further. Let me fetch one of our governors."

After the door closed, Castor asked, "Where are the governors based?"

Rich said, "Their offices are on the other side of the city from here–"

The door swung open again.

"Ah, visitors!" A thin man with a white beard and wearing blue robes of office strode into the room. He sat behind the desk while Moon lingered by the door. "I'm Governor Spalding."

Rich sat back to watch the proceedings. As he'd suspected, this was taking on a flavour of an orchestrated performance. Better compare notes with Castor once they were back at the embassy.

"I thought you didn't have a hierarchy," said Alf, his chin jutting out. "How come you've got a title and fancy clothes?"

"You might view 'governor' as a position rather than a title. The robes are for easy recognition in case any citizen wishes to speak to me while I'm out and about. People know they can approach me with concerns or requests for advice."

"Oh." Alf's forehead wrinkled. "Can anyone just tell you if they have problems? Such as their landlords not fixing broken furniture? Or, say I ran into trouble, I could ask for help?"

"Certainly. In fact, I would encourage it. We are here to serve the people, after all." Spalding turned to Castor. "I'm shocked to hear of your accusations against Mr Bergrim-Hoyt. When he arrived last week, we believed the plans he offered us were his own work. Our scientists were overjoyed at the opportunity to move Calesia into an age of enlightenment."

"I'm sure they were." Rich met Spalding's glance with a bland expression.

"And of course Lesser Grenia, should your fine country wish to unite with us. But you have no interest in the plans, you say."

"We're not *as* interested," said Castor. "But we'd still like them back."

"It's the principle of the thing," Rich added. "Didn't you think it odd that he was offering scientific plans when he's a businessman?"

Spalding raised his eyebrows. "Not at all. His wife might be a brilliant inventor, but Mr Bergrim-Hoyt is also from a scientific background. I assumed he chose to stay out of the limelight after they married."

"Where is he now?" asked Castor.

"As far as I know, he took a room at the Ironfort Society. He mentioned other business interests in Shambito."

"And what about Miss Guinevere Wilson?" Sweat dotted Alf's forehead. "Did she go there too?"

"The young lady who arrived with him? We have accommodated her at the Science Centre. The agreement was that she would work on the invention we believed to be his."

Alf clenched his fists and gazed at the floor. "S'pose it was too much to hope she'd change her mind."

"At least you know where she is," murmured Rich.

Maybe having siblings was a liability rather than a comfort.

"I see," said Castor. "I'll want to interview her as well."

"I'm sorry." Placing a hand over his chest, Spalding smiled apologetically. "Your letter of introduction was very specific. You are in pursuit of one Lesser Grenian national, namely Mr Leo Bergrim-Hoyt. We offer you all our assistance in that regard, including cooperation from our citizens. However, your warrant pertains only to him. Otherwise, you have no right of access to Lesser Grenians."

"What?" Castor's face purpled.

Amusing though it might have been, Rich opted not to needle him about a point of law he'd missed. An apoplectic fit would only cause delay. Instead, he said, "We're very grateful for your cooperation, Governor Spalding."

"You're welcome. Without a formal agreement, we could stand accused of violating people's rights. I'm glad you understand."

"Only too well," muttered Castor. He glanced at Alf. "Wilson, it's just as well I brought you. Do you have something to say?"

"Me?" Alf raised his head, and then his face cleared. "Oh, right. Can *I* visit her?"

"You?" For once, Spalding's face was blank. "Why?"

"She's my sister, is why." Alf glowered. "Don't tell me family need special permission to see each other."

The governor steepled his fingers and regarded the ceiling. At length, he sighed. "You are not barred from seeing her. But she has the right to refuse your visit."

"I'll take my chances." Alf stood. "And I want to go now."

"Good," said Castor. "Remember what I told you yesterday."

"I'd hardly forget, would I? Even though you pretend it was your–"

"Thank you," said Rich before Alf could put his foot in it.

Spalding exchanged a glance with Moon. "Arrange for Mr Wilson to see his sister."

After Alf and the officer left, Rich leaned forwards with a careful smile. "We're grateful for the information about Mr Bergrim-Hoyt. Would you mind also returning the plans? It would be nice if Inspector Castor here could tick off both items on his list."

Castor cleared his throat. "That's right. We'll be in Shambito until–"

"Of course!" Spalding reached inside his robes and drew out an envelope, offering it to Castor. "Here you are."

Castor's brow wrinkled as he accepted the papers. "Is that it? I suppose the plans weren't as valuable as–"

"Thank you," said Rich. "About apprehending Mr Bergrim-Hoyt, we wouldn't want to tread on any toes. Is there anything else we need to be aware of?"

Spalding clasped his hands on the desk. "We are happy to cooperate, but please be reminded that he has committed no crime on Calesian soil. If we were to aid you in his arrest, he would have a right to be tried here."

"Hmm." Castor stroked his straggly beard with a frown.

Better nudge things along. Neither of them wanted to be stuck here for a trial, especially one that might be biased. "I think it would be best all round if we took him back to Ironfort. And hopefully Inspector Castor won't need to request your help."

"Agreed," said Castor, no doubt looking forward to dragging Bergrim-Hoyt home in chains.

"Just one more thing." Spalding drew another paper from his pocket. "One of our representatives in Ironfort sent me this."

Oh, damn. It was a copy of the *Ironfort Guardian* from the day after the kidnapping.

"Your newspaper seems very certain that a Calesian was involved," said Spalding. "But the information was incorrect. Please convey our distress at being so misrepresented."

Rich cleared his throat. At least that edition hadn't printed his face on the front page. "We shall. It was clearly a misunderstanding, and these tabloid papers don't always concern themselves with accuracy."

"That's understandable, but they're worryingly influential, even among our enlightened citizens. How did they conclude the kidnappers were Calesian?"

Castor raised an eyebrow at Rich. "It was in fact Lord Hayes here who was apprehended in the Bergrim-Hoyts' house. The circumstances were somewhat unusual."

Damn the man. Surely he knew they couldn't afford to sully Rich's reputation? "An unfortunate coincidence, and, er, nothing to do with–"

"Is that so?" Spalding studied Rich's face. "Ah, yes. I see how they came to that conclusion. Your family was originally from here?"

"That is so." Rich swallowed, hoping his blush wasn't too obvious. "I was born in Ironfort."

"But what were you doing in the house?"

Rich glared at Castor. The man had better not let anything slip. "A private matter."

Spalding exchanged an amused glance with the inspector. "These nobles, always so discreet."

"I believe the Bergrim-Hoyts have a very pretty maid."

Castor grinned smugly while Rich seethed.

Alf stomped out of the Security Office and into the clean-swept street, refusing the soldier's offer to arrange him a carriage. Bloody Castor, pretending it was all his idea for Alf to seek out Gwen. No wonder Rich enjoyed goading him.

Within moments, he was lost. Not wanting to return to the Security Office and admit his mistake, he stopped and glowered at the imposing stone buildings. The mass of pedestrians split around him with polite nods. They all looked purposeful and well-fed, and he felt very small and out of place in his too-hot borrowed suit.

Across the road stood a fruit seller's stall. Alf allowed a dray horse and a lumber wagon to pass, and then he crossed to ask for directions. In between extolling the delights of Calesian mangoes and offering him samples, the fruit seller explained how to get to the Science Centre. She kept glancing over his shoulder as she spoke—easy at her height—but when Alf turned around, he couldn't see anything amiss.

The Security Office was on the same side of Shambito as the military compound. If he didn't get lost again, he should arrive at his destination within half an hour. Licking tangy mango juice off his fingers, Alf walked out of the main city and along the paved road. The morning was warm and humid, and his strangling cravat was soon soaked with sweat. Added to that, increasing numbers of road apples informed him of horse traffic along the route. Ruts either side of the paving were testament to heavy loads being transported, although beyond them lay an untouched expanse of waist-high grass.

Well, at least his prosthesis was still working perfectly. With the old one, he'd have been limping by now. He jogged a few paces then halted. The day was far too hot for that. Standing on his good leg, he swung his other leg in the air, admiring how the mechanical ankle flexed.

Footsteps marched up behind him. "Lovely morning."

Embarrassed to be caught in such a ridiculous pose, Alf grunted, "Yes," to a black-sashed soldier who was apparently also out walking. He resumed his journey. Couldn't a man grouch to himself in peace?

"Are you visiting the military school?" Damn, obviously the bloke had decided to keep the titchy foreigner company.

"Yes? My sister's at their science place." Alf tried not to stare at the man's scarred forehead. At least a false leg wasn't on display for everyone.

"I see." To his relief, the soldier moved ahead.

When Alf approached the compound gates, his erstwhile companion was speaking to a pair of blue-sashed gate guards. The fatter one's shoulders were hunched, and he gazed at the ground.

"Given other issues, I'll overlook it this time." The black-sashed man glanced towards Alf. "But if you smoke on duty again–"

"I won't, Agent Guthrie! I swear it!" the fat guard stammered while his thinner companion smirked.

What was it to Alf if they smoked? He had other priorities. Fists clenched, he marched up to the gate and said, "I'm here to see my sister. She's–"

"Of course, sir." The thinner guard nodded and pointed at the road that continued past the gate. "Keep going straight ahead for the Science Centre. But please don't cross any parade grounds that are in use."

"Thanks. I'll take care." With his shoulder blades prickling, Alf walked along the indicated route. All these helpful people were grating on his nerves. Not that he minded politeness, but it felt like the Calesians were hiding something.

It was only after the guards were out of sight that Alf realised they hadn't even asked Gwen's name.

The road was indeed straight, with signposted brick-built dormitories lying on either side. Outside one, a beige-uniformed soldier pulled weeds from cracks in the concrete. At another, laughter and a peppery aroma drifted from an open window.

The dome-shaped Science Centre squatted in the middle of an enormous combined parade ground. Several groups of soldiers drilled separately, and Alf took a couple of detours so as not to get in their way.

He circled the concrete building until he reached a heavy wooden door with a substantial iron lock. It was propped open. He squared his shoulders and ventured inside.

In the coolness of the reception area, he wasn't completely surprised to find the soldier he'd met on the way—Guthrie—reading a noticeboard. Well, he'd put up with their games if they let him see Gwen.

"You expecting me?" Alf asked the receptionist, who looked far too muscular to be in a desk job.

The receptionist's gaze flicked to the noticeboard and then back to Alf. "We are, Mr Wilson. Governor Spalding sent word. Your sister is working in the laboratory. Is it essential that you see her right now?"

He wouldn't have come all this way otherwise, would he? "It is."

Guthrie ambled over. “In that case, follow me.”

Alf followed the officer down spiral stairs which ended in a circular hall with a dozen doors, each with a gas lamp above it. One of the doors stood wide open. It revealed an unoccupied room with workbenches lining the walls.

Another door was ajar, and wisps of smoke seeped out along with excited chatter. A bespectacled man staggered out, coughing and laughing at the same time. Sooty smears covered his overalls and horn-rimmed glasses. “If we can trigger it remotely, it’ll certainly obscure vision and hamper–”

“We have company,” called Guthrie in a low voice.

“What?” The man squinted. “Oh.” He scooted back inside his room and slammed the door.

Alf wrinkled his nose at the burnt rubbery odour. “Gwen’s not in there, is she?”

“No, we have several different projects.” Guthrie headed for the door opposite the stairwell.

“Like what?”

“Nothing relevant to your visit.” After a sharp glance at Alf, Guthrie knocked on the door and cracked it open. “Assistant Wilson, a visitor for you.” He swung the door wide.

“Yes, sir!” came Gwen’s voice.

Alf stepped inside and sighed with relief. His sister stood at attention by the far wall, wearing beige overalls in the same shade as the soldiers’ uniforms.

For a moment, she gazed at Alf without recognition. When he drew breath to speak, her jaw dropped. “Alf? What’re you doing here?” She looked him up and down. “And why’re you dressed like a toff?”

“Me? Why’re *you* dressed like a–” Aware of Guthrie behind him, Alf tugged his cravat. “Seemed right since they’re putting me up in the embassy. I've come to take you home."

"Home? What for? I'm busy with this."

"So what?" Alf paused. He didn't want Gwen to kick him out before he said anything, and his brotherly authority probably didn't count here. Spalding had already told Castor where Mr Bergrim-Hoyt was, so there was no need to ask about that. Better pretend an interest in her project and then work up to the more tricky topic of taking her home. "So, what is it?"

After a glance at Guthrie, Gwen patted her slate-topped bench. "Come and have a look."

Alf stepped around the central island and peered at her work surface. Pliers, callipers and other tools were strewn across the work surface, and grubby papers with scribbled-on diagrams. Nothing that made sense to *him*. Odd, he could have sworn she was struggling at college, but maybe she really had talent. "Wow, you're a real researcher now."

"Told you I could do it. Isn't it pretty?" She pointed at a hand-sized wooden box. It contained a jumble of mirrors and wires. Some of them glowed. "A new device for converting energy."

He flinched as a light beam struck his eye, making it water. "Into what?"

"Oh, uh, heat and stuff? Getting it just right is critical. I'm nearly there!"

What was so special about making it in Shambito? Alf ground his teeth. With Guthrie listening in, he didn't want to say anything too personal. "We were all pretty surprised when you left Ironfort in such a hurry. Why not come home again and do your important stuff there?"

She tossed her head, her fluffy hair catching the reflected light. "Why would I want to do that? Here, I'm making an important contribution. And I can achieve my full potential."

That sounded like the baloney they spouted to persuade guys who knew no better to sign up for the really filthy jobs. "But–"

"Which is better than you've ever managed."

Alf gaped. Of course he hadn't! He'd been supporting the family! "What potential? You've only been at college for two months, and you failed half your exams."

Hands on hips, Gwen scowled. "That's because the system was rigged against us poor folks. You don't know anything."

He could have strangled her. "But I'm your brother! And Mum–"

"That doesn't mean you can run my life. This is my big break, so shut yer gob and stop interfering."

"I'm right to! Mr Bergrim-Hoyt is a crook, he is. A thief and a kidnapper. He's filled your head with–"

"What?" She stared at Guthrie with wide eyes. "Is that true? Sir, he's not a criminal, is he?"

Guthrie folded his arms. "I can't speak to the Lesser Grenian system, but Mr Bergrim-Hoyt has certainly committed no crime on Calesian soil."

"Ha!" She pointed accusingly at Alf. "Telling porkies, 'cos you's jealous of my success."

Alf's blood chilled. "No, I'm not–"

"Go away! I don't want to see you again."

Guthrie stepped between them and faced Alf. "Mr Wilson, your sister is an adult. You can't force her to leave."

"But *she* can force *me* to leave," growled Alf.

"The Science Centre values Miss Wilson and will continue to support her for as long as she wishes to work here."

Behind Guthrie's back, Gwen stuck out her tongue. Then she turned her back on Alf and picked up a pair of pliers.

Alf remained silent while Guthrie escorted him to the compound gate. He shook his head at the offer of transport back to the city. As he trudged back along the road, he consoled himself that Guthrie must be getting equally footsore.

Chapter 20

After leaving the Security Office, it gave Rich some satisfaction to lead the way into the Ironfort Society. Castor brushed past him while he paused to inhale the scent of tobacco and furniture polish and to listen to the clink of silverware on plates. Just like his club at home. He wondered if they had a less formal back entrance–a pity the embassy didn't–but on seeing a grime-streaked labourer pick up a room key, he concluded such niceties weren't needed here.

Even Alf needn't feel out of place in such an environment. Considering his humble background, the man had shown admirable fortitude in venturing so far from his home. He deserved to retrieve his sister without incident.

"Hayes, stop lolly-gagging and come on." Glowering at Rich, Castor jerked his head towards the reception desk.

Unfortunately, Rich was stuck with helping the inspector towards success. "Haste maketh mistakes, Castor." He strolled up to the marble-topped counter.

A stocky boy in a pristine white uniform bowed. "Good morning, sirs. How may I be of assistance?" His speech was slow and careful, and his accent redolent of the Ironfort slums.

What an interesting recruitment policy the club must have. "I'm Richard, Lord Hayes. And my friend here is Inspector Castor."

"Gotcha." With a wink, he reached for a key. "I guess you guys wanna–Do you gentlemen wish a double room?"

Castor's expression of horror probably mirrored Rich's

own. Puce-faced, the detective shoved his letter of authority across the counter. "Absolutely not! Hayes and I are investigating a crime."

"Oh." The boy's shoulders hunched, and he stared at the paper. "I better fetch the boss. Sirs." He disappeared into a back room and returned with a colleague.

The manager was plump with a sweaty face. His white uniform was similar to the receptionist's, but with gold trim on the collar and cuffs. He returned the letter to Castor. "My trainee tells me you're on an official investigation, sirs. What do you wish to know?"

"I need information from the guest registers," said Castor.

Rubbing his hands together, the manager bowed. "Of course we would normally exercise the utmost discretion over sharing information about our visitors. But the Security Office has the ultimate authority." He nodded to the boy. "Check the records for Lord Hayes."

The boy obediently pulled a pile of books from the shelf behind him. "Yes, sir. I shall check the records for His Lordship."

Castor scowled. "It's just 'Hayes.' Nothing else. Never mind this 'Lordship' business."

"Jealous?" murmured Rich, lifting an eyebrow. "You'd think a professional–"

"Yes, sir. For Hayes." The boy's fingers flicked through the pages with the dexterity of a pickpocket. He ran his finger along a line of writing. "H-a-y... Hayes. Victoria and Ulfred?"

The smile dropped off Rich's face as his heart thrummed. "*My mother?* And my father too?"

"Sure thing, mate! Unless your mother slept with–"

"No, you dolt!" The scowling manager shook a fist at his trainee before addressing Rich and Castor. "I do apologise most profoundly, sirs. We recruit staff from the Lesser Grenia probation service and it takes time to bring them up to our standards."

"How wonderful." Castor hooted with laughter. "Maybe Hayes could work here until he's reformed."

"When was this visit?" Rich's voice was hoarse.

"Three years ago."

Three years? This must have been their first port of call. Trepidation prickled his spine. What if they'd run into trouble here and never left again? He chewed his lip.

Castor's eyes narrowed. "One might almost think you didn't know. At least, you're putting on a fair show of it."

"I didn't know! Or else I wouldn't be asking."

"Easy to say that, when there's no one to contradict you."

Damn the man. Rich's grip tightened on his cane. "You know nothing of–"

"It's polite to pretend you're not listening," the manager murmured to the gaping boy.

Head throbbing, Rich shut his mouth. It would be beneath him to make a scene.

"Entertaining though this is"–Castor smirked at Rich–"we're getting distracted. I wish to know about Mr Bergrim-Hoyt's stay."

As the manager discreetly stepped back, the boy flipped through the book. "B-e-r-g- Here we are, sirs. He checked in on..." He paused to count on his fingers and then provided a date six days previous.

Castor quivered with excitement. "Which room is he in?"

While the receptionist studied the page, his lips moving, Rich paced up and down. If he didn't work off some energy, he'd yield to the temptation to assault Castor.

The boy tapped a line. "He's not here now. He gave us the dosh–uh, settled his account two days ago."

"Damn!" Castor frowned. "Is there a forwarding address?"

"Moonview..." The boy squinted at the entry, and then he smiled. "No, Mountaintop Hotel."

Alf arrived in central Shambito with his stupid cravat tied around his head as a makeshift sweatband. How did the locals cope in this heat?

Despite his sweat-soaked jacket, the memory of Gwen's rejection was a frozen lump in his chest. Returning to the embassy was out: either Rich would laugh at his woes, or even worse, he'd look on him with pity. Alf glared at the shoppers, their cane baskets piled high with pastries and vegetables, and wrinkled his nose at the aroma of odd spices. How dare they be so cheerful.

A doorway caught his eye. *Workers Respite.* That sounded promising. He could do with somewhere to sit down and have a nice cold drink. The place certainly wouldn't be full of nobs.

He entered, immediately relaxing in the cool dim interior. "What have you got that's strong?" he asked the bartender.

A few locals sat at wooden tables. They chatted over steaming glasses. The fragrant scent of herbs made Alf's nose twitch as he climbed on to a wooden stool.

"Try this." The barman pushed over a brimming tumbler with a gnarled hand. "It's a nice day."

"Too bloody hot." When the fumes hit the back of his sinuses, Alf's eyes watered. He took a slug of his drink and caught the barman's glance towards the door. "It's not illegal to drink alcohol, is it?"

"Not at all. We believe in personal choice." Picking up a cloth, the barman carefully wiped the counter.

"That's a relief." He swigged again. Strong stuff, and with a resinous after-taste, but it started to thaw the block of ice inside him. "This stuff ain't bad. Wish I was back in Lesser Grenia."

The click of heels sounded on the scrubbed wooden floor, and then Guthrie perched on the adjacent seat. "It's a long way to travel, just to see your sister."

"Oh, you again. Yeah. And she wasn't even pleased to see me." Alf waved a finger. "You didn't help either, telling her that Mr B. was all above board. She stopped listening to me after that."

"That's not exactly what I said. But I apologise for causing discord." He flicked a finger at the barman. "My usual. And Mr Wilson could do with a top-up."

"Don't mind if I do." As his glass was refilled, Alf stifled a burp. "Uh, thanks."

"Mr Wilson, are you also from an engineering background?"

"Me?" He snorted. "Nah, no fancy training here. I used to fix some machines, but that was all."

"Hmm." Guthrie accepted a steaming cup from the barman. "You seemed rather interested in our projects."

"Well, sure. Me sister's there. Had to check up on her, even if she don't like it."

"You saw for yourself she was in good health."

"Yeah, but..." Alf tapped his temple. "She's a bit daft.

Not like our mum. Or me."

Guthrie swirled his tea. "I don't see much of a family resemblance between you. When you arrived and claimed to be her brother, I was a bit taken aback."

Alf scowled. Why did Guthrie care that Alf's dad hadn't been married to Mum? "That's none of your bloody business!"

"I can't help wondering"–the soldier's voice was stern–"whether you simply wanted a pretext to inspect our lab."

"Why the blazes would I be interested?" Swaying slightly, Alf slurped his drink again. "I don't care if you guys wanna spy on everyone, or make secret weapons, or steal our plans, I just want my sister back!"

"You're not a typical visitor, Mr Wilson. Inspector Castor's aims appear clear enough. I'm sure Lord Hayes will make his own move soon." Guthrie's lip curled. "Though even here, his title protects him to a certain extent."

"Bloody toff. And after all I did for him..."

"Did you, now? What was that?"

Alf opened his mouth then shut it again. He'd look a right twerp for being taken in like that. "Uh, nothing."

Guthrie shook his head. "I can't believe you're as much a naif as you appear. Barman?"

The barman fumbled with his cloth. "Yes, sir?"

"Would you say Mr Wilson is being disruptive in your establishment? Public disorder, perhaps?"

"Now that you've pointed out to me, sir, I have to agree."

"How unfortunate. I have no choice but to take him into custody. Perhaps he'll be more forthcoming there."

Rich glared daggers as he followed Castor into the embassy. It was hardly *his* fault that Bergrim-Hoyt hadn't checked into the Mountaintop Hotel. Not that Castor was being reasonable.

"… and remember, Hayes, *you* are answerable to *me* on this trip!" Castor stamped the marble floor for emphasis. "That's assuming you value your position in Ironfort."

Rich rolled his eyes and mouthed insults. When he caught sight of the embassy receptionist, he straightened his expression. No need for both of them to look like idiots.

The receptionist held out an envelope. "Inspector Castor? Message for you."

After ripping the envelope open, Castor groaned. "That bloody Wilson! On top of everything else."

"What's he done?" asked Rich, momentarily diverted from his impulse to whack Castor with his cane.

"He's gone and got himself arrested. Wanton drunkenness, behaviour likely to incite public disorder and alarm."

Jailed for being drunk again? Rich frowned. He'd thought Alf more sensible than that, but perhaps something had gone wrong with his sister. The man obviously couldn't cope under pressure, and that might place the girl at risk. "We'd better visit and–"

"No. He's not our problem. We'll need to trawl the city's hotels now, which will take forever. That's assuming he's still here."

"But Alf–"

"Wilson is a distraction." Castor's eyes narrowed. "I notice that you are once again bringing up matters unrelated to the investigation. Given your level of untrustworthiness, I suspect you're trying to sabotage me."

"Of course I'm not." True, he wasn't as obsessed by the mission as Castor was, but that didn't mean–

Castor jabbed a finger towards Rich's face. "And don't worry, I haven't forgotten about your parents. Once I have Bergrim-Hoyt in custody, I'll get to the bottom of their disappearance. It wouldn't be the first time someone decided to take his inheritance early."

Hot blood surged to Rich's head. He raised a fist. "How dare you! Your insinuation of murder is–"

"Dear me," came an amused contralto voice from behind him. "I didn't expect to return to murder accusations."

Rich spun.

In the double doorway stood a slender woman with grey-streaked hair in a beaded chiffon wrap.

By her elbow, Laurence set a travelling bag down. "Inspector Castor, Lord Hayes, may I introduce Her Excellency, Evita Mulgrew?"

Before Castor could move, Rich strode forwards. He took the woman's proffered hand and bowed over it, murmuring, "Enchanted to meet you, My Lady."

When he straightened, Castor bowed awkwardly. "Uh, hello."

"A belated welcome to Calesia." Lady Mulgrew's accent was pure Parlay Square, although Rich didn't remember meeting her in the past. "I hope that your visit is yielding fruit. But I couldn't help noticing a seemingly heated discussion."

Castor fanned his sweating face with the letter and cleared his throat several times. "Yes, we seem to have lost our direction as to which hotel Mr Bergrim-Hoyt might be staying in. Isn't that right, Hayes?"

Rich bared his teeth at Castor. "Exactly. I couldn't have put it better myself, old man. Apologies if our interaction seemed a touch *robust*."

"I'm sure Laurence could help." She inclined her head to her junior colleague. "Or is there someone you could ask who knows Mr Bergrim-Hoyt's habits?"

"Ah." Rich slapped his forehead lightly. "Of course. Why don't I telegram his wife for suggestions? Professor Bergrim-Hoyt must have some idea where her husband tends to stay on his travels."

"What a good idea," said Castor, his face stony.

Laurence said, "The telegram office closes in an hour."

"I'd best be going," said Rich. How excellent. He could drop by the prison and speak to Alf while he was out. If it was within his power, he'd find a way to rescue the man from custody.

Castor glared. "Don't take too long."

Lady Mulgrew chuckled and patted Castor's arm. "Give your young friend a chance to work off some energy. I'm sure he'll be fine."

"That's what I'm worried about," muttered Castor.

Seated on his prison bunk, Alf massaged his scalp. Shouts from the nearby military compound made his head throb, and the odour of pigsties didn't help his mood. What had he been thinking, going out and getting drunk? Castor had *told* him that Calesia's laws were strict. He should have known better.

And what idiotic stuff had he rambled on about in the pub? He had a vague memory of Guthrie prying about Gwen's dad—bloody nosy soldier—but after that everything was a blur.

Under other circumstances, Alf would have appreciated having privacy to recover, but the single-occupancy cell made him feel even more alone. In contrast to Ironfort, there were four stone walls and a tiny glazed window. The solid metal door contained a viewing grille. There was even a sink and toilet in one corner.

Footsteps approached. An acne-faced guard peered through the hatch, a flash of green at his neck.

"I'm not a zoo exhibit," said Alf peevishly.

The guard blinked. "Sorry. Just checking you're alright."

"Of course I'm not alright," grumbled Alf. "How long am I likely to be stuck here?"

"Drunk and disorderly? Normally we'd release you after..." He consulted a notebook. "Oh, that's odd. Agent Guthrie has noted that you'll probably be sentenced to a month's hard labour."

"*A month's hard labour?* For saying something stupid?" What if he'd got into a fight? Would they have chopped off his other leg?

"That's right." Misinterpreting Alf's look of horror, the guard added, "But don't worry. You'll be provided with food and a bed, and appropriate equipment and protective clothing. There's a small stipend, which accumulates until you're released. Some offenders take well to the work and continue on to paid jobs there. The re-offending rate is minimal."

"I should bloody think so!" No wonder the other cells were empty. Calesians probably tiptoed around, frightened of being hauled away.

The guard's brow wrinkled. "Oh, there's another comment here. If you have further information you'd like to share with Agent Guthrie, you only need to say so. That would allow some leniency–"

"Much obliged," called a hearty voice over the sound of

light footsteps in the corridor.

Alf stood with a frown and approached the hatch, craning his neck to see through it. Rich appeared in the doorway, accompanied by a blue-sashed guard.

"Come to gloat?" Alf asked sourly.

"Of course not." Rich wore no hat, although he carried his carved ebony cane.

The two guards stepped back a few paces, the green-sashed one pointing at his notebook.

Alf scratched his chin. "So why're you here?"

"Alf, my friend–"

"No friend of mine."

"–It's the least I can do. Castor says you'll need to serve your time, but that seems rather rough on you. I wondered if there was some way I could help."

"Yeah, great. Don't suppose you got your lock picks, Mr Thief?"

With a glance behind him at the curious guards, Rich chuckled. Beads of sweat dotted his face. "Ever the joker, Alf."

Of course, now the no-good toff would have to act all innocent. "Are you doing anything *useful* here? I'm surprised you're taking time out from living it up at the embassy to come and visit me."

"I'm on my way to send a telegram to Professor Bergrim-Hoyt."

Telegram? "That's a fast message, right?"

"Certainly."

"Uh..." Alf regarded his shoes. If Ina had such a proprietary interest in his prosthesis–and its attached user–maybe she could intervene? After all, Spalding had mentioned how respected she was, even here. It was a long shot, but worth a try. "Could you mention about my arrest? Please?"

Rich raised his eyebrows. "If you wish. What happened, if you don't mind telling me?"

"I couldn't talk Gwen round. It kinda went to pieces after that. And..." Alf squirmed. "Would you mind sending a second telegram? To Sally? How I might be stuck here for a while. She can decide whether to tell Mum. If it's not too expensive."

"Don't worry about the cost." There was an undercurrent of amusement in Rich's voice.

Alf squelched his embarrassment at seeking reassurance. It wasn't as if there were other friendly faces around. "Do you think she'd reply soon?"

Rich snorted. "I'm not going to ask which 'she' you mean. It's unlikely we'll get a message tonight. But I'll drop by again once I've done it. How does that sound? Anyway, I need to be on my way, or else the telegram office will be closed."

"Sorry about being rude," mumbled Alf. "But I'm kind of stuck. You will come back later, won't you?"

"Of course, old man. I'll also see if the ambassador can offer any advice, even if Castor's no help."

"Thanks." Maybe Rich wasn't so bad.

Chapter 21

After a walk brisk enough to work up a disagreeable sweat, Rich was relieved to find the nearest telegram office still open.

The doorman frowned at Rich's cane, probably comparing it to his own cudgel. "We're nearly locking up."

"I shouldn't be long." Tucking the cane under his arm, he entered and scanned the cool interior. The unoccupied customer area held several open-framed benches with no chance for concealment.

Each of the dozen counters was labelled with a regional name. Behind them, harried clerks shoved papers into box files which they then stacked on shelves labelled with dates. A broom-wielding teenager pushed through a swinging gate between the staff and customer area.

Rich smiled at his habitual observations: it wasn't as if he was going to burgle the place. He approached the cubicle at the end which was labelled "INTERNATIONAL."

The nearest clerk paused in her filing and hurried to the counter. "Yes?"

"I'd like to send two different telegrams, please. Both to Lesser Grenia."

"Details for the first?" She reached towards a stack of forms.

"To Professor Bergrim-Hoyt." Rich provided the address and the message:

Need list Shambito hotels LH uses STOP Alf incarcerated

Gwen refusing to return STOP respond soonest to embassy

The clerk read the message back to him, commenting, "We're closing, but if it's urgent, any reply will go through the main office. That's open overnight."

"Excellent," said Rich. "Next message is to Miss Sally Rosely–"

"So it's you!" The clerk sniffed disapprovingly.

Rich blinked. "Sorry?"

"That poor woman's sent so many messages here over the years, and you never replied."

Had he misheard? This was getting stranger by the moment, but best to find out more. He offered an apologetic smile. "Oh, of course. I'm not sure I received the most recent one. When did it arrive?"

"Must have been... ah, it was a couple of days ago." Her face softened. "It was my birthday, and my husband gave me rose water, so I connected the name and date."

Rich retrieved his change purse and laid a coin on the counter. "I'm afraid I never received it. Since I'm here, would it be possible to request a copy?"

The clerk regarded him sharply. "Are you suggesting that we failed to deliver a telegram to the correct address? If so, I need to raise it with the chief–"

"No!" Damn, what now? Stomach quivering, he chuckled weakly. "It's a bit embarrassing. My, ah, wife may have taken receipt of it and then destroyed it before it reached me. She sometimes gets the wrong impression."

"I see." The clerk glanced at his wrist, which was of course bare of a wedding chain. Her voice didn't hold any sympathy. "I'll give you a form to fill in for a redelivery."

Double damn! He didn't know who or where the true recipient was. It was lucky the clerk didn't remember either, even though she'd remembered Sally's name. Rich accepted the form and glanced at the clock. "Oh, is that the time? I don't want to keep you. For now, can we just deal with the message for Miss Rosely?" After raising the clerk's suspicions, he couldn't then change his mind about sending the telegram. He put on his most charming smile. "I'll bring the copy request in tomorrow. And I wish you a belated happy birthday."

Blushing faintly, the clerk took down the second message and slid his change across the counter. Rich replaced his coin purse in his jacket pocket, his fingers tracing the outline of his lock picks. Alf hadn't been entirely wrong.

After strolling out into the early evening heat, he headed for a tea shop across the road. He sipped a bitter brew and pondered. Sally was sending messages that didn't seem to receive a reply. Even if the unknown recipients used a different post office for return communications, the evidence pointed to more than social exchanges. It was most likely that she was reporting to a Calesian party.

How *could* she? And after all the opportunities his parents had given her? Rich bit savagely into a pastry, its sticky sweetness not assuaging his mood. What a trusting fool he'd been. He'd never felt the need to secure the paperwork he brought home from council meetings. It had been Sally who kept his notes tidy, and he hadn't questioned her motives. Was she involved with Bergrim-Hoyt, or was it some totally different scheme?

It was vital that Rich learn who she was communicating with, and what she was telling them. His gaze touched on the telegram office's entrance. The doorman was locking up for the night. Obviously Rich would have to gain entry and then find the telegram in the box.

He nodded. Hopefully, he could handle the matter himself without exposing his gullibility to Castor, but that remained a possibility. It couldn't be helped: Rich was obliged to act. She was *his* maid, after all.

Alf scowled at his empty bowl. Although the barley and peas had satisfied his hunger, annoyance gnawed at his gut. Rich had promised to return, but that had been hours ago. Sunset was approaching and still no sign. So much for starting to trust him. He'd probably got distracted and returned to the embassy for a leisurely dinner.

Maybe he'd also forgotten about the telegram. Almost, Alf wished his message wouldn't reach Sally. She'd shake her head or roll her eyes at his foolishness, and there would go his chances for any kind of future with her.

Footsteps clumped in the corridor, accompanied by a quiet rumble. Alf brightened, then his hopes fell as a guard appeared, followed by a wheeled automaton. The steel contraption was around Alf's height but far more bulky, maybe as wide as a tun. Four serrated arms hung at its sides.

He swallowed. The discolourations on the metal were rust, right?

The guard unfastened the door grille. "Bowl, please."

With sweaty hands, Alf passed it through along with the spoon. "Any sign of Lord Hayes?" He shouldn't have mentioned those lock picks. If Rich had seen this monster earlier, no wonder he'd opted to stay away. No need for both of them to land in trouble.

"Nobody has been by." The guard indicated the automaton. "I am obliged to warn you, this automaton is programmed to attack any non-guard it detects outside the cells. So you'd better not try to escape."

Alf's mouth went dry. "No fear of that. I guess you have them patrolling outside as well?"

"Hardly." The guard chuckled. "It would put the pigs at risk. And anyway, their wheels don't like the mud. Lights out in twenty minutes."

The guard departed, leaving Alf and automaton looking at each other. Definitely no chance of Rich sneaking in to help him escape.

"I guess you're going to have a boring night," said Alf. "I'm not great company. You stay on your side of this door, and I'll stay on mine."

The automaton didn't respond, which was a relief.

A month's hard labour! Odd to think that this morning he was tucking into a cooked breakfast at the embassy, and by nightfall he was in jail. From now on, would a machine be waiting to pounce on him every night if he breathed at the wrong time? He'd better get used to the idea.

Feeling stifled, Alf opened the window, although the outside pig-scented air could hardly be termed cool or fresh. The trees were only vague outlines in the dark.

He inspected the window aperture. It was a mere six inches square, and the wall was at least a foot thick. Unlike the Ironfort cells, the construction was solid and modern. No wonder they weren't worried about people escaping through the wall. Any exit would need to be via the door.

Well, if there were an accomplice outside with a crane, it might be possible... Alf shook his head. That was a factory worker's wishful thinking, and Rich had no way of returning that favour. Might as well go to sleep. Maybe something better would happen in the morning.

He sat on the bunk and rolled up his trouser leg, preparing to remove his prosthesis. As he reached for the release button, he noticed a flap hanging open. A light briefly pulsed inside. There hadn't even been an obvious seam earlier. He pressed the flap, but it wouldn't fit back into place.

A growl escaped him. If he'd broken the casing, that would really take the biscuit.

With his leg still attached, he inspected it further. Something must have got dislodged. Under the flap was a narrow cavity. His probing finger found a pencil-sized rod which flicked out on to the floor before he could grab it.

Bugger! He picked it up. After removing some paper wrapped around it, he inspected the component. It was a silvery rod with a button at one end. Etched into the barrel was a tiny diamond. That would be Ina's logo. Yes, there was "AB," her trademark initials. Though, a second set of initials was intertwined with hers within the diamond. His eyes nearly crossed as he focussed further and made out "LH."

Odd, but this was a needless diversion. What Alf needed was to replace the whatever-it-was. He wasn't sure which way up it should go. Maybe the paper included instructions? Ina didn't think much of Alf's scientific knowledge, after all.

Alf unrolled the paper:

Stolen design is flawed. Unstable on completion, will immediately explode.

Pausing to catch his breath—Shambito was hillier than Ironfort—Rich glanced back along the residential street. There was still no sign of anyone following. He kept his steps sedate and resisted the urge to twirl his cane. The euphoria of his successful break-in earlier was difficult to suppress.

Entering the telegram office had been a trivial matter, and he even knew which filing box to peruse. International telegrams were so infrequent that the address he sought was at the top of the pile. The name of the recipient was "Hedge."

As the telegram's text replayed in Rich's head, his grin faded:

> *R plus two arriving Shambito imminently STOP diplomatic immunity STOP other details remain as in letter STOP suggest you enlist him*

Assuming "R" meant Rich, why would this mysterious faction be interested in him? The unpleasant implications made him gnaw his lip. Thanks to his ill-judged actions over the last few weeks, Sally now knew of his criminal side. Blackmail was a possibility, especially given his social status.

The scent of grilled chicken and herbs prompted him to scan the nearby detached houses. They were modest in size, but clean and well maintained. Overall, an innocent-looking location for whatever plot was being hatched.

Outside the indicated house, Rich paused. The occupants were in, going by the light flickering behind the window blinds. He couldn't exactly stride up the path and knock on the door, could he? That would give the game away. But going back to Castor with an address for the mysterious Mr Hedge seemed a pathetic return for his efforts. He could just imagine Castor's look of contemptuous suspicion, especially when he mentioned Sally's involvement.

A man's silhouette passed across the window.

Rich's breath caught. There was something about that

high forehead and elongated nose... Maybe someone he'd encountered at the Ironfort Society? Or one of the soldiers at the Security Office?

The unanswered questions spurred him to a decision. He'd work his way around to the back door and either eavesdrop or gain entry. It was too optimistic to think he'd find Sally's letter, but he could at least get a clue about the occupants. What *had* she been telling them over the years?

With another glance behind, Rich moved cautiously up the path, twitching as gravel crunched beneath his feet. The side path was paved, and he breathed out in relief at the reduced noise.

Scents of flowering jasmine met Rich's nose. Away from the street lamps, the walled back garden was illuminated only by the full moon. He made out the outline of the back door. Good, no light leaked through the crack, so this room must be unoccupied. He pressed his ear to the wood. Assuming there was silence, he'd use his lock picks–

The door swung open. Rich lost his balance. A hand shot out of the darkness, grabbed his collar and yanked. As he raised his cane, a blow to his thigh made his leg give way.

The cane slipped from his hand. It clattered on the floor. Flailing at his unseen assailant, Rich knocked over a bottle. Glass splintered. The odour of brandy filled his nose.

Another hand gripped the front of his jacket and twisted. Rich toppled over.

He sprawled on the floor and sucked in a breath. "Ow!"

A match flared, and someone lit an oil lamp. "Damn. That was our last bottle."

The voice was a woman's.

Rich squinted up at his assailant. When he saw her exasperated face, his heart hammered. "Mother?"

Chapter 22

Stolen design is flawed. Unstable on completion, will immediately explode.

Design? Explosion? *Gwen's project?* Terror gripped Alf's chest and squeezed until spots danced in front of his eyes. "Gwen!" Visions of her mutilated body threatened to overwhelm him. He strode to the door and shouted, "Help!"

The corridor remained empty, other than the stoically inert automaton. Alf craned his ears, but there was no sound from the prison guards.

"Guard! Guard! Help!"

Stomping up and down, Alf yelled until he was hoarse, but nothing happened. He pounded on the door in frustration, which only resulted in bruised fists.

Bloody automaton. It was there to prevent his escape, not to alert the guards about other trouble. Grinding his teeth, he crumpled the note and threw it at the useless automaton's head.

A metal arm whipped into the air. It blurred in front of Alf's eyes. A snicking noise gave way to silence.

Shreds of papers floated to the floor, surrounding the once again motionless automaton.

The lights went out. A faint blue glow appeared around the automaton's head.

Shit! Alf's mouth dried up, and he panted for breath.

He stumbled to the bed and sat down. Trying to calm his thoughts, he became aware he was still holding the rod.

What *was* it? It couldn't be an essential prosthesis component, or else he wouldn't have been able to walk so easily.

Why hadn't he examined it properly before they switched the lights off? He rolled it in his fingers. It was the length of his hand, and the diameter of his thumb, slightly roughened where the logo was. A bit like a pen, really. The only feature of note was the button at one end. With nothing to lose, he prodded it.

The rod grew slightly warm. From its other end, a narrow beam of light pierced the gloom, barely enough to be visible.

Alf growled under his breath. Bloody scientists and their pointless inventions–

A trickling sound came from the corner.

Holding his arms out, Alf shuffled in the direction of the sink. His foot slipped, and he caught himself on the wall. He bent down and touched the floor. *Wet?* He patted his way to the pipes and found a finger-width leak, its edge warm. On exploring further, a hole of the same size pierced the adjacent wall. The hole was deeper than his probing finger could reach.

Alf could form only one conclusion. That light beam from the rod must have made a hole in the pipe. Like using a magnifying glass under sunlight, but stronger, hotter. More destructive. His head swam. What if he'd pointed it at himself?

He drew a shaky breath. Ina must have hidden the gadget–call it a lightrod–in his leg. Nobody else had been near it. What had been on the woman's mind? He rubbed the stubble on his chin. Something secret, obviously. Even secret from him. She *had* accused him of wearing his thoughts on his face. So, she'd sent him here with a warning and a tool, but no indication what to do.

What did she want? Stuff that, who bloody cared? Whatever Ina's intentions, Alf's priority was obvious. He needed to leave this prison and prevent Gwen from completing that damnable device.

But how? He stood and eased a kink in his shoulders, trying to calm his racing thoughts.

Perhaps he should try to disable the automaton? Even if he did no damage, maybe light from the rod would blind it. Standing by the door on tiptoe, he squinted through the hatch at its blue-hazed outline.

Holding his breath, he aimed the lightrod and gently tapped the button.

"Ow!" Alf sucked a singed finger while he tried to reconstruct what had happened. The light beam had bounced off the automaton's metal casing and back into his cell. He shuddered. This was far too chancy.

He set his jaw. But it was his only chance. If the beam reflected off metal, he'd need to be extra careful where he aimed it.

Alf fumbled his way back to the outer wall. Thanks to his earlier accident, he knew one thing the lightrod worked on. Carving his way through solid stone would take some time.

Lying on the tiled floor, Rich gaped at the patrician face from his past. He must have whacked his head when he fell. "Mother? It's really you?"

"Who else?" Mother huffed. "I don't know why you couldn't have knocked on the door like a normal person."

Her outstretched hand took Rich back to his childhood, to days when she'd lift him up after he'd fallen while playing. But he was an adult now. Trying to calm his racing heart, he stood and bowed. "It's good to see you again."

"Likewise." She presented a cheek for him to kiss. "Your father is in the sitting room."

After retrieving his cane with a shaky hand, Rich followed her down the hallway. Her familiar elegant glide prompted him to brush the glass fragments off his suit, although he couldn't do anything about the brandy stains. His cheeks warmed. Not the reunion he had imagined.

They entered an open-plan living area with terracotta tiled walls. Candles flickered, and Rich caught a whiff of beeswax.

"Ulf," called Mother. "You were right about our visitor."

Father rose from a wooden chair with embroidered cushions, raising an eyebrow over his half-moon glasses. In line with Calesian custom, his greying hair was cropped and his face clean shaven. He laid a newspaper to the side and extended a hand. "Son. I am pleased to find you in good health."

"Father. Likewise." Rich shook the proffered hand, trying not to stare at Father's naked face. No wonder he hadn't fully recognised his profile. "You don't seem all that surprised to see..." As the pieces fell into place, he slapped his forehead. "Sally!"

Seating herself at a dining table, Mother chuckled. "Cottoned on, have you?"

Rich's jaw clenched. "She's been in touch with you all this time, hasn't she?"

"Of course." Father reseated himself and waved Rich to the opposite chair. "Her reports have been invaluable."

"She's been *spying* on me!" His stomach roiled. So much for his fond delusions she'd been ignorant of his activities.

Instead, she'd been so discreet that *he* hadn't noticed *her*. What a fool he was.

"Such an ego, Richard." Mother rolled her eyes. "She primarily kept us updated on council matters, although she also informed us of your behaviour. Talking of which–"

"This thieving business." Father pinched the bridge of his nose. "I thought we'd raised you with more sense of honour. And the last straw was this." He tossed a paper into Rich's lap.

He scanned it, his heart sinking. It was that cursed issue of the *Ironfort Guardian* with a sketch of the so-called Calesian spy. "Damn!"

"You owe us an explanation."

Rich spluttered. "After you left me with no money, how was I supposed to pay the seat tax?"

"What about the farm?" asked Mother.

"It's hardly profitable, with all the workers' pensions and–"

"Fair point," said Father. "But you could have got a job."

"I couldn't! Not and still hold on to the title. You emphasised how important that was before you left. Several times, as I remember." He jumped to his feet. "Anyway, *you* owe *me* an explanation! Vanishing without trace like that! I thought you were dead!"

Mother's gaze fell to the tabletop. "It was necessary. We were in Shambito when Professor Bergrim-Hoyt announced her new invention. Every nation wanted to get their hands on the technology before their competitors did. Immigrants like us would have come under closer scrutiny from various parties, especially given your father's position on the Council of Lords. And that in turn would have jeopardised our delicate, ah, trade negotiations."

Rich threw his hands up. "You valued trade over your own son?"

"It was more complicated than that."

"No doubt." Bitterness laced his voice as he sat down again. "But even if you had good reason to vanish, couldn't you have let me know? You trusted Sally with the information."

"Who would pay attention to a maid?" Father snorted. "And you would have let something slip, impetuous boy. Besides, you started your thieving so soon afterwards, we couldn't risk attracting scrutiny from the Calesian authorities."

"Hang on." Something niggled at Rich's mind. "You passed me the title *before* you left."

Father regarded the floor. "Well, since you'd reached your majority, a temporary transfer seemed prudent. Just in case."

"Really?" They were definitely keeping something from him. Another memory struck him, a barely glimpsed shadow the day he'd found–"Those lock picks in the back garden. I thought a fleeing thief had dropped them there. But they were yours, weren't they?" He surged to his feet again and pointed a trembling finger. "You... you hypocrite! Spouting fine words about honour, and all that time *you* were breaking into people's houses."

"Not stealing," said Mother sternly. "And they were *my* lock picks."

"Yours?" Rich collapsed back into his chair. An image struck him, of his mother gracefully wriggling through an upstairs window. He couldn't help the chuckle that burst from his lips. "So what *were* you doing, if not burgling?"

"You wouldn't understand."

"Try me."

She folded her arms. "People may speak fine words about loyalty and commitment, but behind their front doors they're up to something else. Especially ambitious nobles. Heads of state don't remain so if they're oblivious of dangerous machinations."

"Seriously?" Rich's voice squeaked, and he coughed. "You sneaked into people's houses to check if they were scheming?"

"It's more honourable than stealing, young man!"

"Oh, yes. Totally agree. Just didn't realise people actually did that. And of course you'd have reported directly to..." At her pursed lips, he thought better of suggesting names. "Surely you'd shown your loyalty? I'm sure trade negotiations would have continued. There's something else, isn't there?"

Father leaned back in his chair. "I've always trusted your mother's judgement. It was the merest hint of trouble in the air, but enough for us to cut ties with Ironfort."

"Other than Sally." No, he wasn't bitter.

"There was minimal risk with her, especially after my training." Mother's voice was conciliatory. "You're a little more mature now–"

"Thanks!"

"–and diamond technology has spread, so the potential pressure has eased. Still, it pays to be cautious–"

Rich clutched his head. "Just tell me straight, will you? I've had enough of obfuscation."

"I'm trying to. After your father gained his title, he was occasionally approached by parties who sought insider information."

"And I always refused," grunted Father.

No surprise there. He considered the matter further. "If the stakes were higher, they'd become more persistent, right?"

"Yes, it got worse," said Mother. "During a garrulous moment, His Maj—hints of our covert position reached inimical ears. And with diamond power imminent, we would have faced increasing pressure to yield. For example, threats to those close to us. So we fled back here and cut ties before that could happen. Took ourselves out of the equation, so to say." She cleared her throat. "We hoped Sally would keep you out of serious trouble."

"To be fair, she did get me out of jail. What did you mean about threats to—*Me*?" Rich's jaw hung open before he recovered his composure. There had been *death threats* hovering over his oblivious head? "Oh. I see. Thank you. This is worse than *Inspector Grimley's Casebook*."

"Come again?"

"Nothing." He folded his hands in his lap and suppressed the urge to dance. His parents really hadn't abandoned him! Or they'd only abandoned him for his own good. "I suppose Sally told you I'm here in pursuit of Leo Bergrim-Hoyt?"

Father raised an eyebrow. "Indeed. We wondered if she was mistaken—his actions were unbelievable! But it does seem that you are working on the side of justice for now."

Mother's face softened. "And do I gather she's found herself a young man? It's about time she had some fun."

"Maybe." Poor Alf, no doubt wondering when his noble compatriot would return. Rich was struck by a twinge of guilt. Tomorrow, he'd make up for it by taking him a hamper from the embassy. "But he's in jail here. His sister got caught up in Mr Bergrim-Hoyt's scheme, and..."

After Rich filled in the information Sally hadn't provided, Father sniffed. "I suppose your conduct has been fairly sensible."

"Thank you." Hopefully, they wouldn't ask just how he'd discovered this address. "The trail grew cold at the Mountaintop Hotel. We're awaiting a telegram from Professor Bergrim-Hoyt concerning where her husband might be now. Hopefully she will reply tomorrow morning."

"I see." Father twirled his glasses round by one leg, a gesture that filled Rich with nostalgia. "If that doesn't work, we could make enquiries among our business associates. It might come in useful some time in future if your Inspector Castor is favourably inclined towards us."

Remembering that scene in the embassy, Rich scowled. "You've not met the chap. He grew suspicious about your disappearance. In fact, he as good as accused me of murdering you!"

Mother's nostrils flared. "We'll have to disabuse him of *that* notion!"

"Since we won't make progress on our mission tonight," said Rich carefully, "might you consider accompanying me back to the embassy? It would be nice to put paid to rumours of your deaths." And an ideal opportunity to rub Castor's nose in it.

"It's getting late." Mother glanced at her grey linen dress. "And I'm not dressed for visiting."

"Vic, dear..." Father smiled fondly and took her hand. "You're beautiful just as you are."

Rich squirmed. He didn't remember his parents being so affectionate in Ironfort. "We're likely to be busy with Bergrim-Hoyt's arrest tomorrow, so I'd like to clear things with Castor tonight. What if I return to the embassy now and let him know you're on your way?"

"That would work," said Mother.

"Just one more thing, Mother..."

"Yes?"

"He's not *my* Inspector Castor."

Alf's breath rasped in his chest, and he glanced anxiously up at the full moon. His earlier jog had slowed to a plod on the rutted ground with its waist-high grass. He'd opted to travel parallel to the road in the hope of avoiding detection. If he judged right, it wouldn't be long until he reached the military compound's gates.

For a moment, he grinned. What would his captors make of his escape? An Alf-sized hole in the prison's outer wall and whatever footsteps he'd left behind. Maybe that herd of pigs would obliterate his traces.

The lightrod nestled in his pocket. Thankfully, it was now cool. It had grown uncomfortably hot while he was cutting through the wall. Maybe it wasn't meant to be used for so long.

A glow ahead signalled the gate's position. Lights high on the wall illuminated the adjacent tarmac.

With a quiet grunt, Alf got down on his hands and knees, crawling through the sun-dried grass. His nose tickled, and he suppressed a sneeze.

Once he got closer, he cautiously poked his head up just enough to inspect the guards.

There were two of them, slouching on either side of the gate.

"... and then her father showed up..." The speaker gesticulated, and the other sniggered.

Lying prone, Alf clenched his jaw in frustration. No way

could he talk his way in: he was as conspicuous as a mule on a racetrack. Disable the guards? How? He patted his pocket. The thought of aiming it at people made his stomach roil. These men were only doing their jobs, and they didn't deserve to fall prey to an invisible weapon.

A distraction was needed, one that didn't prompt them to summon help. But what could Alf do? He wasn't a man of action, nor did he have a quick mind. No doubt, Rich would have come up with some clever scheme that didn't involve lying here in the prickly, dusty grass.

The sizzle of a struck match reached his ears. Seconds later, the scent of cheap tobacco smoke made him wrinkle his nose. It reminded him of the lads at the docks, sneaking a smoke when the foreman was elsewhere. Alf raised his head again.

One guard blew a smoke ring into the air while the other muttered and flapped a hand in front of his face.

That was it! Smoking on duty was forbidden. Guthrie had issued a reprimand earlier in the day—or maybe yesterday, by this point. Alf dredged up his memory of lads playing tricks on each other at school. Since the lightrod heated up in use, it made sense it could set things on fire. All he needed to do was wait. He aimed the gadget towards a dry patch of grass near the gate, a few feet away from the guards.

The smoker pinched out his cigarette and tossed it down, grinding it underfoot.

Bingo! Holding his breath, Alf pressed the lightrod's button until a wisp of smoke curled up from the ground.

"Careful!" The non-smoker pointed at the smoke. "If anyone finds out—"

"I've got it." Shaking his head, the smoker strode over

and stamped on the grass.

Alf grinned. This time, he aimed the lightrod at the ground outside the illuminated area.

A tiny flame sprang up. A gentle breeze carried the scent of burning grass towards him.

"Now you've done it! Why did you have to–"

"Just help me, will ya?"

Both guards chased after the flames. Alf laid down a trail of sparks until they were busy with his little distraction. Then, while their backs were turned and they were coughing from the smoke, he stood up and tiptoed through the gateway.

His pulse rushed in his ears as he listened for signs of alarm. After creeping around the first building, he collapsed against its wall, sweat running down his face. All this sneaking around wasn't good for his nerves.

Then he straightened. The job wasn't over yet. He had no idea where to find Gwen. But he *had* to save her life, even if she never spoke to him again. Thinking about it, he didn't need to find *her*. He could simply enter the Science Centre and destroy the device. The lightrod would make entry through its wooden door a straightforward enough task. Leaving might be a different matter, but he'd deal with that when it came.

At the sound of voices from behind, he flinched. But then someone laughed. Three young people strolled into the compound, wearing casual dress in patterned fabrics. Maybe they'd been on a night out? If so, it might not be so difficult to blend in, although he couldn't do anything about his height.

With a gulp, he shoved his hands in his pocket–one clutching the lightrod–and strolled further into the compound. The Science Centre lay straight ahead, but dozens of dormitories lay along his route. He crossed his fingers the occupants were asleep: or at least, that they weren't looking on to the street.

Eyes darting from side to side, he ambled past the residential buildings. Most had darkened windows.

Melodious whistling sounded from ahead. Judging discretion the better part of boldness, Alf turned down a side path and circled the building until he was sure the whistler was gone. Then he resumed his steps.

He was crossing a parade ground when an armed guard stepped out from a side path and headed towards him. Too late to turn away!

Sweat rolling down his face, Alf gave the guard a cheery wave and whistled the first merry tune that came to mind. It was that bloody song Rich had sung after his prison breakout. "My girl, she wears a frock... on her way down to the dock..."

The guard waved back and walked on. Still whistling, Alf mopped his forehead with his grubby cravat. That was far too close.

The muscles in Alf's neck tightened as he approached the open area where the Science Centre stood. The area was unlit, and the building a dark silhouette in front of him. Just a few more steps, and he'd be able to–

At a thump on his shoulder, he squeaked.

"Alf!" hissed Gwen, gripping his arm. "What the bloody blazes are you doing here?"

Chapter 23

Rich nodded at the embassy doorman and jauntily swung his cane. The closing doors cut off the rattle of the cab's departure. He glanced at the wall clock: ten pm. Rather late for dinner, but it was worth missing a meal if he could make Castor apologise for his earlier accusations. He strolled towards the reception hall.

A blue-clad figure barged through a doorway and collided with him. Rich staggered and dropped his stick.

Castor! Rich glared at the inspector. "Excited to see me?"

"Hayes! I told you to return here straight away. Where did you get to?" He sniffed and then glowered at Rich's begrimed suit. "You've been out drinking! And fallen over, by the looks of it."

"No, I haven't!" The defensiveness in his voice made him wince. He cleared his throat. "I was investigating."

"Investigating what?" Scorn dripped from Castor's words. "The local houses of ill-repute? You're no better than Wilson. He practically threw himself into jail."

Rich huffed. "You wouldn't believe me if I told you. Anyway, why are you so concerned with when I return? We can't do anything until Professor Bergrim-Hoyt replies."

"She has!" roared Castor. "She's given us three hotels. We need to leave immediately, or he'll slip through our fingers yet again." He thrust a telegram towards Rich.

Try Cumulus or Mountain View or Haven Hotels STOP

I'll sort Alf

Damn. So much for paving the way for Mother and Father's arrival. "Hold your horses. I can't imagine he'll go anywhere at this time. Wouldn't it be better to wait until morning?"

Castor's eyes narrowed. "You're still dragging your heels. One might suspect you were in league with him. Are you worried he'll let something slip?"

"Are you out of your mind? I'm as keen as you to catch him and keep my title. However, you as good as accused me of killing my parents." Rich took a deep breath and tried to keep his voice calm, clipping off the words. "It gives me the utmost pleasure to inform you that I have now located my mother and father. They are making their way here, so that you can see for yourself that they are alive and well."

"Really? After all those years? Such convenient timing." Castor gripped the truncheon that hung at his waist. "What I can see for myself is that you're causing me even more delay. Now that Professor Bergrim-Hoyt has decided to intervene about Wilson, you're scrabbling for wilder excuses."

Rich eyed the truncheon, which presumably Castor was wearing to make his arrest tonight. He didn't seriously expect Castor to attack him—and in the embassy too!—but some prudence might be warranted. He stooped and snatched up his cane.

The lock picks slid from his pocket and clattered on the floor. Damn!

Castor stared at them, and then he pointed at Rich with malicious triumph. "You can't explain those away, Hayes. Rest assured, the council will hear of this. Meanwhile, I'll arrest Mr Bergrim-Hoyt myself. Maybe he can tell me about your role in the whole scheme."

Was it wise to go visiting without backup? "But what if he–"

"Not another word. I should never have trusted you." Castor strode away.

Served him right if he ran into trouble. Rich smirked then groaned. How was he going to explain this to his parents?

Sagging against a wall, Alf stared at his sister. "How did you find me?"

"Couldn't sleep. And then I hear your out-of-tune whistling, right outside my window. How did you get in?"

"I snuck past the gate guards. Really needed to see you." The back of his neck prickled, and he imagined unseen listeners in the shadows. "Can we mebbe go somewhere less obvious?"

She huffed, then tugged at the blanket wrapped around her shoulders. "Can't take you back to the dorm and wake the other girls. We'd better go to the lab."

With his legs trembling from a mix of stress and previous exertion, Alf crept behind her to the Science Centre. Keys rattled as she opened the door, and they stepped inside.

The interior was unlit, but moonlight came through the high windows. His feet scuffed the hard floor as they headed downstairs, and he wrinkled his nose at the scent of bleach and smoke.

Gwen moved confidently to a door and unlocked it. Once Alf followed her in, she switched on an electric light.

His breath hitched. "Is that safe?"

"Safer than blundering around in the dark. No windows here." She turned to face him, hands on hips. "Now, why'd you trek all the way from the embassy in the middle of the night?"

"Embassy? Oh, yeah. I was worried about you, didn't want to wait till morning." He glowered at her nightdress with its inexpertly tacked hem. It was in the same beige as her overalls and the soldiers' uniforms. She was even bloody sleeping in army clothes! Would she listen to reason, or had she been thoroughly brainwashed by Guthrie and his mates? He pointed at the project's wooden box, still sitting on the back bench. "You've got to stop building it."

"This again?" She strode past the central island, cursing when her skirt caught on a knob, and stood protectively in front of her box. "You're just jealous."

"I'm not! It'll blow up if you finish it! Professor Bergrim-Hoyt told me."

"Ha! You didn't mention that earlier. I suppose she sent you a special telegram."

"Not exactly, she hid a message in my false leg."

"What? That's the weirdest thing you've said so far." She peered at him. "You been drinking? Or did the heat get to you? You need to drink plenty of water, you know."

Alf shook his head dismissively. "Never mind that. The plans are all wrong."

Gwen patted the diagrams on her workbench. "Better minds than yours have checked these out."

"Like whose? Yours?"

Her face reddened, and she tugged an earlobe. "Well, Mr Bergrim-Hoyt. He oughta know what he's doing. The senior guys here had a look too, though he had to explain it to them."

What was he up to? Did he know the plans were so dangerous? "He's a criminal. I told you that. The Ironfort police are on his tail."

"Agent Guthrie said he wasn't, and he oughta know. What happened to innocent until proven guilty?"

"Guthrie said, 'in Calesia.' He kidnapped me and Mum in bloody Ironfort."

Gwen gaped. "What? That's nuts."

"Yeah. And it's true. Really. Seems like a lifetime ago, but it's only been ten days." If even Alf thought the story sounded unbelievable, how could he convince Gwen?

"Lemme see..." She counted on her fingers. "We'd already left by then. So he couldn't have been involved."

"Obviously I didn't mean *him*, I meant his goons. He gets people to do his dirty work for him, just like you're doing here."

Her forehead creased, and then she folded her arms. "You're making all this stuff up."

"No, I'm not. Tell me, why isn't he here, working alongside you? I bet he knows it's going to blow up."

"He's a gentleman! He doesn't do hands-on stuff."

"Ina does."

"Who?"

"His wife."

"Ooh!" Gwen tossed her head and waggled her hips. "You're on first-name terms with her? Pull the other one. I'm not as dumb as you think."

Alf's neck tightened. He'd run out of arguments to bring her round. His only hope was to destroy the device. What was his best strategy without hurting her?

He fingered the lightrod in his pocket. It was reassuringly cool. There should be enough power for a final bout of slicing.

Back in his suite, Rich hastily changed into a clean shirt and trousers. After being caught off-guard at his parents' house, he wanted to present a more dignified face when they arrived.

He reached reception just as the hallway door opened. Mother sailed through, draped in a peacock-patterned silk shawl. Hands in his pockets, Father ambled along behind her. He hadn't bothered to change.

She smiled at the receptionist. "Good evening, Bernard."

"A pleasure to see you again, Mrs Hedge." The receptionist returned her smile. "And good evening, Mr Hedge."

"Do you know *everyone*?" asked Rich, feeling slightly peeved.

Father shrugged bony shoulders. "We occasionally negotiate with the ambassador and her visitors."

"Talking of visitors..." Mother glanced around. "Where is Inspector Castor?"

Rich rubbed the back of his neck. "I'm sorry, he just left. He received information about possible hotels and he's gone to investigate them."

"And you didn't accompany him?" Father sniffed.

Being honest with himself, Castor's rejection had stung. Rich set his jaw. "I was waiting for you. Didn't seem right to hare off when I'd arranged to meet you here."

"Really, Richard." Mother's voice was reproachful. "You've never been very good at prioritising. Of course you should have gone with him. What if he runs into trouble and needs support?"

Rich squirmed at her words, so similar to his earlier concerns. "I'm sure he won't, Mother. At worst, he'll not find Mr Bergrim-Hoyt, and then he'll return here."

Father shook his head. "You assume your criminal is working alone. But didn't you mention he had recruited unsavoury associates in Ironfort? Guards who carried out the kidnappings?"

Spot on, dammit. "You're absolutely right, Father, Mother." On noting their expectant looks, Rich cleared his throat. If Castor did run into trouble, it would be partly his fault. "I suppose I should get after him."

"That's my boy." Mother smiled. "And we'll just come along with you–"

"Mother!"

"–to ensure you don't meet further problems."

How was he going to explain their presence to Castor? "I would be delighted."

"What were the hotel names?"

"Cumulus, Mountain View and Haven." He tried not to sound like a sulky schoolboy reciting poetry.

"Which one's closest?" Mother asked Bernard, who wasn't even pretending to ignore their conversation.

"Haven," he replied. "Inspector Castor asked that too."

"Wait a moment..." Rich didn't want his parents taking over his job. But if things went well, he could vindicate himself *and* leave Castor unable to complain. "The lad who checked the records at the Ironfort Society may have misread 'Mountain View' as 'Mountaintop.' He didn't strike me as terribly literate. Maybe we should try that one first?"

"Good thought," said Father.

Warmth spread through Rich's chest. "Thank you. I hope I'm right."

Alf forced a smile and stepped further into the lab. Even with his improved prosthesis, he couldn't rush her, not with that table between them, dammit. “Sorry. I always think of you as my little sis, and I underestimated you. You must have worked really hard on this project. Did you help with the design?”

She shook her head. “The plans were finished when I started the project. It was easy to follow the instructions, though a bit fiddly. Everything has to connect up just so, or else it’s useless.”

“So, uh, how does it work?” It sounded like even a little damage would make it fail. How could he get a shot at the box before she decided they ought to leave?

“Well...” She picked up the box, flipped open the lid and tilted it towards him. Something glistened inside. “This here’s the diamond. It provides the power. Then these little mirrors, lenses and prisms reflect and multiply that power until it produces a lot of power at once.”

“And I guess that’s useful?” His sweaty fingers gripped the lightrod in his pocket.

“Sure! They want to try it for demolition projects, at least to start.”

“Seems an expensive way of blowing things up.”

“Not *my* problem. Though it’ll work with diamonds too flawed for regular use. Perfect ones are more powerful, of course, ’cos of holding more energy.”

“Oh, I see.” Alf swallowed. He’d run out of things to say. “Mum’s worried about you as well.”

“Is she?” She chewed her lip. “I left her a note. Thought she’d be happy I was going places.”

“Well, she wasn’t. She was really upset to think you wanted to run off. Are they feeding you well? Wherever you are, she wouldn’t want you to starve.”

Gwen chuckled. “It’s different. The canteen food’s

pretty spicy. How about you?"

"I had barley and peas for dinner." Damn, she was still standing too close to his target. Could he pretend to hear something outside?

"Really? I thought embassy food would be fancier."

"Uh, sometimes." His face grew warm. At her curious expression, he chuckled. "Just thinking about your dinner is making me sweat. Oh!" He held a hand theatrically to his ear. "Shh."

"What?" she whispered.

"Someone outside," he mouthed.

Her eyes grew wide. She pointed at the light switch and sidled around the room's periphery, giving him a clear shot at the box.

Alf stabbed the lightrod's button so hard, his thumb cramped. A sizzle marked the beam's passage through his pocket. The smell of singed wool reached his nose. A punched-out hole appeared in the box's facade.

Hoping to melt the components, he kept his aim until the lightrod grew hot. With an upward flick of his wrist, he drew a vertical line through the wood. The box clattered in two halves. Yes! He drew a breath of relief. Easy peasy.

Gwen's head jerked round. "What–?"

"You're too late." Now for the harder part–the argument.

Leaping back to the bench, she wrapped her arms around the wreckage and bawled, "You... you big bully! You've ruined it!"

"I'm sorry. I couldn't think of anything else–" He squinted at a flicker. "Uh, it wasn't glowing before, was it? You'd better step back."

"Why? So you can bash it around some more?"

“It’s dangerous–”

A blinding light seared Alf’s eyes, and he flinched, dropping the lightrod. Spots danced in front of him.

“Ow! My fingers!” came a shriek.

Nausea erupted in his stomach, and he panted for breath. He blinked rapidly until his vision returned.

Gwen huddled pale-faced against the far wall, sucking her–thankfully intact–fingers. With her uninjured hand, she waved at the table. “It burnt me! What’s it doing?”

Alf gaped. The fragments glowed an ominous red, getting brighter by the second. Sparks flashed along the wires and mirrors.

He cleared his throat several times. “I might have set it off. How do we stop it?”

“How should I know, you idiot? It’s not supposed to be stopped!”

Chapter 24

Rich entered the Mountain View Hotel while resisting the temptation to look back. Father had told him to precede them while they paid the cab driver, but he couldn't completely ignore their presence. Raising his chin, he reminded himself he was an adult now. They were *all* adults. This wasn't a practical assessment.

In the entrance hall, he stepped carefully on the rumpled rug. His nose twitched at a whiff of incense. Passing through the bar area, he paused to admire a floor cushion embroidered with a sunray motif. Clearly this hotel catered more to locals than to foreigners. The street door swung open again—his parents—and he hastily resumed his stroll.

Behind the desk, the receptionist straightened from his slouch and bowed respectfully. "Good evening, sir."

"Good evening." Rich slid a coin across the desk. "Is Mr Bergrim-Hoyt in residence?"

The coin vanished. "He is, sir. Top floor, grand balcony room."

"Grand?" It was odd how Bergrim-Hoyt hadn't made more effort to hide his movements.

"They all have balconies, but that one has the biggest." The boy shrugged. "Though not much of a view, if you ask me. It overlooks the military compound."

Rich rolled a second coin across the counter. "Did Inspector Castor visit earlier?"

"Not to my knowledge, but I've only just come on shift."

Excellent. Castor must be trying Haven first. "Ah well,

it seems I may be Mr Bergrim-Hoyt's first visitor this evening."

His tentative glance towards his parents turned into a grin. Father chatted with the barman. In a nearby cubby, Mother divested herself of her shawl, revealing a simple black dress, and sank on to a floor cushion. She caught Rich's eye and made pushing gestures.

With a chuckle, Rich ambled towards the stairs. Not only could he capture their quarry before Castor arrived, his parents trusted him by himself after all.

Or did they? On the top floor, he peered down the stairwell with a frown, but his parents hadn't decided to follow. Reassured, he took a moment to prepare. He had his lock picks in case the man was out, and his cane of sturdy ebony in case he was in. Even that was probably overkill. Only military personnel were permitted firearms. If it came to an undignified brawl, the elderly Bergrim-Hoyt would be no threat.

He knocked.

"What is it this time?" came a quavery voice.

"Open up in the name of the law." Rich grinned. He'd never imagined he'd be saying *that*. What would Mrs Wilson say if she found out?

Halting footsteps approached, and the door swung open.

Leo Bergrim-Hoyt blinked up at Rich before running a hand through white hair too long to be fashionable. His shirt was unbuttoned at the top, and a silver pen dangled from his fingers.

"You don't look like a policeman," Bergrim-Hoyt said breathlessly.

Of course he didn't: he had a sense of style. "I'm

Richard, Lord Hayes. I'm here on behalf of the Lesser Grenian police."

"Have we met before?"

"Not socially, no. I dropped by your house once, but you weren't answering the door." With a touch of pity for the bewildered old man, Rich glanced at the empty corridor. "May I come in? It would be nice not to make a big scene."

"Yes, it would be good to keep our business private." He stepped back and allowed Rich to enter.

While Bergrim-Hoyt locked the door, Rich surveyed the room. Several floor cushions had been shoved against the walls. A sleeping pallet with heaped-up blankets suggested the maid hadn't been in for a while, as did the dirty plates. In the centre of the room stood a knee-high writing desk cluttered with papers: would it be too much to hope he'd been writing a confession?

Wrinkling his nose at the odour of fermented beans, Rich strode to the open windows. They led on to a modest balcony. He wouldn't have called it "grand". Still, a glance to either side confirmed its neighbours to be even smaller. A gentle breeze brought the scent of gardenia, overlaid with a tinge of smoke. Far below, a few lights flickered in the military compound. "Nice view."

"It'll be a nicer view when my plan comes to fruition." The voice now bore a thread of amusement.

The back of Rich's neck prickled, and he turned. "What?"

"You youngsters, so over-confident." With his pen, he indicated the pallet.

Might as well humour him. Rich studied the heap of blankets. As they shifted, his breath caught. "Castor!"

Swaddled in a knotted bedsheet, a gag in his mouth,

Castor glared at the two of them. Bergrim-Hoyt's face bore a faint smile.

Could the detective not even manage a simple arrest? Never mind, this was an opportunity to show him up. Stepping forward, Rich raised his cane. "Did you catch our detective off-guard? You won't find me such an easy–"

A two-foot length of ebony clattered on the floor. Rich gaped at his abbreviated weapon. "That was my father's!"

"Is that so?" Bergrim-Hoyt pointed his pen–surely no pen–at Rich. "Stay there, Lord Hayes. I don't want to harm you, but you can't interfere with my plans."

He's an inventor, you fool. Just like his wife. As a glow from the pen's tip faded, Rich licked his lips. "And what plans are those?"

"Why, blowing up the Science Centre."

"I beg your pardon? You kidnap your own wife, steal her plans and deliver them to the Calesians. And *then* you say you want to destroy their research building?"

Bergrim-Hoyt glowered. "They threatened her. Nobody does that with impunity."

"You did all this to *protect* her?"

"That's right. I'm sure she'll have deduced my reasons by now." A fond smile curved his lips. "How is my dear Ina, by the way?"

"*Dear Ina?* You almost got her killed!"

"What?" Bergrim-Hoyt swayed on his feet, but as Rich stepped forwards he raised his weapon again. "No. You can't trick me that way. Her rescue made the *Guardian*'s front page, after all. It even merited a paragraph in the *Shambito Daily Intelligence*."

Damn. Why had that article suppressed so much, but emphasised her full recovery?

Rich spread his hands and stepped back. Whatever the mysterious weapon was, it seemed prudent to keep his distance. If he leapt for the balcony, could he reach the adjoining one before his adversary reacted? Unlikely. "I still don't understand."

"The Calesians contacted me, demanding Ina's latest plans. They threatened to kill her if I didn't hand them over." Bergrim-Hoyt bared his teeth. "They've brought this on themselves."

Sweat chilled on Rich's back. Was this the type of pressure his parents had fled? "But why did you kidnap her?"

"Even if I acquiesced, I couldn't trust them to leave us alone in future." His tone suggested he didn't think much of Rich's obtuseness. "They told me not to contact the police, so I arranged a... less direct method. No doubt she's heavily guarded now. Am I correct?"

"You are indeed." Not wanting to provoke an attack, Rich kept his voice gentle, although his legs quivered with tension.

"As agreed with my blackmailers, I brought her latest set of plans for an explosive device to Shambito."

"Giving them what they wanted, in return for her life. And simultaneously ensuring her protection." Rich sighed. Given the choice, he would have opted for flight. "But what did you mean about blowing up the Science Centre?"

Bergrim-Hoyt's smile was cold. "The plans are flawed. Ina spent weeks trying to pinpoint the problem. Once the components are assembled, even a tiny application of energy will trigger an irreversible reaction."

"Wouldn't their people realise that when they study the plans?"

"Lord Hayes, you do not realise how brilliant a scientist

my wife is. Her diamond project barely challenged her. It was just like using concentrated coal."

Rich dipped his head. "Is your pen one of her inventions too?"

Bergrim-Hoyt's face softened. "A joint project. We indulged ourselves in a matching pair for our fortieth wedding anniversary."

"How touching."

He waved the pen while Rich fought the urge to duck. "Her true legacy will be her wireless remote devices. Just imagine, controlling items when you're nowhere near them."

"And what might that be used for?" If he could keep his quarry talking, help might arrive. How long would his parents wait before growing concerned? Unfortunately, with Castor already captive, they'd need to fetch the Calesian authorities. But diplomatic negotiations could wait until everyone was safe.

"It's proven its worth already." Bergrim-Hoyt chuckled. "When my assistants kidnapped Ina and tied me up, I didn't want to be left there all night. So I reactivated our automaton remotely, just in time to catch some idiotic thief who'd blundered in. A lucky piece of misdirection."

"What a fool he or she must have been," Rich murmured, his jaw clenching. "But other than those peculiar circumstances, it seems excessive to use a device when you could just walk down the stairs."

"True, but she aims for far greater distances. However, I digress. You probably tire of listening to an old man's ramblings." He glanced at Castor. "And the good inspector too."

"Not at all." Rich swallowed. "I find it all rather educational. You were saying how the Calesians won't realise the plans are flawed."

"Exactly. And I brought a young student with me–"

"Gwen."

"Yes, Gwen. The uneducated girl hung on to my every word, and she jumped at the chance to travel here. Grateful as she was for my interest–not to mention her generous stipend–she was easy to mould to my purpose."

"But why involve her?"

"Verisimilitude." Bergrim-Hoyt barked a laugh. "It would look suspicious for me to offer personal input after being blackmailed. Anyway, why are you so concerned? She's only a low-class child."

Of all the patronising–Rich ground his teeth. "I owe her brother a debt. And in fact, the reason for *that* is because of your plans as well." He took a breath. Better not get side-tracked with thoughts of Alf's grievances. "So. When she completes the device, it will explode almost immediately, destroying the building–"

"With all their other projects. Hopefully an even wider area."

"–and killing anyone within range. Am I right?"

"Well done. You're not quite as frivolous as you look. It will set back Calesian military endeavours by, oh, decades. And, diplomatically speaking, they can't retaliate because they shouldn't have had the plans in the first place."

"And what of Gwen?"

Bergrim-Hoyt shrugged. "She'll die satisfied. As will I, knowing I've had my revenge."

"We don't want to kill you." Rich might have laughed, reassuring the man who held a deadly weapon.

"Oh, not *you*. The Calesians will send someone, sooner

or later." For a moment, he looked wistful. "I've been waiting here so I can enjoy the results of my plans."

"Very clever," growled Rich. How could he overpower this madman and get to the military compound in time to prevent such wholesale destruction?

"I'm afraid you and the inspector will have an uncomfortable stay. But Gwen should finish up tomorrow, and then... we'll see what happens."

Rich's hand crept towards his pocket, and he stilled it, not wanting to draw attention to his lock picks. Surely Bergrim-Hoyt had to sleep sometime? Keeping his tone light, he said, "I'm sure we've both overnighted in worse places. Thank you for your hospitality."

There was a knock on the door, and a woman's voice called, "Room service."

A fist of anxiety battered inside his chest. *Mother.*

Shards of broken glass and mirrors surrounded Alf and Gwen as they stomped her equipment to pieces. How many people would be caught in the destruction if it exploded?

Alf squinted, a hand protecting his eyes from the scattered lights. The red glow had turned orange a minute ago, and was now changing into yellow. "We need to leave."

"Just one more go," pleaded Gwen. "I'll be in awful trouble if it blows up."

"No! Trouble will be the least of it." He'd been mad to think they could stop it.

He grabbed her hand and stumbled through the door. A high-pitched whine followed them as they raced up the stairs and outside.

Gwen's foot caught on the hem of her nightdress, and she tripped. Scooping her up in a fireman's hoist, Alf staggered away from the building. An alarm bell sounded from inside.

"Let me down!" Gwen wailed, making his ears ring. "You'll make me throw up, you bloody great oaf!"

"Intruder!" came a shout from ahead.

A chance to warn someone. Alf accelerated into a jog. How far away would be enough?

Two guards appeared on the main street. "Hey, he's kidnapping someone!" one yelled.

"No, I'm not!" With Gwen still bouncing on his shoulder, Alf raised his hands. He ran towards the guards. "Out the way! It's going to blow up!"

"Halt!"

"No bloody way!" yelled Alf, barrelling past them and paying no attention to their firearms. "Explosion! Fire! Help! Anyone!"

"Intruder alert!"

He gulped for breath, feet pounding on the tarmac. In the dim moonlight, several figures converged on him. Gwen pounded her fists on his back. He didn't care. He lopsidedly ran on.

Behind him, the building roared.

Sweat trickled down Rich's neck as Bergrim-Hoyt glanced at the door.

"Room service," came Mother's voice again. "The champagne you requested."

What was she playing at? At least Rich could warn her he'd run into trouble. Nerves twanging, he raised an eyebrow and smirked at his captor. "I arranged a little celebratory drink, though I rather expected it to be for me and not for you. Well done, sir. But they'll grow suspicious if we don't answer."

Bergrim-Hoyt tossed the key over and aimed his pen at Castor. "Open the door and get rid of her. No funny business."

Rich carefully crossed the room, exchanging a helpless glance with the trussed-up detective. It *might* be possible to flee, but that would mean abandoning his unwanted colleague. Letting him down again. For all their disagreements, they were on the same side.

Conscious of Bergrim-Hoyt's gaze, Rich opened the door. His eyes widened.

Mother stood outside wearing a maid's apron over her plain dress. On top of her serving trolley stood a bottle of champagne and two flutes. She bobbed her head and said in a thick Calesian accent, "I'll just bring these in and then leave you gents to your evening."

"No, that's fine," said Rich hastily. He lifted the bottle and glasses, mouthing, "Trouble. Fetch help."

With an expression of concern, she grabbed the bottle he held. "I should really bring it in for you."

No! Rich couldn't provide Bergrim-Hoyt with even more hostages, especially not his mother. After a brief and silent tussle—had she always been that strong?—he stepped back triumphant. "Thank you so much! I hope the rest of your shift is quiet." He kicked the door shut in her scowling face and locked it, his shoulders easing. Now, he just needed to keep Bergrim-Hoyt occupied while his parents sought help.

Placing the key and glasses on the table, he offered his captor a weak grin. "They're certainly conscientious."

A prolonged boom sounded from outside.

Rich glanced at the window, where a red glow lit the

sky. Gwen! Outrage burned in his chest. Stuff waiting for help, he would have his revenge.

Bergrim-Hoyt started, lowering his pen. "Already? But they never work at night–"

Hurling the bottle at his hand, Rich tumbled out of the way. He landed on top of Castor, who grunted. The pen clattered against the wall.

Rich scrambled to his feet. Skidding on the wooden floorboards, he launched himself towards Bergrim-Hoyt and bore him to the ground. He slugged the old man with all the force he could muster.

"And that's for Miss Wilson," he growled as Bergrim-Hoyt slumped.

Momentarily ashamed of himself, Rich massaged his stinging knuckles before checking that his former captor was truly unconscious.

"One moment," he told Castor.

Best not leave a dangerous weapon lying around. He retrieved the silver pen, stowed it with his lock picks and used his cutting tool to remove Castor's gag.

"Thanks," said Castor gruffly while Rich unwrapped him from his bonds.

"You're welcome." It was a surprise to mean it. Maybe shared peril had some benefits. "Did he get the jump on you?"

Castor's lips twitched. "My visit was much the same as yours. Came in thinking my truncheon would be enough. Though he didn't expect a second visitor."

"I guess it was lucky, the way things worked out."

"I suppose so–" Castor's eyes widened. "Behind you!"

Footsteps scuffed on the balcony.

An accomplice! Turning to face this new opponent,

Rich whipped the silver pen out. How the blazes did it work? Its end had a–

Pain seared his cheek. "Ow!"

"Richard?" called a familiar voice.

Rich's heart nearly stopped. "Father!"

Father stood on the balcony, untying a rope from around his waist. "Who else? We did say we'd keep an eye on you." He surveyed the room. "Though it seems that everything is under control."

Rich's cheeks burned, and not just from his self-inflicted injury. How close had he come to killing Father? He'd never live it down if they found out. He slipped the lock picks back in his pocket. "Indeed we have. Though it wasn't easy–" A horrible thought struck him. "Gwen!"

"Calm down, son." Father retrieved the key, opened the door and let Mother in. "Everything's fine, Vic. Richard didn't do badly at all."

"Everything is *not* fine! Gwen can't have survived–" Rich's eyes pricked. "What will Alf say?"

Mother knelt and aided Castor to free himself. "He'll understand you couldn't be in two places at once."

"But if we'd come earlier..."

"There's no way we could have known," said Castor as he stood. "Did I hear right, and these are your parents?" At Rich's nod, his face went red, and he tugged his sleeves back into place. Then he bowed to each of them in turn. "I owe your son a debt of thanks for his help. His behaviour has been commendable."

"That's my boy," said Father.

Rich barely heard him as he ran out. He called over his shoulder, "I have to get to the prison!"

Chapter 25

Bleary-eyed, Alf folded his arms and leaned on the table in the interrogation room. He couldn't stop shivering after their near escape. Gwen huddled in the seat beside him, rubbing a graze on the back of her head. She'd been hit by a flying piece of debris. Bloody soldiers, they hadn't even provided a bandage.

Still, it could have been so much worse. By the snatches of conversation he'd caught, the patrols had all been chasing him when the Science Centre blew up. Nobody was caught in the initial blast radius. What if the explosion had happened in the daytime when the building was full?

Raising his eyes, he met Guthrie's glare. The officer had appeared shortly after Gwen and Alf's arrival, muttering something about conspiracies. That man had a right bee in his bonnet. Prompted by Gwen's anxious expression–at last, she'd stopped blindly trusting Guthrie–Alf hadn't spilled the entire story on the spot. Instead, he'd demanded Governor Spalding's presence before he said anything more.

"After all," Alf had said, "he did tell me he was here to serve if anyone needed assistance."

In the silence while they waited, Gwen's clammy hand crept into his. He squeezed it. She'd be fine. It had been worth it.

Footsteps sounded in the hallway, and Spalding strode in. He wore his blue robes and seemed far more perky than a man of his age had a right to be after midnight.

"Mr Wilson." Spalding sat at the head of the table. "I gather from Agent Guthrie that you wish to confess."

Alf blinked. "It's not a confession, not really. But I guess you chaps want to know what happened."

"We do," said Guthrie grimly. "Now, start talking."

"He *what*?" came a shout from along the hall. "Where is he?"

Rich? Alf shook his head. Trust him to show up after the danger was over.

Light footsteps approached at a run. Rich skidded to a halt in the doorway, his silk shirt smeared with dust. A green-sashed guard panted up behind him, uttering remonstrations.

"What're you doing here?" Noticing a trickle of blood on Rich's cheek, Alf half-rose from his seat. "And what happened to you?"

"I came to–" Clutching the door frame, Rich pointed at Gwen. "You! Are you Miss Gwen Wilson?"

Alf leaned slightly in front of his sister. "Yeah, she is. So what?"

Rich threw up his hands and beamed. "You're alive!"

"Of course I'm bloody alive." Gwen shoved Alf aside. "Who're you, mister?"

Gah, toffs attracted her attention, even when they were grubby. "This is Rich. A nob from Ironfort."

"Him, a nob?" Incredulity laced her words.

"I apologise for not introducing myself." Rich clicked his heels together and bowed. "I'm Richard, Lord Hayes. Delighted to be at your service."

"Wow." Pink touched her cheeks, and she turned to Alf. "You're on first-name terms with nobs?"

Alf could have laughed. "Just this one."

Spalding raised an eyebrow. "Lord Hayes, why did you think Miss Wilson wouldn't be alive?"

"Ah..." Rich tugged his collar. "We witnessed the explosion from the Mountain View Hotel. Knowing she had been working in the building, I feared the worst."

"So you happened to connect–"

"I am also pleased to inform you that Inspector Castor has taken Mr Bergrim-Hoyt into captivity."

Gwen's mouth dropped open. "You really arrested him?"

"Told you," muttered Alf. "He didn't just kidnap me and Mum, but his own wife as well, so he could steal her plans."

"I mean, he was always muttering about weird stuff, but I'd no idea he–"

"So why didn't you bloody listen to me?" Alf shoved her arm, and she shoved him right back. "Because I'm your brother, so I can be ignored? All you did was whine and yell and..."

Rich's smirk was oddly comforting in its familiarity.

Alf exhaled. "Anyway. Yeah, that's why Rich and Inspector Castor came here, and I tagged along to make sure you were alright."

"Oh." Gwen hunched her shoulders.

Spalding rapped the table. "Now that you have restored familial harmony, why don't you tell me everything from the start?"

Rich opened his mouth, but Spalding held up a hand. "I'd like to hear Mr Wilson's account of events from his own mouth. You may sit in, Lord Hayes. But only if you remain silent."

While Rich slid into the remaining empty seat between

Guthrie and Spalding, Alf shrugged. No skin off his nose if Rich and the governor wanted to argy-bargy over diplomatic stuff. Alf had nothing to hide. He waved a hand at Guthrie. "So, he was there when I spoke with Gwen and she refused to return to Ironfort with me. I went into a bar and... got drunk? My mind's a bit hazy on that. Anyway, he'll remember, 'cos he was there too. Asked me a load of questions. I guess I got noisy, and they put me in jail. Guard said I'd get a month's hard labour."

"A month?" Spalding frowned slightly.

Rich gave him a sharp glance. "Isn't that usual?"

Guthrie tugged at his uniform sash then stroked his lapel while meeting Spalding's gaze. Bah, all this palaver, and the soldier was more interested in his appearance than the explosion.

"Sometimes," said Spalding blandly, "a senior officer judges it necessary to diverge from the usual routine."

Leaning back, Rich folded his arms. "I see. Thank you for the clarification. I apologise for the interruption. Go on, Alf."

What was all that about? Alf studied his face, which bore its usual expression of mild amusement. Embarrassing though it was to admit it, Rich's presence was a comfort.

"Anyway," said Alf. "My false leg started playing up. I found a note from Professor Bergrim-Hoyt saying her plans"—he prodded Gwen, who scowled—"that Gwen was working on were flawed, and that the device would blow up."

Guthrie's jaw clenched. "Who passed you the note?"

"Nobody. It was in my false leg. I did yell for help, but nobody came, so of course I had to escape and warn Gwen." He pointed at Guthrie. "And *your* guard automaton destroyed the note, else I'd have left it for you."

At Spalding's enquiring look, Guthrie muttered, "We wondered why there were paper shreds on the floor. And just how did you escape, Mr Wilson?"

"The professor hid some gadget in the leg too. A kind of cutting thing? I'd no idea it was there until the cover opened."

Suddenly pale, Rich opened his mouth, but Spalding wagged a finger. "Don't interrupt."

Despite the serious situation, Alf suppressed a grin at the sight of Rich being told off. "You should be glad I escaped, else you wouldn't have got warning of the explosion."

Guthrie extended a hand. "Hand it over."

Alf huffed. "I don't have it, do I? It got blown up in the Science Centre. You could always try digging through the rubble." He was pretty sure that even if they found it, it wouldn't be of use to them. An image of Ina's grouchy face arose in his mind. Would she be really cross he'd lost it?

"So," Alf continued, "I sneaked into the compound."

"And you somehow found Gwen among the thousands of residents, even though you claim it wasn't a prearranged meeting."

"We got lucky." It *had* been luck, in retrospect. Or was it? There had been a story in *Inspector Grimley's Casebook* where... "Maybe one of them mysterious family instinct things. She *is* my sister, you know."

"Yeah." Shrinking under Guthrie's dark look, Gwen clutched Alf's hand. "I couldn't sleep and noticed him going past me window. So what could I do but go out and nab him?"

Guthrie grunted in displeasure. "Why did you take him

into the Science Centre?"

"Where else were we to talk?" asked Gwen defiantly.

"That's right," said Alf. "I know how strict you lot are. I tried to convince Gwen her device was dangerous and that she should stop working on it. What were you planning to use it for, anyway?"

"Never mind that," said Spalding.

Alf paused. Maybe it would be better to omit his deliberate attempt to destroy it. "And she was showing it to me, and all of a sudden it started glowing–"

"Gave me a right turn, it did." Gwen widened her eyes. "I thought mebbe Alf was telling the truth about it being flawed, after all. And it looked more dangerous than I'd expected. So we scarpered."

"And just in time," concluded Alf. He glowered at Spalding. "Now tell me, why did you let my little sister work on such a dangerous experiment?"

"I do wonder," murmured Spalding. "We didn't tell him to bring–Ah, Agent Guthrie, any comments?"

"She came highly recommended by Mr Bergrim-Hoyt." Guthrie's brows drew together. "On reflection, that's suspicious. I think you two and Mr Bergrim-Hoyt were in this destructive plot together."

"No bloody way!" Alf shook a fist. "He's a thief and kidnapper. And a traitor, selling you his plans."

"Rub it in, why don't you?" said Gwen, but without much heat.

"Are you saying our 'plot' needed me to be jailed?" asked Alf. "You put me there yourself."

"And for a month's hard labour," murmured Rich. "Convenient for questioning, maybe?"

Spalding held up a finger. "Silence, Lord Hayes.

Though I appreciate your point." He folded his hands and considered, exchanging a long look with Guthrie. Finally he said, "The fact of the matter is that you and Miss Wilson have destroyed years of research, whether or not you were conspiring with Mr Bergrim-Hoyt."

"Sorry about that," said Alf. Served them bloody right.

"I have no choice but to incarcerate you both for life."

"What?" Alf's heart lurched. He wasn't sure what he had been expecting, but the pronouncement still came as a shock. "Is there no alternative?"

Guthrie's lip curled. "There's always capital punishment."

Gwen paled.

"That's not fair!" Alf thumped the table. "Gwen had no idea what was happening. Uh, neither did I, really."

"That's not the point," said Spalding.

"What about Mr Bergrim-Hoyt? If he planned all this, doesn't he deserve an even longer sentence?" If Alf was going down, he wanted to see justice done to the kidnapping bastard.

Spalding said, "He has committed no crime on Calesian soil. He is now in Inspector Castor's custody, and his case falls under Lesser Grenian law. Unlike yours."

Bugger!

Chapter 26

Rich's perplexity turned to horror as Alf dug himself deeper into his pit. Did he have no sense of discretion at all? Or self-preservation, even?

Alf's shoulders sagged while Gwen clutched his arm. Obviously the man had run out of arguments. Rich had better intervene. It would be so unfair if the siblings were jailed for life because of Bergrim-Hoyt's maniacal scheme. They were unwitting pawns, no more.

He coughed. "Governor Spalding, now that Mr Wilson has made his statement, I'd appreciate it if you could satisfy my curiosity. I may have misunderstood."

"Go on." The governor's lips tightened.

"As I gather, the main charge against Alf and Gwen is that they conspired to destroy your research building."

"Exactly."

"Although the building was destroyed, by some miracle there were no fatalities or serious injuries. Detonating the device at night saved lives."

Spalding tipped a hand from side to side. "True, but–"

"Breaking things down further, an uneducated labourer broke out of your high-security prison unaided, and then infiltrated your military compound. His actions were coordinated with his sister, whom you had already permitted free access to the Science Centre. Correct?"

"It wasn't quite like–"

"Additionally, the plans were provided to you by a man we know to be a thief and kidnapper. Someone whose reliability might be called into question." With a faint smile, Rich held up a hand. Was this how Pettigrew felt when mediating appeals? "To be fair, you had no way of knowing about Mr Bergrim-Hoyt's crimes until the Lesser Grenian police contacted you."

Spalding and Guthrie exchanged glances, and then Spalding cleared his throat. "I suppose if we had questioned his motivations earlier, we might have been more suspicious."

"I'm sure the *Ironfort Guardian* would have a field day with this." Rich's smile widened, and he folded his hands on the table. "I learned something rather interesting earlier."

"Do tell."

While studying his hands, he watched Spalding out of the corner of his eye. "Mr Bergrim-Hoyt was under coercion from a Calesian group who threatened to kill his wife unless he handed over her plans."

The governor's face froze. So he *had* known of the plot. Probably he'd been behind it.

"What?" Guthrie's outraged tone surely couldn't have been faked. Interesting.

"You're having us on," breathed Gwen, her eyes wide.

"I assure you, Miss Wilson, it's the absolute truth." Rich regarded the ceiling and shook his head sadly while carefully selecting his words. He didn't want Calesian assassins seeking vengeance. "He capitulated and handed over the plans, arranging her kidnap in the process. I'm not sure why he brought Miss Wilson, but perhaps it was because he knew her as a diligent student."

Gwen prodded Alf and whispered, "See? Even Lord Hayes thinks I'm good."

Rich smiled inwardly at Alf's glower.

Guthrie's lips flattened. "How do you know the group was Calesian?"

"He said they were. I didn't press him for details." He met Spalding's gaze. "Obviously such a group must be hardened criminals, working without any official sanction. I suspect they've tried this before. But whoever they are, this time their plans were knocked awry."

"So it would seem," said Spalding.

"And it's very unfortunate," concluded Rich, "that the plans happened to be flawed, and that you made use of them in good faith. The professor must have known about the problems–no doubt she's developed her plans further by now–but her husband didn't. Hmm, I wonder if his blackmailers had an inkling too? We could hypothesise that they were a rogue faction. Perhaps their plan was to sow chaos and trigger war between our nations. Obviously none of us would want that."

Spalding's hands curled into fists. "Obviously not."

Guthrie set his elbows on the table, his scar pale against his red face. "This is appalling. I'll need as much detail as Mr Bergrim-Hoyt can provide. Whatever their reasons, it's a matter of national security."

Rich shrugged. "If you wish to speak to him, you'll have to ask Inspector Castor for permission. Though he isn't obliged to grant it." Better have a word with Castor as soon as possible. And Bergrim-Hoyt too, if he agreed to cooperate. "Agent Guthrie, it's none of my business, but I am concerned. This secret group has successfully evaded your intelligence network's notice. Once word gets out about your vulnerability–"

"You're right." Guthrie bit off each word. "I'll need to

divert more resources to rooting them out."

"It seems you've hit upon something close to the truth," said Spalding. Rich could just about hear him grind his teeth. "To sum up, some mysterious group pressured Mr Bergrim-Hoyt into giving his wife's latest plans to our research institution. We unknowing Calesians were delighted with his gift. However, it turned out the plans were flawed and posed significant danger on completion. Fortunately, Mr Wilson received a warning from Professor Bergrim-Hoyt, and he managed to save many lives, even though our building was destroyed."

"I didn't plan it like that," Alf muttered. "Just wanted to save Gwen."

"So modest, my friend." Rich grinned. "Just think, it'll make a great story to tell your grandchildren. And I'm sure Sally would love to hear about it too."

A goofy smile crossed Alf's face. "D'you think that would impress her?"

"Alf's got a gi-irl!" Gwen snickered.

Guthrie asked, "Do you know why Professor Bergrim-Hoyt chose such an unusual way of communicating with you?"

"Dunno," said Alf. "Mebbe it's just that she likes her gadgets?"

"And she's a proud woman," said Rich, considering the uses of wireless remote controls. "Perhaps it was simply too painful for her to openly admit to a mistake. Of course, she didn't expect the plans to be stolen in the first place. We should just be grateful she sent a warning." Her reasons for *that* remained opaque. If she knew her husband's intentions, surely she would either have gone along with them or opposed them straight away?

"I suppose so." Guthrie looked sour.

"Under the circumstances, I believe it would be massively unfair to penalise Mr Wilson and his sister. They were simply victims of circumstance. And they're heroes, not criminals." Rich waved towards Guthrie. "I believe Agent Guthrie should be lauded as well, for re-establishing order so quickly in the chaos."

Guthrie glared. "I was only doing my job."

"I agree," said Spalding, "that your interpretation of events is most likely to be correct. Mr Wilson, Miss Wilson, you are both free to leave."

"Thank you." Rich stood. Best get the pair back to the embassy before Alf stuck his foot in things.

"Oh, phew," said Alf. "But do I still need to do a month's hard labour?"

Guthrie glowered. "No. I'll see you to the door."

The black-sashed officer stomped beside them to the reception area before disappearing down a side corridor. Rich strolled towards the desk, and his eyebrows rose. Mother and Father stood chatting with the on-duty guard.

"Success?" asked Mother.

"I think so." Rich introduced everyone.

Father bowed to Gwen and inspected Alf. "That jacket looks familiar."

Alf winced. "I hope you don't mind. I borrowed your old clothes. Uh, and sorry. I put a hole in one of the pockets."

Father chuckled. "Don't worry."

"And you're Sally's young man?" Mother took his hands.

Alf cleared his throat several times while Gwen smirked. "I hope so. But she didn't seem that keen on me, and..."

Mother kissed him on the forehead. "Things will work out wonderfully. I'm sure of it. Richard, are you ready to go back to the embassy?"

"I am." He thought a moment. "Do you know of any furriers who do short-notice work? There's a collar that needs repaired."

The passenger deck shifted under Alf's feet as *The Ascending Queen* lifted off the ground. Keeping half an eye on Gwen, Alf drank in his final view of Shambito. The embassy had been a real introduction to the world of luxury, but he looked forward to returning home for a decent plate of sausages and mash.

Rich's parents had been surprisingly down-to-earth people. Mrs Hayes–or was it Hedge?–had quizzed Alf about Sally. She was obviously invested in her former maid's well-being, and Alf could appreciate why Sally had been so loyal. It must have been tough on both sides, having no communication for a whole three years, until Rich tracked his folks down.

Alf grinned. Of course he'd tell Sally all about meeting them: they'd also asked him to deliver some presents. And he could mention, casual-like, the grand sights he'd seen in Shambito. Or maybe refer to the fancy furniture. He wouldn't mention the sets of cutlery, however. Sally might start asking questions, and it would become obvious he hadn't managed to keep track.

Rich strolled up and bowed. "Enjoying the view, Miss Wilson?"

She grinned up at him. "Yeah, and this airship's really nobby compared to the one we arrived in. I'm going inside so I can make the most of my suite."

"Good girl." Alf watched her departure with relief that she wasn't hanging around Rich, all starry-eyed.

Rich joined Alf at the railing. "She's taking it pretty well, the loss of her project."

"She had quite a stroke of luck. Professor Bergrim-Hoyt said she can make some arrangement among her contacts. Something suitable for her skills."

"Really? No offence, but the professor doesn't strike me as kind-hearted. Or is it that she feels guilty about what her husband did?"

"Don't think so." Alf scratched his head. "I'd assumed it was because she and Mum got on so well. Being locked in that vault together, they got pretty chatty..." The back of his neck heated as he remembered their topics of conversation. "So, yeah. They kinda became friends."

"Ah," breathed Rich, his eyes wide. "So that's why she did it. Lucky, that."

"I just said that, didn't I?"

"Oh, so you did. Looking forward to seeing Sally again?"

"Yeah. I guess I'd better be careful what I tell her."

"Oh?"

"She'd be shocked at how sneaky some people can be."

"How–How true!" Rich's lips quivered. "Though she's had to put up with *me* for years."

"You're different. I'm surprised you're coming too, now that you found your parents."

"Oh, I'm sure we'll keep in touch. And... perhaps I appreciate them more in small doses."

"What're they going to do?"

"They'll continue their business developments in Shambito. Father asked me if I'd act as their representative in Lesser Grenia. The title will be useful for that."

Alf snorted. "Toffs."

Rich smirked. "Castor's promised to give me a good report. And once he delivers his prisoner, he'll get that promotion he's so set on."

"I can't believe this was all because some secret group was blackmailing Mr Bergrim-Hoyt."

"I know!" Rich laughed. "If you told anyone that, they'd accuse you of making things up."

"I bet the explosion gave Mr Bergrim-Hoyt a nasty shock. Though he'll be glad nobody was seriously hurt."

"I'm sure he is," said Rich. "It turned out for the best, I suppose. Calesian military developments will have been delayed for some time. Perhaps business people like my parents can continue to push for peace."

"That would be something." Alf gazed at the city as it shrank in the distance. "Funny how I never considered all this stuff before I met you. I can be proud I'm now a man of the world."

Acknowledgements

I owe enormous thanks to everyone who helped while I was writing *The Diamond Device*. Special thanks go to Philip Folk, as well as to my other critiquers and writing buddies on Scribophile.

Mistakes and inaccuracies are my own.

If you enjoyed reading this, maybe you'd like to take a few minutes to leave a review on your favourite book website. I'd also really appreciate word-of-mouth recommendations to any friends who might enjoy my writing.

About the author

M. H. Thaung works in a pathology laboratory in London, England. When not supporting patient care or biomedical research, she revels in throwing fictional characters into challenging situations and seeing how they react.

Website: mhthaung.com

Twitter: @mhthaung

Other books

A Quiet Rebellion: Guilt

A Quiet Rebellion: Restitution

A Quiet Rebellion: Posterity

A Quiet Rebellion: Short Tales – Flash fiction from the world of Numoeath

Printed in Great Britain
by Amazon